THE FIDDLER'S LEG

Also by Ann Lingard

Figure in a Landscape

THE FIDDLER'S LEG

Ann Lingard

HEADLINE
REVIEW

First published in 1996
by HEADLINE BOOK PUBLISHING

A HEADLINE REVIEW hardback

10 9 8 7 6 5 4 3 2 1

British Library Cataloguing in Publication Data

Lingard, Ann
Fiddler's leg
1. English fiction - 20th century
I. Title
823.9'14 [F]

ISBN 0-7472-1662-2

Typeset by
CBS, Felixstowe, Suffolk

Printed in England by
Clays Ltd, St Ives PLC

HEADLINE BOOK PUBLISHING
A division of Hodder Headline PLC
338 Euston Road
London NW1 3BH

ACKNOWLEDGEMENT

I am indebted to Paul James, of the European Union Baroque Orchestra, for the helpful and amusing insights that he gave me into the workings and jargon of a baroque band. Any musical inaccuracies in the text are my fault, not his!

Chapter One

Julian was in the bathroom when Mrs Knight arrived, so he didn't hear the doorbell. But she let herself in, anyway, with her key, and shouted, 'Morning!' as she shut the inner door. Julian leapt in shock and banged against the washbasin, then yelped in pain and swore. Hell! Mrs Knight! He'd forgotten it was her morning; now he wouldn't even be able to eat his breakfast in peace. It was tempting to stay where he was and lock the bathroom door, but he peered out into the hall instead.

'Morning,' he said noncommittally.

'You only just up, Julian? Good gracious me. Look at me now – soaked!'

She trundled up the hall towards him, square and stocky. He thought of her as a tank, gliding relentlessly in pursuit of prey, perhaps because she walked with the short steps of a many-legged caterpillar. Her bent legs and short stature indicated a wartime childhood in a poor area of the city, and a shortage of vitamins and nutritious food, but she was as relentless in her optimism as in her progress.

'I'll tell you why I'm late, Julian. I'll tell you why I'm wet.' Julian stood at the bathroom door, unable to escape. 'I'm going to write and complain. That number 23! I was waiting by the stop, had my hand out –' she swept out her arm, brushing Julian's stomach '– you shouldn't be walking round like that, you'll catch cold – and do you know what he did? He just speeded up and went right on by. Grinning, he was! Grinning. And right through the puddle, just on purpose. Look at this!'

Julian had such a clear image of the dirty water spraying up beneath a grinning face that he almost grinned himself.

But he said, 'I'm sorry. How unkind,' and reached out to help her out of her spattered blue mackintosh, holding it while she unknotted her headscarf and tucked it into the large, tapestry-covered bag that she had put down on the floor. She grunted upwards into a vertical position again.

'Go and put some trousers on, your leg's turned blue. Now, I'll just hang this in the kitchen and then I'll be getting started.'

Julian looked down. Only his calves and bare feet were showing beneath his nightshirt, but the scarred and wasted pallor of his right leg was visibly darkening with the cold. Mrs Knight was completely pragmatic about his disability, referring to it openly whenever she felt it necessary. There was no subtlety, no averting of the eyes; she said what she felt or thought – on any topic. He grimaced, and as he went into the bedroom to dress, he heard the squeal of the pulley on the overhead drying-rail.

'I saw Michael, too,' Mrs Knight said from the kitchen. Julian had to stand near the bedroom door to catch what she was saying. 'He was waiting at the traffic lights – big new car, one of those BTMs or BMWs, or whatever they call them.'

'Uh-huh,' Julian shouted, desperately trying to remember who Michael was. Oh yes, the Professor of Botany. Mrs Knight liked to refer to all her employers – her 'clients', she called them – by their first names. She enjoyed 'doing' their houses and being on first-name terms with professors, opera singers and the wives of important men in the city. But they all referred to her as Mrs Knight. It seemed improbable that she even had a first name of her own.

'He tooted his horn at me, cheeky devil! I was crossing with Lizzie Campbell – she's got a job at Tesco now – and she said to me, "Who's that good-looking bloke waving at you?" she said. "Oh, that's just Michael," I said.'

Julian pulled on a navy Guernsey sweater and ran a hand

over his hair before he limped back into the kitchen. He wished he had already had some breakfast to give him strength for their usual battle of wills. This time, though, he would prevail!

'I'd like you to do the oven today, Mrs Knight. It's been needing a good clean for some weeks.'

'This floor's all sticky here, Julian. What have you been doing, spilling things? Now I'll just start on the front room. If I've time I'll have a go at this with bleach,' and she touched the imagined sticky patch with her shoe.

'And the oven, too. Perhaps you could do the cooker with bleach?' he suggested, hoping that the lure of another bleachable surface would encourage her, but with the skill developed during twenty years of cleaning other people's houses she swiftly blocked his advance.

'I doubt I'll have time for that today, but I'll see how I get on. Now, I'll be getting the vac out . . .' and she trundled past to carry out her usual, unvarying circuit of the flat.

Julian felt angry helplessness at his defeat. Perhaps she thought such jobs beneath her. But it was more probable that she couldn't bend over. She was like a tree-trunk, he thought as he savagely hacked off bread for toast. The blue mac hit him in the face as he turned to fetch the filter coffee, and he stabbed at it viciously with the bread knife.

He put coffee, and toast spread with thick, dark marmalade, on a tray and carried it back to the sanctuary of his bedroom. The room was light, and sparsely furnished, the shelves and hanging space tucked away behind cupboard doors in a recess. The silky, deep-piled Kazakh rug, whose dusky brick-red and dark blue patterns provided a rich pool of colour against the beige carpet, had been chosen by his mother, and the fine walnut desk at which he now sat had been owned by his grandfather. The room was his, in a way that the front room was not. The front room was the music room, for pupils and members of the Ensemble, but his bedroom was private, for him alone – and this made Mrs Knight's weekly intrusion all the more distressing. The vacuum cleaner thumped against something solid, the piano or the doorframe, in the music room, and he shuddered in exaggerated horror.

While he ate, Julian looked through the papers that the Ensemble's treasurer, an accountant and the principal cello, had sent him. There was a small amount of extra income from the sale of their new recording, but the last couple of concerts had been poorly attended and that had made a dip in this month's income. So had the invoice for the maildrop of the handbills, but the extra advertising should bring in a bigger audience. He scribbled a note to the librarian about some music they would need, and took an envelope and a stamp from the top drawer. Subconsciously, he registered that the vacuum cleaner had changed in tone from A flat to D, and he wondered what was plastered against its nozzle – probably a sheet of music, but hopefully just a duster.

Mrs Knight had moved into the hall, and the vacuum cleaner was scraping and sucking against the skirting. (God! What disruption and irritation she created!) But now, at least, he knew the noise would temporarily stop.

'Julian? Julian, I'm just going to make a cup of tea. Are you wanting one?'

'No, thank you,' he shouted back, feeling as though he were cowering in a corner. 'I'd rather die,' he added quietly, baring his teeth and snarling a little. He rather enjoyed the idea of himself snarling and wondered what he looked like, but the mirror was in the bathroom so he just practised curling his upper lip for a few seconds, trying unsuccessfully to see his reflection in the window. A curtain flicked open in a window opposite, but there was no one to be seen except a square-faced tomcat, who stared arrogantly up at him from a wall in the back lane.

For a while, there was silence, then the noises resumed, this time from the bathroom, splashings and flushings. He knew that a thick blue sediment of scouring powder would be lying like an evil, immovable growth at the bottom of the lavatory. At first, he used to try to dislodge it with a stream of pee, but it wouldn't move and lay there like soft, wet concrete for a day or two, slowly disappearing down the drain. The bathroom wouldn't take Mrs Knight long; she'd be coming in here in a few minutes. The invasion was imminent! He quickly pushed the papers into a drawer. As he stood up he heard a yeowling screech and saw a snarling, screaming ball of ginger and black rolling in the back lane. Then, as abruptly as it had begun, the fight stopped and the cats slunk off in different directions.

The kitchen, when he returned the tray, smelt strongly of bleach. He touched the front edge of the sink and sniffed his finger: he had once had to throw away a pullover that had developed a pale bleached band at waist height, exactly where he propped himself against the sink or worktop. No, it seemed to be safe; she must have wiped the floor instead.

Mrs Knight looked in at him.

'I wiped the floor. I'll be doing your room now, Julian, if you've finished.' She paused and looked at him. 'Are you feeling all right today, then, Julian? You're looking a bit tired. You could do with some good fresh air, you're too much indoors.'

'What am I supposed to do?' He couldn't help snapping; the noise and clatter, the stuffy confines of the flat, the intrusion, were suddenly too much. 'Go skiing in Austria? Surfing in Australia? Climb a few Munros?'

'No need to be touchy, now. I just thought you didn't seem quite yourself these days. I said to Zoe the other day, I said, "Julian's not looking quite himself these days . . ."'

'I'm fine, Mrs Knight. I'm sorry. You're right, I do need some air. Your money's on the table, I'm going out.'

He pushed past her to get his coat, taking his letter, his car keys and his stick, and breathed out a huge sigh as he let himself out of his front door into the communal hall. He didn't know where he was going to go – but he was out!

The terrace had its own narrow private road, separated from the public highway by a line of red hawthorn trees and a thin strip of grass and shrubs. Once, a family with at least a cook and a live-in maid would have occupied each house, and small carriages or hansom cabs would have waited by the wide sandstone steps. But now each house was divided into four flats (or eight, or even sixteen rooms in less prosperous streets) and the narrow drive was made still narrower by a multicoloured line of close-parked cars. Julian's car sat right outside the front door in a specially delineated space. His space was occasionally encroached upon by visitors, but no residents repeated their mistake unless they enjoyed having their callous unconcern advertised by a politely worded but garish notice tucked underneath a windscreen wiper. Today, though, his car was where it should be. But what should he do? Where should he go? He rested his arms on the steering wheel and looked out bleakly. He ought to go to the swimming baths to get some exercise, but his swimming trunks were still inside the flat. Perhaps he could hire some at the pool. He slotted a cassette into the player and opened the window so that the music blared out into the street as he drove.

There was no one by the postbox so he waited, engine still running, tapping his fingers on the steering wheel in time to the beat. Soon, a teenage schoolgirl, wearing an *interesting* variant of her uniform, her short brown skirt all but hidden by her long black pullover, slouched towards him. He allowed the window to glide down further and leant out, hoping that his smile was the boyish, embarrassed one that he sometimes practised in front of the mirror.

'Excuse me! Would you be good enough to put this letter in the box for me?'

He held it out towards her, conscious that she was now enveloped in the heavy beat of the music.

'Do it yoursel'!' She said it without rancour, looking

sideways at him, consideringly. 'Lazy bugger!'

But she had stopped, prepared to be distracted. Julian rested one arm on the window and let his smile become more knowing. There were goose pimples on her thighs and her calves were thick and broad above her ankle socks.

'What's that music, then?'

'Come a bit closer and you'll hear it better.' He turned the volume down and adjusted the tone until the melody was nearly lost but the bass was heavy and insistent. 'Do you like it?'

'Can't hear it now, can I?'

'You can come and sit next to me if you want to hear it better. But you'll have to post this first.' And now he grinned at her knowing sneer. 'I'll drive you up to school then, if you're a good girl. Or anywhere else.'

Now she really looked at him, no longer smiling but biting her lip, assessing him. 'Never accept lifts from strangers' was clearly not part of her personal code of safety. He looked steadily into her eyes.

She made her decision, serious and suddenly nervous.

'OK. Give it to me then, quick!'

'Oh, with pleasure. But we can take as long as you like.' But she slid her eyes away.

He waited until the letter was in the box, then reached up and tapped the 'Disabled Driver' sticker on his window, waiting just long enough for the significance to hit her.

'Thank you, my dear. That was most kind.'

And he released the handbrake and accelerated across the road and down the hill. He hoped she wasn't the type to set fire to the contents of the postbox, out of spite.

The picture of pale, goose-pimpled flesh made the idea of swimming abhorrent, so he drove instead to the covered market, with its crafts and second-hand *objets* and antiques, to buy a birthday present for his mother.

* * *

It was nearly half-past four when he returned home, skidding the converted Mini round the corner into the road in front of the terrace, and he was angry with himself for his unprofessional tardiness. It had been a good day, after all: he had found a small, beaded Victorian bag for his mother's birthday (pretty, although not functional, but she had, in any case, almost everything that she could need or want) and he had encountered a friend, also browsing amongst the market stalls. They had eaten lunch together in a wine bar that served good seafood, in the warren of narrow streets at the edge of the city centre, and had driven in Julian's car, with its coveted and permissive sticker, to the large bookstore, where the minutes had passed faster than Julian thought.

Next to his space on the terrace was parked a dark blue Volvo, containing two women and a boy. As Julian manoeuvred into his space, the driver and the boy simultaneously got out; the boy was carrying a violin case.

Julian swept the carrier bag of books and the bag with his mother's present on to the floor out of sight before the woman reached his car. He turned off the ignition and sat for a moment, slumping slightly, then slowly opened his door.

'Julian! We've been waiting nearly half an hour!' The woman's voice was loud and indignant.

He looked up at her, his expression weary, and half smiled as he turned his body in the seat and reached into the back for his sticks, the one he had brought with him this morning and his spare. Carefully, grunting slightly, he pressed the ends of the sticks into the gutter and hauled himself out of the car.

'I'm sorry,' he said, heaving himself on to the pavement. 'Robbie, the keys are still in the ignition. Could you lock the door?

'These wretched hospitals . . .' his voice trailed off. 'One waits and waits . . . I keep wondering if I could go privately, but one has one's principles, and the consultant does seem to know what he's talking about . . .'

'Yes, it really is most inconvenient.' She was only slightly mollified. 'I assume you'll still take Robbie for an hour, Julian. But his father will have to collect him, I've got a meeting.'

'Of course, we'll manage something, won't we, Robbie?'

Julian had by now negotiated the three shallow steps, and leant against the doorframe to catch his breath and unlock the door.

'Come along then, Robbie. You go first.'

Zoe Lutyens had almost been on the point of leaving when Julian's Mini turned on to the terrace. Her son had fidgeted and grumbled, but had eventually taken out some school books and had started to do his prep. Margaret Gillespie, who had been helping Zoe at a charity tea, had also grown impatient, not because she needed to rush home but because Zoe's increasingly fractious remarks had begun to set her teeth on edge. She had just decided that she would make an excuse, get out of the car and walk the short distance home, when Robbie said, 'There's Mr Kersland's car! Mummy – please don't make a fuss!' and had begun to pack away his books.

'He really is the *end*!'

Zoe was becoming ever more tense, and she had opened the door before the approaching car had stopped. Poor Mr Kersland was for it now, thought Margaret, interested to see the confrontation. She was puzzled that he seemed to remain in the car so long, but then she saw, beneath the open door, the rubber ferrules of two sticks, placed firmly and supportively in the gutter. The windscreen of his car reflected moving clouds and, unable to see him, she expected someone old and arthritic to emerge. So Julian's dark hair, and his thinly handsome, ascetic face (but a face that was gaunt with pain or effort) surprised and intrigued her. She hadn't realised that Robbie's teacher was so young – or crippled. She watched how Robbie rushed to help, hovering uncertainly around his teacher, and she was puzzled that Zoe seemed unbending in her irritation, apparently unmoved by the young man's difficulties. She wondered what was wrong; the hospital, he'd said . . .

'What's wrong with Mr Kersland?' she asked when Zoe returned. 'I hadn't realised – Oh, are those Sunday concerts – yes, of course, the Kersland . . . Ensemble, I think it was. There was a handbill through the letterbox. Are they to do with him?'

'Yes.' Zoe was short. 'How he can possibly organise a whole gaggle of musicians when he can't even organise himself to be here on time, I cannot imagine!'

'But he was held up at the hospital. Isn't that what he said? You know what those waiting rooms are like. They give everyone the same appointment time from what one hears.'

'Not any more. I think it far more likely, my dear, that Robbie's illustrious teacher had been held up by his lunch!'

'Zoe!'

'The smell of alcohol is unmistakable. But I suppose it's uncharitable of me to doubt him. He *is* a very good musician.'

And Zoe reversed her car out of the drive with much sound and vigour.

Chapter Two

Sunlight was forming parallelograms on the wall, slanted bleached rectangles on the pale Wedgwood-green paint. The plaster leaves and flowers of the rose in the centre of the ceiling trembled in the reflection from the birdbath on the front lawn. Margaret Gillespie paused for a long moment, oblivious of the cushion in her hand, and stared out of the bow window, seeing nothing, merely pulled briefly out of the action of tidying the room.

Consciousness of the cushion returned, infinity became invisibly distant, and she realised that she was focusing on the tulips that stood on the delicate Regency table near the window; yellow tulips in a clear glass vase, the petals opened to expose the flowers' black throats, the stalks curved and dipping in stooping grace. She put the cushion down, automatically arranging it to best advantage on the chair, and walked over to the table to touch the broad, curved leaves. The water was faintly brown and she could see a dust of pollen on the stamens; the flowers were ageing, but supple and more pleasing in their age. Smiling to herself, she raised her arms above her head and stretched over to one side, then leant forward and swept her arms round in a curve, bending her back so that her thick brown hair flopped over her face like a curtain. Her figure was still good, despite her forty-three years, but the suppleness was going. For a moment she longed to discard the elegantly simple clothes of the middle-aged wife of a successful solicitor and to wear instead the casually

comfortable clothes of young people, leggings and a floppy
pullover, so that she could sit cross-legged on the floor. Perhaps
she should join the Fitness Centre and go to aerobics classes
or practise yoga . . . Perhaps she should help at the University
Nursery, where she could wear slacks and sit upon the rug in
the reading corner, surrounded by fascinated children hanging
on her every word. A petal dropped on to the polished table,
a golden-yellow boat, and she sighed impatiently and picked
up the vase; but the telephone rang so she put it back again,
knocking off more petals and pollen.

'Hello. Margaret Gillespie.'

'Margaret dear, I'm so glad to have caught you.' Zoe's clear,
confident tones rang out, and Margaret held the receiver away
from her ear: Iain always said Zoe didn't need a phone, you
could hear her well enough without. 'Look, lovey – the hospice
coffee morning. It's on Thursday. I know you put it in your
diary but I'm just phoning round to check. Can you be a love
and bring a cake or two? Nothing fancy – you know the sort
of thing.'

'Oh . . . I don't think—'

'*Do*, lovey. You've probably got something tucked away in
that marvellous freezer of yours, haven't you?'

Margaret was cross with herself; why didn't she refuse
outright? She knew she had already lost.

'Well, I probably can . . .'

'Oh, you *are* good. I knew you wouldn't let us down.' Zoe
dropped her voice slightly, indicating confidences to be shared.
'It's such a *relief* to know there are some people that one can
rely on. And you will come and help, won't you, love – ten
o'clock, as usual?'

'I think that will be fine.'

'Iain all right? We haven't seen him for ages. We simply
must all get together soon.'

'Yes, thank you, he's—'

''Bye, lovey. Nice to talk to you. See you Thursday, then.'

'All right. Yes. Thank you.'

Zoe rang off, leaving Margaret helpless and resigned. Of course there was nothing suitable in the freezer, and she disliked making that kind of cake, Victoria sponges, lemon- or coffee-flavoured, with thick squishy icing. Perhaps some scones would do instead. Why had she thanked Zoe, for goodness' sake, as though Zoe were doing her a favour? Sometimes she despised herself for her weakness. (But at least that was Thursday morning accounted for, a small, treacherous voice whispered inside her head.)

The hospice was the new good cause: coffee mornings, bazaars, collecting tins to be jangled in the street, even a poetry recital with blunt, incomprehensible local poets. And there were other good causes, too: Save the Children, clothing for refugees, food packages for starving African states – all causes that were either suitably sterilised and civilised or else so far distant that there was no personal threat to those involved in raising money or collecting goods. This area of the city was bursting with financially secure middle-aged wives who had no other outlet for their considerable intellect and energy than charities and good works, and entertaining friends or their husbands' business associates. Their children had left home, their houses were furnished as they would wish, and there was an insidious, usually unacknowledged, fear of appearing redundant in what had once been a stimulating and busy partnership. There was so much creative intelligence going to waste, such a huge resource of experienced management.

Margaret had herself been hard-working and committed, pushing her way up through a firm of provincial accountants; so hard-working, in fact, that neither she nor her previous husband, working equally busily at his own advancement, had had sufficient time or energy left to relax with each other, to forget about the household chores and weekly shopping, and to sit and talk or share a companionable silence. Divorce had finally seemed the obvious option. She had met Iain

Gillespie at the start of her divorce proceedings. She had gone
to his office to ask him to act on her behalf; he had agreed, but
had later inexplicably abandoned her and passed her over to
a partner. On the evening of the day on which she heard she
was officially unmarried once more, a messenger rang her
doorbell and presented her with a single, boxed red rose.
Inside was a note from Iain Gillespie, asking her if she would
honour him by dining with him the next evening.

He was ten years her senior, had two teenaged daughters,
and had recently been made a widower. He had been gentle
with her, persuasive, considerate, but nevertheless in charge,
and she had been glad to find a safe haven in which she knew
herself to be cherished and apparently, to her surprise, loved.
Her gratitude and her pleasure in his company turned slowly
into love and, despite her unfamiliarity with parenthood, she
was pleased, indeed desired, to give up her job and care for
her new husband and his daughters. The younger daughter,
only recently a teenager and deeply unhappy at her mother's
death, had been unwilling to accept a substitute and their
relationship had been stressful and unhappy. The elder girl
had been more tolerant, perhaps intrigued to have a confidante
who was ten years closer to her age than her mother had been.
But it was not many years before both girls became legal adults
and left home for university and student flats, holiday jobs
and long, rambling trips abroad.

Margaret had wondered then about obtaining part-time
work, but she knew she was out of touch and she lacked the
courage to return. It was so comfortable here and Iain had
seemed happy that she should be at home. Sometimes he had
found time to come home for lunch; she would start preparing
an hour or more ahead, eager for his company and the change
in her routine. Even though she knew their lunch would be
rushed, she would feel a small thrill when she heard his key
in the front door lock, and she would come out of the kitchen
to greet him. Once, he had watched her for a few moments as

she stirred the soup – home-made asparagus, she remembered even now – and then he had suddenly put down his sherry glass and had come over and turned off the stove. They had made love upstairs, on the bed, still partly clothed, and he had been quick, impatient with preamble, but had soothed her afterwards with tender hands and words. She remembered how she had laughed when he had slapped thin slices of cold smoked turkey between hastily cut bread, and had left hurriedly, nearly late, eating his sandwiches as he drove. They had eaten the soup with their evening meal, and for a while thereafter 'asparagus soup' had held a new meaning in their private jokes.

It had been about that time, too, that Iain had bought a weekend cottage. It was a traditional, stone-built house with gabled roof and dormer windows that overlooked a secluded inlet of a sea loch, a long-fingered loch that pointed so far inland that only its brown rim of seaweed reminded them it was the sea. That had kept Margaret busy, planning the necessary renovations and the furniture to transfer or buy. They had redecorated most of it themselves, going up there at weekends, working hard but fortifying themselves with wine, and opera on the tape recorder. They had shared in the creation of the cottage together, in the choosing and making of its interior, and the result was, like this house, an elegant and comfortable home. Like this drawing room . . .

Margaret yawned and stretched, and wondered what she had been thinking about for the past ten minutes. When she stood up, her buttock and thigh tingled where the edge of the sofa had dug into them, and she massaged her leg gently, picking a thread of cotton off her skirt. The room felt peaceful. Her life, too, felt peaceful, well ordered, though a little dull.

She wandered round the large, airy room, tidying into piles the books and newspapers that lay on the floor beside the two soft wing chairs. The rich golden-brown of the rug glowed warmly against the polished wooden floor and a complicated arrangement of dried flowers and grasses in an earthenware pot contrasted with the white marble of the fireplace. Delicate watercolours of seascapes and a couple of modern prints hung on the walls. She was particularly pleased with the painting opposite the fireplace. It was a view of cliffs and low islands, a grey sea lit by silvery-yellow light beneath a layer of beige-grey clouds, that she had bought several years ago as an anniversary present for Iain. Although, for her, it was an achingly empty picture, she had known that he would recognise its strength. It also fitted the colour and style of the room. Her own inclination then had been towards a powerful gouache of a woman carrying two heavy baskets of shopping along a crowded street. At the time, the bold strokes of colour, contrasting with the woman's apparently placid acceptance, had caught Margaret unawares, and she had found herself continually wondering about the picture. More disturbing was the recognition that her tastes had not, as she had then supposed, merged with and become indistinguishable from those of her second husband – Iain would definitely not have liked or have been moved by that picture, it would have been too brash and disordered for his taste. Would *she* still like that picture now, she wondered, or had that version of herself disappeared for ever?

Iain Gillespie's meeting had gone well and had ended early. He unlocked his car and, as he leant over to put his briefcase on the floor, he realised that he had nothing scheduled for the remainder of the afternoon, and was not expected to return to the office. He would go home instead. Meg would be surprised to see him. Pleased with the idea, almost skittish at the thought of a few extra hours of leisure, he slotted a tape of Brahms' Violin Concerto into the player and turned the volume a little higher, wanting to fill the car with sound.

The traffic was surprisingly busy as he crossed town; the vehicles on his side of the road were almost stationary, moving forwards in fits and starts. He had plenty of time to look around, at the small, run-down shops, the end-of-winter potholes in the street, the dirt and rubbish on the pavements and in the gutters. A line of traffic moved towards him, travelling quickly as though glad to have escaped the blockage, and the gust of wind caused by a passing bus stirred the litter so that a sheet of newspaper whirled up and was slapped against the windscreen of the battered Escort that was ahead of Iain in the queue. Its driver, whose bare arm was propped on the open window despite the cold, reached out and pulled the paper in, smoothing it and holding up the spread page.

For a moment, a Page Three girl, kneeling, holding melon breasts, smirked provocatively back at Iain, but then was gone, crumpled and thrown out of the window. The ball of paper rolled and was trapped in a black puddle by the kerb, but the young man didn't notice because he was laughing and leaning across to a girl in the passenger seat. Iain watched idly as the newspaper began to soak up water, blackening to soggy pulp. The traffic began to move again, slowly at first, then more confidently, the stream continuing brazenly through a red traffic light so that pedestrians, about to cross, stepped back hurriedly. An untidy blonde girl gesticulated and mouthed something indistinguishable as Iain passed; 'well stacked', the Americans would have called her, he mused, although he preferred the French himself, 'tout le monde sur le balcon'. There wasn't room for more. All the world, all the world and his wife. All aboard.

The traffic had become stationary again ahead. He sighed, and rubbed the creases around his eyes with the finger and thumb of one hand; the weatherbeaten lines on his face sagged with weariness and irritation. At the first opportunity, he accelerated out of the queue, exhilarated by the Rover's sudden burst of speed, and swung the car into a sidestreet on his right, manoeuvring through the network of backstreets, narrow with lines of parked cars. There were crocuses on the embankments and catkins on the hazels in the Botanic Gardens, and that promising sight increased his own elation. He turned quickly into his own gateway, spraying up a shower of gravel, and noticed that his garden had crocuses too.

Margaret, meanwhile, had been baking; golden-topped fruit scones were cooling on a wire rack on the table. She washed the bowls and cutters, checked the plants on the windowsill for water, and noticed that the primroses were in flower beneath the south-facing back wall. She drained hot frothy water from a saucepan that had been sitting on the hob, and tipped the cooked smoked haddock on to a plate ready to tease apart the pale yellowish flakes. She cracked eggs against the rim of a bowl, separating yolks and white; a piece of shell glistened in the clear gelatinous albumen and she picked it out with a pointed fingernail. She melted butter in a pan until it bubbled, then added flour to make a roux, then milk. She drew the pan away from the heat and beat in the yolks and folded in the fish. The white soufflé dish would provide a better contrast than the brown, and she transferred a bottle of white wine from the refrigerator to the marble shelf in the pantry so that it should not be too cold. The rest could wait until later; she would go up and have a shower. But the sweet smell of scones tempted her and she quickly cut one open, plastering it with butter that melted on the still-warm cut surface and glistened on her fingers. She cradled one half in her hand as she walked upstairs, smiling guiltily as she bit into the other.

Margaret's shower was brisk and efficient, but her camisole was white glossy silk and her tights were sheer and free from snags. She chose a dark red polo-neck jumper, and a bottle-green straight skirt, applied a little make-up, discreet blusher and lipstick. She turned her head in front of the mirror, frowning at the few grey hairs that were becoming increasingly visible, and inserted a small pearl stud into her left ear lobe. As she picked up the second stud she heard a car and the spattering of gravel on the drive. Flustered, she couldn't fix the earring in place, the clip wouldn't hold, and she pinched her ear lobe in her haste. When she heard the front door open she gave up and left the stud on the dressing table. Why was Iain home so early? Something must have happened, he must be annoyed, she thought, to have driven the car in like that.

'Meg! I'm home! Are you upstairs?'

She walked nervously to the top of the stairs and looked down at her husband's upturned, smiling face.

'I'm playing hooky,' he called, grinning at the phrase.

'Did you just walk out?' She shook her head slightly in amazement, watching him take off his coat.

'No. I was across at Easterton, and the meeting finished early so I thought I'd come home. No, don't come down – I'm coming up to change.'

He came up the stairs towards her, almost jaunty, and kissed her on the cheek. She waited as he went into his study to leave his briefcase, and then followed him into the bedroom.

'Shall I make you a cup of tea? And there are some scones, too.' She looked quickly at the dressing table to see if she had left crumbs to tell the tale of her earlier gluttony.

'Scones! You must have known I was coming home early!'

She grimaced slightly. 'Zoe phoned. They're supposed to be for the hospice coffee morning.'

'Oh dear! You've been dragooned, have you? Stay and talk to me. You look nice.'

He had hung the jacket of his suit on a clothes-hanger and was taking off his trousers. She sat on the bed, uncertain what to talk about and slightly unnerved at this change in their routine; it was strange to sit there and cold-bloodedly watch her husband change. His shirt hung down over his underpants and his legs were pale, scattered with dark hairs. She felt sudden, amused affection at the sight of him in his socks, and smiled.

Glancing into the mirror, he saw her smile. The unaccustomed view of her, the way the smile warmed, transformed the mirror image of her face, surprised and pleased him, so that he turned quickly and took her hand, pulling her gently upright towards him.

'Meg,' he said, 'let's go to bed.'

'What, now?'

Her startled response sprang into the air and she glanced briefly, helplessly at the bed, as though trying to assess the extent to which the lace bedspread would be crumpled. That glance chilled Iain's desire instantly, and for a moment he wished their lives were more spontaneous, less well ordered with everything in its proper place at the proper time. He pushed his hands gently into her hair, tucking it behind her ears.

'It's all right,' he said, 'it doesn't matter. Make me some tea instead.' He held her to him, for a moment, and kissed her flushed right ear lobe.

Margaret glanced up at his kind and battered-looking face.

'We can, if you like,' she said, even though she knew it was the wrong thing now to say, the wrong way to say it. But he merely smoothed her forehead with his thumbs, smoothing away the anxious lines, and went to the wardrobe to fetch his clothes. She saw her pearl stud on the dressing table and slipped it into her pocket.

'Did you see the crocuses everywhere? It made me think of that little rhyme, do you remember – "De spring has sprung"?'

'Yes.' Margaret tried to smile. '"De spring is sprung, de grass is riz—"'

'"I wonder where dem boidies is!"' they both chorused together, and laughed, and the awkwardness had disappeared.

* * *

When Iain came downstairs, wearing comfortable corduroy trousers and a flecked woollen pullover, there was a mug of tea waiting for him and a warmed scone. Margaret was slicing a lemon, her hair tucked back behind her ears; he noted the new symmetry of the pearl studs and wondered whether they were protection against impulsive kisses but, when he looked at her enquiringly, she said, 'It's to go with Ogen melon – there's a small one each. I was quite lucky to get them.'

'Sounds good.'

He visualised the olive-green and yellow warty surface of the fruits, their tops cut off to reveal soft yellow flesh, but the word associated itself with a picture, black and white that had turned blacker still. He imagined the photographic print, lying in developer, left too long, turning black, overdeveloping and blotted out. Margaret was still occupied in preparing salad, her hair swinging down across her cheeks.

'I'll just check that the latest film's all right,' he said, and went to his own well-stocked darkroom in the annexe to the rear of the kitchen. He unclipped the film that was hanging from the drying line and held it to the white light, examining critically the ribbon of black-and-white landscapes. He tried, for a moment, to imagine what it must be like to photograph people and Page Three girls, and shook his head wryly. He had enough to do with people and their difficulties in his work – inanimate objects were a blessed relief! The dry-stone wall with the dead holly bush looked as though it would print up well. Meg would like that one. He took the strip of film out into the kitchen to show her.

Chapter Three

Julian listened. This was one of the moments that he most enjoyed. He liked the rising tension, the constricted muscles stifling his breath, the pulsing of warm blood in his neck and temples. He breathed deeply several times and listened again for the familiar noises: scattered coughs, a chair scraping on the wooden floor, and the clang of a bow against a metal music stand. He tucked his violin under his arm and closed his eyes and imagined the next few minutes. He would sweep smoothly into the concert hall, almost gliding, twisting and bending his body lithely, swiftly, through the thicket of bows and stands. He would stand at the front, with the merest acknowledging smile for the applause, and then he would sit down and instantly plunge the Ensemble into the opening bars. This dream of the Entrance of the Star was usually able to sustain him until he was seated, until the music took over and displaced the present.

Today, though, he didn't seem to be able to pull the pictures into focus, perhaps because the inside of his head felt fuzzy and his neck muscles ached. He became aware that the silence in the hall had gone on too long, and he was still unable to put the images in place.

The rasp as his right foot scraped across the floor echoed repeatedly, magnified by the admirable acoustics of the renovated church. He bumped against a chair in the second desk and then sat down heavily on his seat at the front and lifted his right leg into a comfortable position with his hand.

The leader of the second violins gave him a quizzical look, but he ignored her and glowered briefly at the smattering of applause. Rosemary sighed to herself. She was never certain which was cause and which effect – the ill temper or the painful leg – but those days on which Our Leader's Leg (as she privately thought of it) was assigned a *dramatis persona* of its own were usually days on which she had to work very hard as mediator and mollifier. There had been ample time while she waited for Julian's entrance to survey the audience. It was, as she had expected, small, and that would not please Julian. There were the usual 'Kersland groupies', those middle-aged and retired ladies who came alone or in twos and threes to enjoy safely predictable music in pleasant surroundings, followed by a predictably tasty lunch. It was likely that many of them came rather for the company, to be able to watch the Kersland Ensemble and each other, and to enjoy the mellow Sunday ambience of the converted church: partly deaf, they were spectators. There were fewer of them today, but there were more young people, up there in the gallery. Music students, Rosemary guessed, who had come to listen critically, perhaps to sit with their eyes closed so that they could listen without the distraction of seeing – with the exception, perhaps, of that boy in the front row, who was resting what could only be a score on the balustrade in front of him. She wondered which piece he was going to follow, and sighed again, thinking of the potential difficulties that lay ahead and wishing it were all over and time for lunch. Perhaps she was getting too old for all this!

Julian stared coldly at the audience, indicating his wish for silence, then nodded to the harpsichord to sound an A. There was the usual brief, related cacophony of plucking and bowing and blowing, and then his bow beat crisply in the air to indicate the tempo, and they were off, into the short Bach sinfonia that was to set the mood.

The second work, by Hellendaal, was more unusual, and gave the violas and second violins a chance to shine. Unfortunately, the bassoon player was apparently so entranced at the principal viola's virtuosity that she missed her cue and came in late. Her cheeks turned pink and Julian swung in his seat and glared at her as he played, hoping that the audience hadn't heard the mistake; thus he didn't notice the young man in the balcony who straightened up and shook his head. Instead, as he turned back to his music, Julian was briefly distracted by a flash of yellow in the corner of his eye, as a large girl in the gallery flicked her long blonde hair behind her shoulders. Her mouth opened in an enormous yawn, that she didn't trouble to hide, presumably imagining herself unseen.

Isobel yawned again and impatiently pulled strands of hair from the corner of her mouth. She shifted her bottom on the bench and clapped a few times, perfunctorily.

'There's no such thing as a free lunch,' she whispered. 'We're paying the price for this one!'

David looked surprised, then smiled.

'Oh, I don't know. I'm quite enjoying it. Hey, did you see that woman playing the bassoon – she must have made a mistake, they were all grinning at her.'

'You didn't tell me he was lame, Dave. I wonder what's the matter.'

'Who? Oh, Kersland. I don't think I noticed.'

'You wouldn't!'

'Well, it was crowded, and everyone was standing around drinking. You don't notice people's legs in that situation. Why, do you want to go and examine him in the back room?'

Isobel smiled, looking sideways under half-lowered eyelids, and gripped David's leg, her fingers pressing his inner thigh. He jerked back on the bench but he managed not to shout, and his pale face crumpled in a grin of complicity as the pressure of Isobel's fingers crept up towards his crotch.

'Sssh! They're starting again,' Isobel whispered, staring down at Julian Kersland, who was poised like a puppeteer, bow raised and ready to jerk the waiting musicians into life. She could feel David's tenseness, his thigh pressed tightly against hers. She wished that they had stayed in bed. She surreptitiously slid her hand a little higher and David clasped it in his, trying to make it look as though they were merely holding hands. Isobel wished that they were sitting in the back row so that they would be unobserved if she seized David's hand and pushed it down inside her too-tight jeans. She squirmed, and swallowed, and David frowned and looked pointedly away.

Isobel made herself observe the hall instead – the curved white ceiling ornamented with plaster medallions depicting angels and roses and strangely interwoven garlands, the white walls contrasting with the dark wood of the pews and balustrade. Although it was midday, the grey, wintery light failed to excite the rich dark reds and blues of the windows, but the huge brass chandeliers sparked off their own reflections from the glass.

She hadn't been to a concert before and was not stirred by classical music. She had certainly never imagined that concerts could be like this – informal midday affairs, where people wore their normal everyday clothes and appeared to have wandered in off the streets, even to have brought their children. There was a family at the front of the gallery, near the group of students: the mother, frizzy henna-haired, had been reading the programme notes to the children, who could have been only eight and ten. She pointed out the instruments and occasionally nudged her daughter to indicate something special. ('Now watch the double bass, see how the oboes and bassoon answer each other; look how they're plucking strings, that's called pizzicato.') The father, bearded and in a baggy pullover, had found his own inner beat, his half-bald head shining irregularly as he moved it to some insistent rhythm that was all his own. Behind him, a digital watch bleeped the half-hour and its elderly owner checked the time, then took out his diary to study the world map. Isobel could see the blocks of colour, pastel blue and pink and green, in great detail; late-night parties in Australia, with Vegemite sandwiches and Fosters lager, breakfast in New York, with blueberry pancakes, melon and hot Danish, Sunday lunch in Britain, with a lame violinist playing to rumbling stomachs and fidgeting children.

She could still be wallowing under her duvet in her bedsit, pushing David out of bed to put the kettle on for coffee. They could both be lolling around reading the papers and listening to her tapes. But David had been given tickets for this concert by the Professor of Biochemistry, who had thought, mistakenly, that David was acquainted with Julian Kersland. It was true that David had met Kersland for perhaps two minutes at a party at Professor Smith's house, one of those gatherings of apparently randomly collected individuals with a range of age and status and background for which his research supervisor was notorious. David had been pleased to meet a non-academic who was well known, and he had wanted to talk more but had not known what to say, and Kersland had instead been captured by a confident woman with silver hair.

Now Isobel stared down at the small orchestra and watched how Kersland kept them together, accelerated or slowed them down, encouraged them to play louder or more softly; how he made them pause as though for a comma in a sentence read out loud, then resume again in unison. Suddenly she became aware that the music was not just background noise for wandering thoughts. She winced at the howling discords, and then looked at the programme notes in surprise. Farina? *Cats?* She grinned and looked down again at the orchestra; the players were grinning, too – and the students at the front were sitting forward and glancing at an open book. When the piece ended she took her hand away from Dave and clapped enthusiastically.

Julian had noticed the students' critical interest in the Farina. That's presumably what they've come here for, he reflected, something unusual in the baroque repertoire. It had woken up the rest of the audience, too – briefly. And now back to sleep with Bach. Those students won't come again, either.

His irritation simmered to the surface once more, and he had to force himself to smile and bow to the applause as he turned to acknowledge the skills of the semicircular group of musicians. At the end, careless in his haste to lead out, he caught his right knee against his chair.

'Shit!' he exclaimed, and it was fortunate that his face was turned towards the vestry door.

'The Führer's out for blood,' an oboist muttered to one of the violas in the vestry. They kept their backs to Julian as they cleaned and stowed away their instruments with the spare, practised movements of itinerant musicians.

'Oh no! That's going to be a big mistake! Look at that!' the viola player said softly.

They watched surreptitiously. Julian, standing by his open instrument case, was wrapping his violin in its soft old Paisley shawl, ignoring everyone, but the bassoon player, holding her instrument across her chest as though for protection, had gone to stand beside him. Her face was pink and shiny.

'I'm sorry, Julian,' she said. 'I just . . .'

He stared at her for a moment.

'If you kept your mind on the job instead of smirking across at –' he'd been going to say 'your boyfriend' but he caught himself just in time '– at the violas, you'd be a bloody sight more use to us.'

He jabbed the heel of his bow in her direction so that she stepped back quickly, shocked. The girl's husband looked bemused as he packed away his cello; her viola player busied himself with strapping up his case. Rosemary, as usual, was instantly there, seemed to have been there all the time, interposing her comfortable, firm figure between the swordsman and his prey.

'I don't suppose anyone realised, dear,' she comforted the girl. 'And if anyone did notice, they'll have forgotten it by now.'

'There was nobody much *there* to notice, was there?' Julian attacked her as though the sparse audience were her fault.

'There were some new faces today.' Rosemary was patient. 'It's good to see some young people, there were quite a few in the gallery. They'll probably come back.'

'And most of the regulars were here – perhaps they'll bring some friends next time,' someone else chipped in, and added under his breath, 'to hear the menagerie!'

'Yes. With an average age of sixty-two and not the slightest bit of musical imagination amongst them.'

'Julian, that's quite unfair! It's unlike you to be so condemnatory.' Rosemary's tone was firm, even though she knew such judgements were fairly typical.

Julian snorted and turned away to finish packing up.

'Did you see that old guy at the back, reading his paper?' the oboist whispered to the viola player. 'I hope the boss didn't see that or he'll get really constipated! Ah well, I'm off – I've got a date to do the Bach oboe on Wednesday, but I'll see you Thursday as usual.'

The others were ready now; they were used to Julian's outbursts and knew he would calm down, that Rosemary would cope. They began to chat, to exchange remarks about the weather, gardening and Sunday afternoon plans, and to drift out of the doors. The bassoon player alone was silent, and she left protected by the bulk of her unimaginative husband and his cello.

'Are you coming down to lunch?' Rosemary asked, as she sorted the music into piles. Julian was sitting on a bench, absently feeling his knee and staring across the room.

'No. I can't face it.'

'Come on, come with me. You look as though you need some food.'

She smiled at him. Julian often found it irritating, the way Rosemary reduced his emotional states to mere by-products of physical needs.

'Some of the groupies are here. That'll cheer you up!' She stood in front of him, half teasing, cajoling, wanting him to be a normal, tolerant and tolerable human being. 'Come on, dear leader. I don't want to eat on my own.'

Julian sighed, not entirely mollified; he felt tired and drained after his admittedly childish outburst, and his knee was aching where he had banged it, but there was nothing at home that he could be bothered to eat. He felt ashamed of himself, and sorry for himself, and suddenly he just wanted to put his arms out and rest his head against the firm, asexual shelf of Rosemary's bosom, and have her comfort him like a child. For a second, the need must have been reflected in his face, because Rosemary had to stop herself from stroking his hair and touching his forehead to see if he had a fever, as though they were both twenty-five years younger, and she was a mother comforting a child.

'You're the only one that cares,' said Julian, and the hint of self-pity, rather than praise for what was undeniably her great attribute, her good-humoured patience, restored her to brusque practicality and a hint of laughter.

'Come on, Julian,' she said. 'You can mingle sociably and I'll get your food. You can jolly well pay for your own, though.'

'None of us will be able to buy a crust if the audiences stay this small,' he grumbled, but he stood up, grunting, and followed her across the hall.

There were still a few people standing near the entrance, chatting and tying on woollen headscarves, adjusting gloves or umbrellas, and one or two people smiled vaguely in Julian's direction as he and Rosemary went towards the crypt.

The stone steps were worn and scooped, narrow triangles spiralling clockwise, so that he found it difficult to position his foot. He slipped slightly and had to grab the rail. At the bottom, an elderly man and woman stood back to give him exaggerated space for his descent. They smiled and nodded politely, and he saw the concern in their faces, and didn't want them to speak. But Rosemary was there, greeting the couple as she passed, and leading Julian to the restaurant door.

The room's low ceiling trapped the warm, damp smells of cooking and of people in outdoor clothes – garlic, and cooked cheese, coffee, tweed coats and talcum powder – and the clatter of plates and cutlery and the buzz of conversation mingled and were inseparable from the smells. Already, most tables were occupied or at least claimed for future use by outspread coats or hats or programmes. There was still a queue, moving slowly past the counters where deep quiches, terrines, cold meats and glass bowls of unusual, often unidentifiable, mixtures of fruits, vegetables and cheese offered themselves as colourful salads.

'Morning! Interesting menu you had for us today!'

The balding, bearded man beamed cheerfully, his glasses misted with enthusiasm, or perhaps merely dirt, and Julian realised the man was talking to him, commenting apparently about the music programme, not about the mounds of mixed beans and grated carrot and spinach quiche that almost hid his plate.

'I'm glad you liked it. We'd begun to feel we had all become a little too stereotyped. It's good for us all, audience included, to be shaken out of our Sunday somnolence now and again, don't you agree?'

The man's wife nodded vigorously, and restrained her son from making music with his knife against his glass of water.

'It's encouraging to see that you're bringing up your

children to appreciate classical music. Your son seems to have been inspired.'

'Oh yes!' The woman's anxious, earnest face lit up. 'He's really into music-making, aren't you, Timmy? We've got boxes of instruments that we've made at home, drums, rattles, a whole range of—'

'Wonderful! How exciting! I'm sure he'll be starting on the marimba soon.'

'Oh well, actually we'd been wondering about the violin . . .'

'Good to talk to you. I do hope we'll see you all again next time. Do excuse me, won't you?' And Julian briefly smiled his charming smile, focusing it on the woman, easily resisting the urge to pat the boy on the head, and moved away.

He felt like a vicar greeting his Sunday flock, offering encouragement to newcomers and a few words of greeting to the faithful. There was one of the faithful, two tables away, waiting rather tensely for her food. Her gloves were laid possessively on one chair, her handbag on another, and she was looking towards her friends in the queue, shaking her head, mouthing words around her nervous smile.

'No. No lettuce.'

Julian made his way towards her, lurching clumsily between the tables, and Rosemary, who was simultaneously filling two plates, talking to the couple behind the counter, and observing the eating audience, caught his eye and smiled complicitly.

'Good afternoon, Mrs . . . er . . . how very nice to see you and your friends.'

The woman jumped slightly, and turned towards him, flustered.

'Oh, Mr Kersland! I'm sorry, I—'

'Did you enjoy Carlo's cats? You look like a person who is fond of cats!'

'Oh dear, well, it was a bit of a *surprise*, Mr Kersland. But very clever. Most unusual . . .' Her fingers waved above the table and came together in an anxious clasp. 'We're all very fond of that Bach suite, though. I'm really glad you included that.'

Julian felt as though those delicate, bony hands had prodded him in the chest, but he continued smiling into her elderly kind face, which was framed by waved white hair and a rather daring dark blue beret.

'I'm sorry to have surprised you. But now you can relax over your nice lunch, which I see your kind friends are bringing you. Telemann and Vivaldi – a Vivaldi violin concerto – next time. And I shall look for you in the audience!' He leant forward, breathing in her dusty smell of age and cleanliness and Chanel No. 5, and gently touched a blue and silver butterfly brooch on her lapel. 'What a very attractive brooch. The blue matches your eyes!'

He smiled warmly into them, gratified to see her lined, sallow face flush pink at his close attention. He rested his hand briefly on her shoulder as he said goodbye, and nodded across the room to Rosemary, who indicated that his food was ready. If he moved quickly, he'd avoid those students who were sneering at him from their shared plate of food.

His hip knocked against an umbrella that was hanging on the back of a chair, and he saw that it belonged to the blonde girl with the yawn and wayward hair. As she bent down to retrieve the umbrella he wondered that she didn't overbalance; a pity *she* isn't wearing a brooch, he thought. I wouldn't mind patting that lapel. But her boyfriend was staring at him with a strangely intent look, and he hastened by, towards his lunch and safety.

Isobel watched Julian's legs go by, then she straightened up awkwardly, her face red with the effort of scrabbling for the umbrella beneath her chair. She made a face and wiped the soup off the ends of her hair with a paper napkin, and adjusted her blouse. For a moment she had thought that creepy cripple had been going to insert his ever-so-sensitive musical fingers inside her cleavage. Poor David had looked like a puppy waiting expectantly for a biscuit as Kersland had come towards them. She had watched David sit up, ready to acknowledge his acquaintance, but the violinist hadn't even recognised him, too busy trying to charm old ladies and avoid the music students. She had heard the students whispering, seen their nudges and oblique, knowing looks as Kersland fingered that old dear. The one with the book and the black cap didn't seem to think much of the music either, as far as Isobel could tell. What *was* wrong with Kersland's leg? She wished she could ask, and look it up when she got home.

'Dave!' She slid her foot across and hooked it round his ankle. 'Don't look so sad! These musicians are terribly Important People, love. We can't expect them to remember mere mortals. What do you think this green stuff is in this soup? It looks like sputum to me.'

'Ugh!' David's face screwed up. 'Medics are so disgusting.'

They finished their meal quickly, bored with the sounds of elderly ladies, and David took back their trays while Isobel put on her coat. She watched with mild surprise as the boy with the small black cap and the white but handsome face, who had earlier seemed so critical, walked over to where Kersland was still eating and said, with the brave familiarity of youth, 'Great concert, Julian. The Farina was really cool . . .'

Chapter Four

The terraced house in which Isobel lived was in a less prosperous street than Julian Kersland's. Its peeling paint and the crumbling sandstone parapet above the bay window were fairly typical of the area and if one walked past at night, when the lights were on and the curtains were still open, it was possible to see that the large ground-floor reception room of Victorian times had been divided vertically and horizontally to create several of the sixteen bedsits whose black-and-white plastic bell pushes glowed faintly orange by the door: an ornate cornice bisected by a wall, a bed-balcony above a tiny kitchen and, a sign of multi-occupancy everywhere, overflowing dustbins and several padlocked bicycles in the paved front garden.

Isobel lived right at the top of the house, in a low-ceilinged room that might once have been a temporary home for two maids. It was mid-morning, and she had already been working for four hours, seated at the table by the window but occasionally getting up to stretch and pace around the room. Her table was covered with an assortment of scribbled pages of filepaper, screwed-up tissues and used coffee mugs; the medical textbooks and files of notes were piled on the floor and on the unmade bed, several sprouting torn white paper markers like Buddhist prayer flags.

Her back ached and her eyes felt bleary. I've got to have a break, she thought, there's no point panicking. Tidy up, have a bath! She stood up and stretched, and wrinkled her nose at

35

the stale, stuffy smell of the room. The small sash window was crooked and swollen with damp, but she thumped on the horizontal bar with the edge of a textbook until it came unstuck and the window grudgingly slid down a couple of inches. The gust of cold air made the paper globe around the ceiling light swing, so that a dead fly and matted grey dust drifted down on to her chair. 'Oh God, this room is a mess. *I'm* a mess, bleah, feel that greasy hair, oily nose, spot on my chin. What a sight! Bloody books, always in the way. Bloody exams, anyway.' Muttering to herself, *enjoying* muttering to herself, Isobel stacked the books and files into careful piles, made the bed, washed up the mugs and filled the kettle at the basin that, by some miraculous network of noisy pipes, was provided in every room. Need more teabags, need to go to the launderette, need more filepaper, need a bath and need to wash my hair! Ugh!

She opened the door and went to the top of the stairs. The door of the bathroom below was ajar so she should seize her chance. Quickly she gathered up her towel, shampoo, sponge bag and a mug of tea and – just remembering her key before she slammed the door – hurried down to occupy the bath. It was filthy, as usual; the tides, neaps and springs, were marked by an adherent sticky slick of flotsam, and a pubic hair lay coiled at one side of the plughole. As usual, there was no cloth and the tin of cleaner was empty. Improvise, Isobel, or you'll come out dirtier than you went in, she murmured. But the wadded toilet paper that she smeared with soap merely disintegrated as she rubbed, and threatened to block up the drain, so she had to be content with swilling the bath with hot water and shampoo before she let it fill.

At least the water was hot! She bent her knees and let her body slip down so that her hair was beneath the water. Bubbles sang past her ears as the trapped air escaped to the surface, and blonde fronds floated around her face. It took two more submergings to shampoo and rinse her hair, and the water was soon milky with herb-scented bubbles. She took a gulp of cold tea and then half stood and threw the slops into the toilet. Now came the difficult part, mixing clean hot and cold water in the mug to rinse her hair, not too hot and not too cold. If only there were a shower. She soaped herself and shaved her armpits, then ran in more hot water so that steam rose and condensed on the cold tap and the shiny yellow walls. Her breasts were pink with heat, and buoyant. 'Take the weight off your breasts, dear!' 'Give your breasts a rest!' It was a family failing; she and her mother and her sister had a total circumference of nine-and-a-half feet, almost the length of a British Leyland Mini, as her father never failed to point out. Her breasts embarrassed her; and with her blonde hair and occasional apparently vacant expression – when her mind had not vacated her body at all, but had in fact withdrawn to puzzle on more complex matters, to leave her features smooth and her eyes unregistering of external affairs – she knew her intelligence was frequently underrated, more usually unacknowledged. She was slotted into the pigeonhole of 'dumb blonde', more lately 'bimbo', 'more boobs than brain', and could therefore be treated accordingly. After all, you didn't expect a woman to have brains. Even the undeniably intelligent women like that lecturer in Physiology, nice-looking, too, were the victims of disparaging colleagues. 'She was only appointed because of her cleavage,' Isobel had heard one of the lecturers say. And the man he was talking to had *laughed*! Isobel had buttoned up the front of her lab coat and thereafter tried to keep a low profile, to work quietly and efficiently without drawing too much attention to herself.

She worked hard. At school, it had become obvious to her and to her teachers that her academic strength lay in the sciences; moreover, she was practical, a gift not possessed by every practising scientist, and she enjoyed the atmosphere and the organisation of the laboratory. But she was badly advised. And there were so few precedents: the school sent so few pupils to university that an academic career was not an accepted path to follow, either in her family or in the community. So her parents, slightly bewildered, supported the school's suggestion that she go to the local college and learn to improve her technical skills.

It was difficult now, looking back, to know whether the years had been wasted or not. If she hadn't become a medical laboratory technician, she would never have had the stimulus or the courage to want to become a doctor; she would not have had (briefly, until her time for study became too precious) a medical student as a boyfriend and been able to listen to his conversations or, at first, to riffle through, then later to delve into his textbooks. She became proficient at routine preparation and histology of suspected pathological tissue and she was interested in the reasons for the pathological change, the name and cause of the disease. Her interest was appreciated and, more importantly, encouraged by more senior members in the rigid hierarchy, and so she was gradually moved sideways and upwards to learn and understand new techniques. Her name appeared (at the end of a list of five or six contributors) on posters she had herself helped prepare to explain the group's work-in-progress at several conferences. Many of the senior staff were medically qualified; in her job and social life she came frequently into contact with medical students and junior hospital doctors. Wearing a clean white coat, she could go almost anywhere. There was nothing very *special* about medics, after all.

She had been working in the darkroom, scanning slides of fixed, preserved cells using ordinary bright light, then ultraviolet. Her eyes were tired from staring down the microscope and the room was warm, but she moved the slide, focused on a clump of cells then switched the filter to UV. A pattern of bright fluorescing dots, an instant constellation, dazzled her eyes. A positive! The fluorescently tagged antibody had combined, the cells were positive. And pride in her achievement, in her own understanding of the rationale behind this test, of the results and consequences of this test, suddenly thrilled her. She even knew what the owner of these cells would be prescribed: these cells had been derived from a human body, the body of a real, living person. She wanted to be able to see the whole person, to understand and perhaps to try to control, or at least ameliorate, what was happening to that person's body. As Isobel switched off the lamp, and turned on the room light and wrote her notes, she was suddenly convinced that she could do it, if she had the chance. She would make the chance, she was confident that she could make it happen.

It turned out that the decision had been the easiest step in the process. She hadn't then understood about student quotas and mature students and student grants, or the necessity of obtaining top grades in certain subjects. But no, the years had not been wasted. The experience had taught her to be thrifty with her income (to help pay her fees) and to work with great concentration even when she was already tired. And if, at twenty-four, she was several years older than the other second-year medics, well – she had Dave.

They had met at a MedSoc Burns Night dance. She had physically assaulted him during an eightsome reel, when her hands, slippery with the heat, had become detached from her partner's as they swung each other in a tight circle. She'd left the orbit of her eight on a trajectory that had coincided, heavily, with David's. He said later that the impact had registered on the seismograph in the Geology department, but perhaps that was merely his own anthropocentric interpretation.

'Christ! Are you all right?'

David's tall, thin body had buckled under the impact, but he had kept his feet and now found himself holding a dishevelled, half-laughing, half-crying human cannonball.

'I don't know. I think I've ruptured my spleen. Did I kill you, too?'

Isobel's depleted eightsome were calling urgently for her to return, but she shook her head.

'I can't. Oh, I need a drink!' She looked up at her victim and liked the appearance of his hot, slightly anxious face. 'At least let me get you a drink as an apology. Please, I'd like to. I'm Isobel Hutchison, by the way.'

'OK, thanks. I'm Dave MacIlvanney.'

They took their lagers and moved to safer, cooler quarters outside the door. Isobel held the cold, moisture-beaded glass against her burning cheeks; sweat trickled down her back.

'Are you a medic, too?'

'Not likely! I'm a biochemistry postgrad. Are *you* a medic, then? I thought maybe . . .' He shrugged, suddenly realising what he was about to say.

'That I was someone else's guest, maybe? Actually, I'm a mature student. Received the call a bit late in life, but at least it stopped me blundering around in the wilderness!'

'You must be good, then. I thought they hardly ever took any oldies.' He grinned.

'Well, they took me. I had to go to night classes, and I mostly finance myself.'

'You should have let me buy the drinks, then – or are you rich?'

'I'm an Easton Scholar, isn't it grand? A beneficiary of Dr Easton's benefice!'

'Full of Easton promise.'

Isobel snorted and grinned.

'Sorry. Bad pun.' David had rather surprised himself. 'What's an Easton scholar, then? Sounds posh.'

'Local girl makes good. He was the minister of our village church in the nineteenth century and left a load of money in a social fund. I have to "improve myself with the aim of benefiting others". The trustees don't have many suitable candidates, so they were quite glad when I applied. I hope what I did to you won't be counted against me.'

'It's fine, Dr Easton.' Dave raised his glass and looked upwards at the ceiling. 'We're fine down here. I'm already benefiting greatly.'

He had surprised himself again; he thought he was becoming rather witty. Isobel might be quite good company, once she relaxed a bit; that had been quite some impact, though.

'Listen! They're playing something a bit quieter. Would you like to dance?'

Isobel would, she decided, very much. David seemed quite fun, in a surprised sort of way. He was nearer her age, too; she was bored with the raucous, coarse humour of the medics, and they were all so young. Also, it was good to dance with someone tall, and she had no objection when David put his hand on the small of her back, even though that point of contact became warm and clammy, and pulled her body as close as her generous bust would permit. He walked her home, and they had talked and laughed and become easier in each other's company. She had not asked him in because her wariness about motives was still too deeply embedded, but there had been no fumblings or squeezings; yet there had been enough excitement and the promise of lust in their kisses to convince her that this relationship might develop into something good.

That had been a year ago. Their relationship was good, and comfortably casual, each sure of the other, sure enough now to know that they need not see each other every day or night. David shared a flat with two other postgraduates. It was undeniably more convenient and comfortable than Isobel's bedsit – there was a shower, that worked; no more scooping water in mugs to clean one's hair – but there was also a resident landlady on the floor below. And Isobel felt that she herself intruded on the privacy of the flatmates. They felt they had to modify their behaviour, however slightly, when she was there. David frequently stayed here, instead, in her bedsit, despite the lack of space for two people and the medical texts.

Isobel pulled a face as she thought of the cluttered room upstairs. She picked at the chainless plug with her fingernails, wishing, as always, that she had remembered to bring a knife, and she stood up in the bath to dry her hair and back, the floor reminding her of athlete's foot and verrucas.

'Izzy, are you there?'

The tap on the door, the muttered question, made her jerk in surprise, so that she almost slipped.

'David!'

'Can I have the key? I'll wait upstairs.'

'Oh, hang on. I'm still in the bath!'

She was startled and flustered, and didn't want to let him in. The bath was still scummy with froth and hair, and her underclothes, piled on the floor, looked, well – used. But she wrapped the towel around herself and leant forward to open the door.

'Quick! The key's there on the floor. Don't open the door so wide!'

'How can you breathe in here? It's like a sauna. Have you been steam-cleaned? Hurry up, we're supposed to be meeting the others in the pub for lunch.'

'Oh, Dave! What others? I thought we were going to have a quiet lunch. I've been working all morning.' For a moment she was quite upset.

'You need a break. Please,' he wheedled, 'then we'll come back here. I've got some reading to do and I can do it while you work. Hey, give me a cuddle!'

'All right!' Isobel bent down to kiss him and her wet hair flopped forwards around his face. 'There! And you needn't pretend your hands need drying on my towel!'

David laughed and picked up the key.

'I suppose your room's a pigsty, as usual?'

'Don't you touch a thing! I'll be up in a minute.'

* * *

On their way out, Isobel searched through the pile of circulars and free newspapers that were piled on the floor inside the front door.

'No discount tokens or special offers. Pity!' A narrow handbill with a red border caught her eye. 'Look! The Kersland Ensemble. There's another of their concerts today. We've missed it though.'

David laughed. 'The Prof asked me if we'd liked it. Do you know, he admitted that his wife had bought the tickets and then they couldn't face it. And I thought he was doing us a favour!'

'The food was all right, though. I don't mind free tickets that include lunch.'

'No. Oh, by the way, I asked him about Kersland's leg – you remember you were being nosy about it? Apparently he had some sort of accident when he was young. He was helping someone who was in trouble and got hurt himself, or something like that. The Prof didn't know any details, but thought it was something vaguely heroic.'

'Did you notice he banged his knee against the chair when he was going out? I forgot to mention it then. He said, "Shit!" It was quite obvious. He's rather good-looking, though, quite interesting. Why are you walking like that?'

'I'm being *interesting*. Interesting, handsome cripple, that's me. And almost a PhD, too!'

Chapter Five

These staccato, almost rough, scrubbing notes were not what he wanted to play; even as he started on the Mozart sonata, Julian was dissatisfied. Technically demanding, yes, good for bow control, precision, but not what he wanted this morning. He skipped to the second movement, enjoying instead the delicate, pianissimo legato, the lightest of caresses into which his fingers poured a flood of notes. *There* was the challenge, *that* was what he had been seeking: the emotion that could only be hinted at, in a whisper. There was none of the lush obviousness of, for example, Brahms, about this music; he knew that the feeling had to be sought within himself and somehow transferred from his mind into a physical act that would in turn reach out and transform the minds and mood of the listener.

Except that there was no listener, and he delighted in filling his own room with sound, for himself alone. There would be a pupil at lunchtime (a girl who rushed across from her independent school, hurriedly eating her sandwiches as she walked and arriving warm and crumb-spattered to play with earnest competence) and there were several pupils to come in the late afternoon and early evening, but otherwise he was free to play whatever he chose.

Julian supposed that he was fortunate to have this freedom. He had no financial worries, he was a man of private means with a comfortable 'financial cushion' that could be relied upon to support his bodily needs and his surroundings, like the

45

albumen that cushions the chick within the egg. There was no question that his parents would not provide for him when necessary: it was an assumption that required no discussion. His mother, who was French and had a considerable income of her own, was elegant and disciplined, a charming and energetic woman who had been a great help to her husband during his years in the Scottish Office. It was from his mother that Julian had inherited the narrow nose, thin bony fingers, and thick, dark hair. When he was young he had, too, her energy, in its youthful, undisciplined form. But after his accident that energy had been transmuted into an irritability that had struggled to find a positive outlet. His life was divided into before and after the accident, which was the way it was always referred to, and when he was younger he had privately enumerated the weeks, then months, then years, with the suffix BJA or AJA. Now, in his early thirties, he no longer remembered or recognised his young, intact self.

He was a fluent French speaker, if not bilingual. His mother had ensured that right from babyhood, switching from one language to the other within a conversation, and she had frequently taken him, and later sent him, to visit her family. It had always been his parents' intention that he should spend a year doing the modern equivalent of the grand tour, visiting their friends and colleagues around Europe and learning at first hand how Europe worked. This would be followed, of course, by university, to read Law, and the natural progression upwards through the Diplomatic Service in which, with his fluency in French and German and his understanding of who makes things work and how, he should easily reach the upper echelons in Brussels. Julian's future was planned out in his parents' minds.

But the aftermath of his accident had altered that. It was not until nearly two years after the accident that it had become clear what Julian intended to do with his life. The intention astonished and worried his parents, because the path he wanted to follow was so alien to them, so mystifying, and so devoid of informed or influential acquaintances, that they felt themselves redundant and bereft of their ideals. It had always, however, been assumed that he would share in and inherit their wealth and material possessions; now the unspoken assumption was that he would need a larger share, and earlier. Indeed, once she had become used to the idea, Mrs Kersland rather enjoyed the novelty of having a son who was a music student, a would-be concert violinist. She imagined him in the future, elegant in black and white, bowing to the packed concert hall at the end of a dazzling performance of – oh, something powerful and romantic, the Beethoven, say, or the Tchaikovsky – and she imagined how her warm maternal pride would flow out towards him – for, despite the cool efficiency with which she normally treated her son, she cared very much about him and had been privately and deeply unhappy that the path his life would take had had to be revised so completely. She also acknowledged to herself the other, realistic image of him, where he stood awkwardly and lopsided upon the platform.

So she had helped him, later, to find and buy an easily accessible ground-floor flat with a space to park his converted car, and she and her husband provided a source of income, which was augmented by his earnings from teaching and from the Ensemble's concerts and recordings.

The Ensemble had actually been Rosemary's idea. She had long had an interest in baroque music and she knew a little about Julian's background. She was acquainted with his mother and, initially together, and then with Julian's increasingly dominant help, they had put together a plan for the creation of a baroque chamber orchestra. Rosemary hadn't minded that it had become the Kersland Ensemble: he was the star player, he had the charisma. She felt happy and fortunate – she had an important role in the orchestra, and she could play as much baroque music as she liked in a professional capacity.

Julian, too, was fortunate. Unlike most members of the Ensemble, he could spend his mornings doing as he wished instead of driving round the region as a peripatetic music teacher, or spending today and every day teaching in the same school, or working in an office, or even, as in one case, in a university laboratory. Two of the group had full-time employment with the opera orchestra, but the Ensemble suited them because it gave them a chance to play baroque music on period instruments, although their free time was short and their schedule often erratic.

At first the diverse backgrounds of the musicians had worried Julian. The Ensemble seemed to be such a precarious structure, so small and fragile, that any absence or dissension would cause it to collapse; but the unusual nature of their concerts, both in the content and the ambience, had quickly brought acclaim and, with that, a feeling of unity within the group. He knew that the others were quite often united against him, but he knew, too, that that in itself created a different kind of bonding, and his confidence in his group's survival, and in his own survival as their leader and director, had increased. For he was sufficiently cynical and realistic to know that he imparted a very distinctive stamp upon the Ensemble.

He sorted through the rows of music on the shelves, searching for a particular Mozart concerto. He knew he ought to be working on the soloist's part for the Bach violin and viola concerto that they were to play next month, but he was still in need of subtlety rather than precision. He propped the music on the movable arm of the mahogany reading stand that he preferred to use instead of the flimsily treacherous metal music stands, and sat down to play.

After a few moments an almost forgotten sensation began to creep over him. This is it! The thrill of recognition was tight inside him. The creature was back, taking him over; not an

48

intrinsic part of himself, but a creature apart, invading, almost as an alien, uncoiling within him, expanding . . . gently, softly, achingly. His body was poised, his fingers feather-light; he closed his eyes because the black notes, the room, were an intrusion.

The only thing that was important was the emotion, that had to be sought for within himself, and that was only rarely found, but was now *there*.

It *was* there, it had returned, all-pervasive, embodying perfection, demanding worship . . . liberating, transcending . . . for the spiritual enrichment of others: the *meaning*.

Julian played. He played without seeming to do so. He felt disembodied, a spectator, and a great, undescribed joy – indescribable even to himself, because he *was* that joy – filled him. As he played, his leg ached and throbbed, but the pain was itself a part of that joy.

'MORNING, JULIAN!'

Mrs Knight partly opened the music room door and called, in not quite a shout, 'It's only me!'

Out of the corner of his eye, Julian saw the door begin to open and his gut clenched with fear. In the instant of Mrs Knight's greeting he jerked violently upwards, so that the neck of his violin caught the heavy reading stand with a clattering jolt that jarred his neck.

'Aagh!'

He grunted with fear and pain.

Mrs Knight's truncated head appeared around the door, and her eyes and mouth were wide.

'What's happened? What did you do?'

'Don't . . .' Julian could hardly speak. He gulped. 'Don't ever do that again!'

'I was only letting you know I was here. I'm doing extra today, you must have forgotten. Because I didn't do last Friday. I did tell you.' She was unrepentant, accusing.

'No!' Julian put down the bow and stood up quickly,

holding his violin tightly by the neck. His loss was so great, the pain so acute, that he thought he was about to cry. He had found it again, he had been – flying! And she had banged in and—

'No what?'

'No. I don't want you here. I can't stand it. I can't stand the noise . . . the interruptions!' He moved towards her, becoming angrier and more determined as he regained his breath. 'The *hassle*! There's no peace. I have to . . . to *work*!'

Mrs Knight had opened the door wider. She watched Julian's advance and her expression turned from self-righteous justification to hardened belligerence. Who did this laddie think he was to order her around? Spoilt kid! He'd been a difficult one from the start, anyway, always going on about the bog and the bleach.

'Work, you call it! Nothing but play as I see it. Playtime all the time. Well, I can't stand it either, Julian. Always carrying on about the oven and the toilet. It's not what I'm used to, I can tell you. That's it then, Julian. I only took you on as a favour to Zoe. No more, my lad. I'm done!'

'You can leave the keys.'

'That's exactly what I'm doing.' She stumped into the kitchen, and he heard the keys clatter on to the table and a drawer open, then slam shut. 'These are my dusters. And I'll be needing paid for Friday.'

She stood back and waited while Julian pushed past to fetch his wallet, erratic in his haste so that he banged his shoulder against the doorframe.

'Here! That's for two weeks.' He was reckless, pushing the money into her hand, ready to shove her from the flat.

'That's small thanks, if I may say so, Julian, for all I've done for you. But I suppose I might have expected that!' Unhurriedly, Mrs Knight tucked the money away in her purse, which she then replaced in her tapestry-covered bag. 'But there you are, you see, that's what you get for trying to come and do a little extra. Lucky I only do you as a favour, Julian, or I'd be having to worry about my rent.'

With great dignity she adjusted her headscarf and went to the door. Throughout the business in the hallway she had avoided looking at Julian directly, but now she turned and looked at him calmly.

'Go on then, back to your playing.' She paused, for dramatic effect. 'Goodbye!' she said, and left, closing the door softly so that the tone of her departure was quietly aggrieved: she was walking out of his life for ever.

Julian went back to his bedroom to fetch his violin. He sat down on the bed because he suddenly felt slightly sick and clammy. His hands were shaking, and he squeezed them together between his thighs, waiting for his heartbeat to return to normal. It had all happened so quickly, he thought he must be suffering from shock. A few moments ago he had been possessed, and yet, it seemed, all-powerful – then suddenly he had been assaulted by his own violin and the doorframe, and had sacked his one-and-only cleaning lady. She'd even taken the dusters – he'd have to use his dirty shirt.

He couldn't help it, he started to laugh; the picture of himself hobbling around the flat with a balled-up shirt, patting ineffectually at the shelves and the top of the piano, was too absurd. It doesn't matter, he thought, I'll manage. There's no one else here. I'm free! He tried an experimental 'Yahoo!' still laughing hysterically, and then another, louder.

'YAHOO! FREEDOM! *LIBERTÉ! UHURU!'*

There'd be no more intrusions, no more vacuum cleaners, caterpillar tracks or questions about cups of tea. He could leave private documents lying around in here or in the kitchen. He might even clean the oven – once a year. No slovenliness, though; he could cope on his own. He should do something to celebrate, tip brandy in his mid-morning coffee and leave the bottle on the kitchen table in full view. *His* full view! No one else's.

But he felt drained. It was too much effort and, without even questioning what he was doing, what he was hiding from, he stretched out on the bed, pulled the duvet around himself, and fell asleep.

The doorbell woke him. For a moment he didn't understand that it was late morning and that he had, for some unaccountable reason, been asleep. He was cold and disorientated. His leg felt strangely, deeply, bruised, almost with a memory of a bruise; a memory. A memory of a doorbell? He looked at the clock: it was too early for his lunchtime pupil. It must be Mrs Knight, come back to collect the bleach – or to apologise. Well, let her ring! He stood up and went into the bathroom to scoop cold water on to his face. The bell rang again and, dabbing his face with a towel, Julian went cautiously into the music room, hoping to catch a glimpse of her retreat. Footsteps – well-heeled footsteps, not the pad of rubber soles – tip-tapped down the steps and Julian moved hurriedly into the bay. Rosemary! He knocked on the window and waved the towel to catch her attention. She looked up and smiled and raised an eyebrow, pointing interrogatively towards the door.

'Yes, come on in,' Julian mouthed, and beckoned.

It would be good to talk to Rosemary. There was something very reassuring about her.

'I decided you weren't in. Did I get you out of the bath?' she asked, as she let him hobble in front of her along the hall.

'Oh, no, I was just washing my face. This is a nice surprise, though. What brings you up here?'

'Just some odds and ends of business. And I wanted to walk around the Botanic Gardens – do you know, the daffodils are out now? And I thought, well, I'll drop in and see how Julian is.'

'Here, let me take your coat. What will you have to drink? There's some new Colombian coffee I'm trying out.'

'Just tea, thank you, dear – black, with lemon, if you've got it.'

Rosemary waited while Julian hung up her coat, and then followed him into the kitchen. Her smile had gone and her face sagged into sad, downward-leading lines. Julian, turning to pick up the kettle, saw the momentary slump in her features and thought, almost with irritation, that she was suddenly getting old. His mother was older than Rosemary, and yet she still looked superb. But then Rosemary was smiling again, asking him the name of the plants on the kitchen windowsill, commenting how nice and bright the kitchen looked.

'Shall we sit in here or go into the music room?'

'I would just love to sit down on a comfortable chair, dear. To tell you the truth I've done a lot of walking this morning. Shall I carry the tray for you?'

'Thanks. You go on through. I'll just get my fiddle. I left it in the bedroom.'

'Was it asleep?' she laughed.

'No. But I was. It was quite strange really. I was feeling a bit odd so I sat down on the bed – and went to sleep. That's why I nearly missed you. Won't be a minute.'

Rosemary went through to the music room and was sitting in one of the armchairs, sipping her tea, when Julian came back. She nodded towards the reading stand.

'What are you playing?'

'Mozart. The slow movement. I—' he frowned. 'I found its voice, I *touched* it – but there was an interruption. Perhaps I'll tell you about that later. Perhaps not. And now I'm not sure if I can quite touch that again. In the music. Sorry! I don't even know what I'm trying to say really.'

'Would you try again now? I would love just to sit here and listen. I won't interrupt. Aaah, it's just good to sit.'

She stretched out her short, sturdy legs and crossed her ankles, holding her cup and saucer on her lap. Her head rested against the back of the chair and her eyes were closed. Julian felt the stillness within her and there was a need for him to reach into it and to make her understand what he had been trying to say. He tuned up quickly and sat down, waiting for a few moments, trying to recall the creature, yet also fearing its return because its joy brought pain. But it was still there, hovering in his mind and wrists and fingers, so that the printed black stream of notes was almost an intrusion, almost unrelated, and yet the source. The delicate high notes whispered so that they barely stirred the air, and Julian's face was closed as though he had retreated inside to listen to the currents in his brain.

Rosemary opened her eyes and watched him, and was surprised at how different he looked now that he was playing, really playing. He was a stranger, and for a moment she felt lost and disorientated; but when she looked around the room, the details were comfortingly familiar. The music flowed over her and she relaxed a little, then found that she had relaxed too much because the aching purity of the notes had penetrated her fragile mental shield and her eyes had filled with tears. She slowly reached forwards to put down her cup and find a handkerchief, but the movement distracted Julian. Briefly his glance flashed across, and he saw the misery in her face, and stopped at once, instantly dispossessed.

'Rosemary! What's wrong?'

'It's nothing. I'm so sorry. Do carry on!'

But he put down his instrument and came over to stand by her chair. He was embarrassed to see her cry; women like Rosemary didn't cry, at least not in public. He tried to joke with her.

'I don't think my playing has reduced anyone to tears before.'

'I'm sorry. I was just feeling a bit depressed and, oh Julian, I'm so sorry. Let me go to the bathroom and tidy up.'

Her tears were flowing freely now and Julian held her arm when she stood up, her face averted. He could feel the sobs within her and felt his own throat tighten, and he put his arm around her awkwardly.

'Don't worry, I don't mind. Please don't cry, you'll make me cry too! Would you like to wash your face? Can I get you something?'

What did one do? How did one comfort an older woman? She usually comforted him! It was as though his mother had cried in front of him. He was almost frightened, but at the same time felt tender towards her. What could be wrong, to make her so depressed? Then another thought struck him: she wasn't going to leave, was she, to leave the Ensemble, even to leave the city? He needed her, the group needed her, she couldn't go. But now she was regaining her control. She patted his arm and bent to pick up her handbag.

'I *will* use the bathroom, if I may. Don't forget your tea, it's getting cold.'

Julian fidgeted anxiously, and waited for her return. She came in briskly and he was almost relieved at what she had to say.

'Silly of me. I had some bad news this morning, a letter from my ex-husband's wife, telling me that he'd died.'

'Oh Rosemary! But I thought you hadn't seen him for years?'

She almost smiled at Julian's callous naïveté.

'You are, of course, right. We've been divorced for fifteen years. But we shared a lot together, Julian. We made children together, don't forget, and shared much of their upbringing. I did love him – and although I'll admit I was very bitter when he left me, it's hard to forget that he was once very much a part of my life. We were married for a long time. So it came as a bit of a shock.'

'Yes. I can see it would.'

'Anyway, I'm sorry, dear. I was rather overwrought. To tell you the truth, I went to the Botanic Gardens to be reminded of him – we spent a lot of time courting in the banana house.

There's a bench hidden in amongst the ferns and palms. I'm surprised it hasn't been taken away, really.' Rosemary sat down again and smiled at Julian. 'I remembered it as being really hot and steamy, but it doesn't seem like that now. I wandered round there for quite a while and then I found myself just walking round the backstreets, remembering. I think I just wore myself out, Julian. Silly of me. And I needed some company, and I'm afraid I've been a nuisance.'

'I haven't been any help at all. Merely made you cry!'

'I'm glad, really, though it's selfish of me. Everything already looks better. But I'm afraid I didn't concentrate properly on the Mozart. Would you like to play it again?'

'No, it seems to have a bad effect on everybody. It caused Mrs Knight – you know, my housekeeper, cleaner, whatever you choose to call her – to walk out this morning. Thank God. I couldn't stand having her about the place any more, she was like a steamroller.'

'How, in goodness' name, did the *music* drive her out?'

'Mozart was an indirect cause. Anyway, I don't want to bore you with that. Shall I make you a fresh cup of tea? I still have half an hour before Elizabeth comes.'

'Elizabeth? Oh yes, the infamous sandwich-eater.'

They exchanged smiles, and the mood lightened.

'No, I'll be on my way. I'll see you on Thursday evening.'

Julian helped her on with her coat. 'Take care of yourself. I couldn't do without you, you know.'

'Well, I'm not going anywhere, my dear, you needn't worry. You take care, too. You're looking a bit pale. I don't like to hear that you fall asleep in the middle of the morning. Extra vitamins, my dear, iron tablets. And I suppose we'd better try to find you another cleaner, too, or your mother will make a fuss.'

'Don't even think of mentioning it to her! And I'm always pale, Rosemary darling. It's a sign of my artistic sensibilities. Hadn't you realised?'

'Did you know that George Eliot referred to Oscar Wilde as a "great white slug"? Now go and get yourself something sensible to eat before that girl arrives.'

Julian laughed, and watched as she let herself out of the front door. He went back into the kitchen and ate, without enthusiasm, a few biscuits and a chunk of Stilton cheese, and was glad when Elizabeth arrived.

The sense of unease, disorientation, had persisted throughout the afternoon. Julian had found it hard to concentrate. Once, he had become aware that the sandwich-girl was giving him a very accusing glare, and he wondered if he had been picking his nose or pulling strange faces at the wall. She had played that difficult Kodály well, too, now that he bothered to think about it; he should have been more enthusiastic. Ach! What did it matter anyway, just one more eccentricity of behaviour to add to the doubtless growing list? He was expected to be eccentric; he was, after all, incomplete, weighted towards the left. Sinistrally orientated, lighter upon the right. Off centre, no centre. No core, just an emptiness, an empty husk. Shake me, fool, like an inflated pig's bladder upon a stick, a walking stick, and I'll make music, of a sort. He took a sip of his brandy. And there had been Robbie Lutyens, too: 'What's the matter, Robbie, why have you stopped?' 'I was telling you, Mr Kersland – I can't get this fingering right. Should I try it in fourth position instead?' 'In whichever position you find it most comfortable, dear boy! It's up to you to choose.' When you are alone, you choose your own position. But in a duet, you must take your partner's views into consideration. Take your partners for a waltz. Partners? Take two, a trio, one-two-three, one-two-three. When you are disabled, when your knee won't bend, you take a stick, in a three-legged race. And as for the position, there are few choices. I have no choice at all. Ah yes, young Lutyens, you'll have had plenty to discuss this evening. 'Honestly, Mummy, I think Kersland's cracking up.

He just fidgeted and stared out of the window, and made strange remarks. He was even grinning to himself.' 'He really is becoming quite extreme. And when you think how much he charges, too. Poor Mrs Knight. I shouldn't tell you, darling, but he sent her packing today. She came round here in quite a tizz, poor old thing. Did Mrs Gillespie come inside when she came to collect you after music? I must give her a ring and find out what she knows.'

Ha, but there's nothing yet for Mrs Gillespie to report, is there? No tumbleweed blowing down the hall, no quagmires in the bathroom, nor sticky grey spiders' webs to ensnare the incautious snooper! Nor would there ever be. No empty husks.

Emptiness. If you removed the musical clutter from this room – the pile of stacked chairs, the music stands and piano – the room would be empty. There'd still be the armchairs and the table, but there'd be no core. It would be a room without a past or a future, just another characterless large Victorian room – tastefully furnished, of course, Mother had seen to that – but devoid of purpose.

Julian sank down further in his chair, cupping his glass of brandy in his hands, and grimaced at the piano. Thirty-three! He could live at least as long as this again, even longer. What in hell's name was he going to do with the next thirty or forty years? This morning was the first time that he had really thought about his music-making, really striven for something that was almost unattainable in – how long? I can't remember, he thought. I can't remember when I last wanted to play like that. I've been coasting along for years, not really stretched or even very involved. Were Farina's cats the best I could do to get myself out of a rut? Make a break! Schoenberg *à la baroque*! Make or break. Break out of the old mould where I'm mouldering away. I could go on like this for years, but to what purpose?

He took a long gulp of brandy, and choked slightly at the fumes. The debonair and talented Julian Kersland, growing maudlin with the booze. It wasn't as though he were alone or a social outcast, either. Only this afternoon, he'd had two phone calls inviting him out to dinner. He had a huge circle of friends, his own friends, family friends; well, close acquaintances, really. Rosemary was a friend, she cared about him – in a motherly way, admittedly, but she cared. And what a help he'd been to *her*! He'd not even noticed that she was upset until she'd cried, and then he'd made that crass remark . . . And that poor bloody Mrs Knight. God, he was glad to be rid of the noise; but she was a person, wasn't she, and he had treated her like bloody hell. Like shit, actually. Considering. Hell's bells, though, she'd interrupted, hadn't she? Just when . . . Just when I was, at last, belatedly, beginning to search once more, trying to use my gift properly. My Gift. The Gift. Ach, hush, no! Not that. Gift-wrapped Talent – I should advertise it as such.

Chapter Six

'Cup of tea for you!'
Margaret rolled on to her back and shielded her eyes against the bright glare that haloed Iain's body.

'Mmm. You *are* good. What time is it? Can you see the hills?'

'Eight-ish, a beautiful morning.' Iain turned away from the window and Margaret shifted her legs to let him sit down on the bed. 'The tops are clear. Still a few patches of snow in the gullies, though.'

'Isn't it good to be back? I slept so well, too. It must be the sea air.'

'Gently rotting seaweed! There are piles of it along the shore.' Iain smiled down at her where she lay, totally relaxed, her face slightly flushed and crumpled from sleep. 'There must have been quite a storm to throw all that up here, so far along the loch. But I've checked round the house and there don't seem to have been any leaks.'

'Have you been up for ages, then?' She knew that Iain hated to waste precious moments at the cottage by staying in bed unnecessarily.

'Hours! I went fishing and caught a pair of kippers for breakfast. Come and eat them with me.'

He leaned forward and kissed her. She smelt his clean, washed and toothbrushed smell, and was conscious of the stale taste in her mouth and the slightly fusty smell that her hair had picked up from the pillow.

'Ugh! Not kippers, especially for breakfast. I don't know why I buy them for you! Toast! Hot toast, and more tea . . . and orange juice.'

She smiled and stretched and groaned. Then, as Iain went downstairs, she slid out of bed and went to stand in the window recess. It was a beautiful morning. The surface of the water poppled gently, as though this were a peaceful inland waterway. Mallard rooted amongst the shallows as in any farmyard pond. Only the hills indicated the scale, but this morning even they were calm, their quartzite summits soft and pink and gentle, pushing coyly out of the horizontal bands of mist that hid their lower slopes. The surface of the water at their feet blushed rosily back as though embarrassed that these harsh, uncompromising hills should so dissemble. Margaret's held breath sighed out. Yesterday evening, when she and Iain had arrived, the hills had been missing, rubbed out by darkness. Knowing that they were there, anticipating their re-emergence from sleep, made her restless. But today they were back; it would be a good day.

She changed quickly, putting on trousers and a striped cotton shirt, and she was annoyed with herself for forgetting her red pullover, especially since she had dithered so long yesterday over the packing. The Aran pullover might as well stay here, as they would probably be coming up most weekends from now on. Today might be a good day to air the bedding – it smelt as though it needed it – and she mustn't forget to check whether they needed more containers for dry food; and she should remind Iain to look at the boiler . . . She caught sight of the hills again, and laughed at herself. 'Oh, hills! I'm so stupid, aren't I? What does all that matter?'

'Your toast's ready!' Iain shouted.

Warmth and breakfast smells drifted up the stairs from the kitchen, so she threw a pullover around her shoulders – the navy one would do – and went down.

Iain was eating kippers and reading. His book was propped

against his side-plate and his half-moon glasses had slipped to the end of his nose. He looked up as she came in.

'Sorry – I couldn't wait. I was slathering at the smell.'

'You'll get bones in the Boswell. I thought one had to concentrate on kippers.'

'I just eat everything. Did you know that kestrels can digest bones but owls can't? Actually, this is Alice Munro, not Boswell. I wanted to check up on something.'

'Was she that incredible woman who travelled round Scotland last century?'

'Yes, 1820, or thereabouts. She explored all over the place. There are some interesting stories about the west coast.'

'There's nothing left to explore now, is there? There are so many people and it's so easy to get everywhere. Besides, everyone was always so terribly well behaved in those days. All those intrepid Victorian ladies seemed to go striding through the countryside and managed to persuade the natives to make them cups of tea and pancakes, or row them miles through hazardous whirlpools to look at basalt pillars. Perhaps they got their feet wet occasionally or their skirts a little muddy, but that just improved the story, didn't it? – more tea? – and they were never sexually harassed, let alone raped and left for dead on a lonely moor.'

'But they were so tightly corseted and covered up. It's all these wonderful bits of elastic and zips and open-necked blouses that are so enticing these days . . . so *quick*!' Iain peered over his glasses at his wife, a forkful of kipper halfway to his mouth. 'Very distracting, really. Can I row you over to the island, madam?'

'You see what I mean? How can I possibly be intrepid with people like you around?'

'I see exactly what you mean, you've proved my point entirely. Your case for the prosecution wouldn't stand up because I would now argue that the victim had brought it on herself by exposing parts of her body to a lonely man who had seen nothing but kipper-flesh for weeks. Well, we've seen it happen, haven't we? There have always been cases where the judge has more or less let off the accused on that basis. Anyway – shall I eat that piece of toast? – going back to Alice Munro and her ilk, nobody would have dared harm her because everyone within a radius of fifteen miles would have known that she was around, and what she was doing, and with whom.'

'You mean the fear of being found out was what prevented her potential attackers? It wasn't the whalebone and bombazine after all? Merely death by hanging! What a disappointing insight.'

Iain laughed. 'So really you are arguing for reintroduction of the death sentence. Then intrepid female explorers will be found striding fearlessly through remote areas of the Highlands, clad in free and scanty costumes! What a terrifying thought.'

'It would select for toughness and endurance. Not to mention unresponsiveness to midge bites.' Margaret leant back. 'Talking of which, let's walk out to the point after breakfast. Just look at that blue sky!'

She stood up and leant on the draining board to get a better view. A ewe that was grazing by the back fence saw the movement; its black face shot up, and it stared at the window in surprise.

The tide was quietly going out, as though somewhere a plug had been pulled, and several sheep had come down to the bay to browse on seaweed. As Iain and Margaret wandered along the shore, the sheep moved slowly ahead of them, their shaggy coats bobbing absurdly above their spindly, fragile legs. Iain poked at the piles of torn bladderwrack with his boots and wished he had been here to experience the storm. Usually their bay was well protected from the full force of the swell, and the more interesting debris was thrown up against the promontory around the corner. Today, though, there were even large flat fronds of laminaria amongst the rotting tangle, evidence of a deep disturbance, and he pulled at one of the long, rubbery stems, remembering holidays by the sea and how his daughters had galloped along the shore, holding the flowing weed against their bottoms like horses' tails.

Margaret was squatting down near some rocks. She was staring, puzzled, at the almost intact orange sphere of a large sea urchin shell. It was surprising to find one on the shore that was so nearly whole – only its teeth and a small section of one side were missing – but it was not that which was puzzling her. Julian Kersland: it made her think of Julian Kersland. But why? She stared hard at the empty skeleton, trying to unravel the hidden association. Of course! The table lamp in Julian's music room! (She thought of him as Julian, even though she scarcely knew him.) Yes, there was a lamp with a spherical porcelain base, a sort of peachy-orange colour; she had noticed it when she went to collect Robbie Lutyens from his violin lesson. (Zoe had phoned and asked if she could possibly be a *dear* and collect Robbie, something had come up suddenly, she didn't know *how* she was going to get away on time, and Robbie got terribly upset, poor child, said he got in the way of the next pupil, and so would she mind *awfully* . . . ?)

Margaret hadn't minded looking after Robbie for an hour or so. She had collected him two or three times now, and he was very polite and diffident, and quietly got on with his homework while he waited for his mother to reappear in his life. In fact, Margaret enjoyed collecting Robbie (and she had an uneasy feeling that Zoe knew this) because it gave her another chance to visit Julian's house. The first time, she had not even entered, because Robbie's lesson had ended and he came to the door when she rang. But the second time she had arrived early and the boy had been sent to let her in, so that she could sit in the music room and listen to the end of his lesson. There had been time to study Julian and his surroundings.

The table lamp that had been bothering her was on top of the broad bookshelves beside the fireplace, shelves that were filled with boxfiles and sheet music and books about composers and music. Did he not have other sorts of books – novels, racy bestsellers, crime or science fiction? What else did he do, she had wondered, as she sat by the door and listened to Julian explaining the timing of a particular passage, tapping the note sequence with his pencil on the edge of the music stand. What did he do when he was on his own? How, and what, did he cook? She had watched his face and his bony fingers and – she couldn't help her curiosity – his damaged leg; not that there had been much to watch, as he had remained seated the whole time. Once, he turned away from Robbie and had smiled warmly at her.

'He's beginning to play this Bach very musically, Mrs Gillespie, don't you think?'

Had there been just a hint of mockery in those dark, deep-set eyes? She could not be certain; but the eye contact had made her awkward, and she had thought of nothing sensible to say.

On this most recent visit, two days ago, she had again arrived early, but by design. She hadn't been able to help noticing that the flat showed some signs of neglect. Indeed, if she were honest, she had looked for it, primed by Zoe's tale of Mrs Knight's dismissal. There were fluff-balls under the bookcase and armchairs, opaque dust dulling the surface of the piano. She tried to imagine Julian using the vacuum cleaner or a duster, but found she couldn't. Perhaps it was physically impossible; if you needed to support yourself as you walked, could you manipulate a vacuum cleaner? Well, probably you could if it was the vertical sort, but probably not if it was the horizontal sort like hers. Absent-mindedly she stroked her finger along the top of the skirting next to her chair and examined the grey powder on her fingertip.

'My cleaning lady walked out on me. As you probably know.'

'Oh, I'm sorry, I don't know what I was thinking about.' Margaret blushed deeply. 'How annoying for you. The city air is so dusty, isn't it?'

However, Julian had turned back to Robbie, who was kneeling on the floor, packing away his violin, and had handed him his music.

It was this memory, Margaret realised now, that had been quietly nagging away at the back of her mind. Something concerned with Julian Kersland was bothering her, and had been brought back to mind by the sea urchin shell.

'Meg!' Iain was looking over to where she squatted, holding a sea urchin skeleton. 'Hah! Are you going to make one of those revolting table lamps?'

She stared at him in surprise, and then her serious expression lifted and she grinned.

'Catch!'

She threw the urchin towards him, but it fell and shattered on the pebbles.

'It was broken anyway. What have you got?'

Iain was pulling aside heaps of weed, and he pointed to where a white skull lay partly buried in the debris. Sandhoppers flipped across the sand.

'I think it's a gannet's skull, isn't it?' He scraped the sand out of the eye sockets and held the skull up for her to see. 'It's a good one – look at the beak!'

'Poor thing!' Margaret touched it gently. 'It's so empty, isn't it? You know, empty of life, I mean.' She looked quickly at Iain, aware that he might think her fanciful. 'Don't you feel, too, that you, the real part of you, is in your head? The rest of your body is just there to keep you, in your head, alive – to carry you round and feed you and so on.'

'A very cerebral point of view! No, not really – but I can

see what you're getting at. But the skull, the empty skull, seems particularly uninhabited. Perhaps that's just because it's hollow. What about the sea urchin shell? Almost all of the animal is enclosed in that shell. Do you feel the same way about that? That the essential urchin has moved out?'

Margaret looked over at the shattered orange fragments and frowned.

'No. But that's because the skeleton enclosed all the animal, not just its brain. If it has a proper brain. That seems a bit of a contradiction, doesn't it? Think what it's like when you get a headache – you can't get away from the headache because it's in there, with you. But if you hurt your knee – no, you'll argue that that's geographically distant in any case – your shoulder then, that isn't so all-involving, is it? You can feel separate from that pain, if you try.'

Does Julian Kersland feel separate from his pain? The sudden question in her mind made her shudder.

'Are you cold? Some cannibal tribes used to eat human brains, of course. They thought that was where the spirit was housed. I suppose that's a similar idea.'

'"Spirits" are what other people have, people you don't know well. I'm not thinking about my spirit—'

'What about your immortal soul?'

'– but about the living, thinking me. And the essential me lives up in here,' she tapped her head, 'and the essential gannet, and all his gannet-ness, lived in there.'

'Somebody once told me that gannets run the risk of going blind. Apparently they dive with such force that their retinas can get damaged from the pressure increase. I wonder how biologists know that?'

'That's awful. So they would just die of starvation. Or of blundering into a cliff. I wonder why this one died?'

'Old age. Or oil pollution. Or perhaps it just couldn't stand the taste of fresh fish. It hankered after Finnan haddies.'

Margaret was not to be distracted. 'Imagine being blind,

Iain. You wouldn't be able to appreciate all this. And by not being able to see out, you'd be trapped inside your head.'

'I don't suppose blind people feel like that,' Iain said reasonably. 'Going back to your earlier idea, perhaps you would learn to extend the location of yourself – to your fingertips, for example, by reading Braille and feeling the shape and texture of things. Perhaps you might start to reside in your fingertips as well.'

He looked at Margaret and thought how his wife's cranial residence seemed to have become more securely shuttered against him in recent years, so that it was difficult for him to read her thoughts. He suspected that most of her activity went on in her mind. Hospices and cooking! If only there was more for her to do! Perhaps if they had decided to have children . . . ? But no, Margaret had had her hands full with his daughters, and she had not been keen.

He took her hand, and tugged it gently and squeezed her fingertips.

She smiled reluctantly. Then, purposely breaking the mood, she asked, 'What are you going to do with the skull? It will clean up nicely.'

'I'm going to photograph it.'

'On its own?'

'Yes. But here, too, in the seaweed on the sand. In fact – I've had this idea for a while – I want to do close-up studies, black and white, of objects thrown up by the sea. Look at this holdfast –' he pointed to the knotted base of some kelp '– barnacles, worm tubes, tiny bits of shell. All ending up on an alien shore.'

Margaret gently picked at one of the shells.

'Perhaps that's too detailed. It depends on the point you want to make, I suppose.'

'Do I have to have a point? It would be nice just to look at objects for their intrinsic pattern – patterns on a stone, the white of the skull against the black strands of weed, and so on.'

'Very arty-farty!' She suddenly grinned. 'But very striking, too. And what about that plastic bottle there? Is that to be included, or will this be an essay about natural organic debris?'

Iain looked around at the various bits of plastic and polystyrene that littered the shore.

'Don't mock! I imagine that it will be about anything that takes my fancy. I might even take one or two photos of you, floating ashore, standing on a scallop shell.'

'My hair's the wrong colour. And I'm not taking my clothes off in this breeze. Let's go and look at that side of the bay. Then you can go back and get your camera.'

She linked her arm through his and they scuffed through the pebbles towards the narrow path.

Margaret rolled up her sleeves and lay back on her spread pullover, closing her eyes against the sun. The early mist had burnt away from the feet of the hills, and they were now fully revealed, but softened by a faint blue haze. She had found primroses in a hollow and small, short-stemmed violets, and the sun beat down with a summery intensity, making up for its feebleness in the winter months. She sat up again, unwilling to miss any detail of the perfect view. There was Iain, his white hair shining, as he strode over to the other bay, the sun glinting on the tripod that he carried. Further down the loch a small boat was bustling around the fish pens, where she knew salmon were packed in by their thousands. The water was busy with birds – a pair of oystercatchers trilled as they flew along the bay and turnstones poked in the newly exposed shore, hastening to catch their food before the tide turned. Gulls flew around the small island and perched on the white-streaked whalebacked rocks, and she wondered if she should persuade Iain to help her uncover the boat and drag it out of the back garden down to the shore. But the sun was too warm and the feeling of peace too great to contemplate too much activity. She watched Iain position something on the shore, then return to his camera and tripod. He was so absorbed. He's such a complete person, she thought, everything fits so neatly around him and into his personality: his job, his hobbies, his houses, me. He even has his children. But she didn't feel any resentment; rather, it made her more aware of what she felt to be her own incompleteness. She had no children of her own, no job, no hobbies – the hospice hardly counted as a hobby, and it certainly wasn't a job. She stared blankly at the salmon farm and pulled at the short, cropped grass next to her.

Julian Kersland: that's what she was wanting to think about. Somewhere there was an answer to this restlessness. She had told Julian that she would ask among her friends about cleaning ladies. Why not help him more directly? Why not do it herself? Voluntary work, her own good cause. She exhaled sharply with excitement. Then immediately she doubted the wisdom of the idea. It wasn't quite the done thing, was it, for someone in her position to work as a cleaner? She tried to imagine herself, instead of Julian, cleaning the bath (and the lavatory? – oh, surely not!), dusting, and washing up dirty coffee cups. She was much easier with the image of herself using the vacuum cleaner, bringing in small bunches of flowers or tasty casseroles, perhaps hanging up freshly ironed shirts to air (he had some rather smart shirts, she seemed to remember). Also, if she were honest, was there not a rather pleasing intimacy about those scenes that made her feel that she would be useful and a welcome part of the life of someone who obviously needed help? She was both excited and nervous about the idea. She would think about it again (especially, perhaps, about the bath and lavatory) and she knew she would enjoy bringing out the idea and examining it at odd moments.

Perhaps, though, she would not discuss it with Iain just yet. She looked for him again, and waved her pullover when he seemed to look in her direction.

Chapter Seven

Julian had arrived late, bringing with him a handsome paper bag that contained a peace offering of flowers and chocolates, and a package of several books. He had not been allowed to explain the details of his misadventure until the main course had been reached, but now his hostess pressed him to tell the tale.

'Now, Julian! Your taxi had an accident, you said. I hope nobody was hurt?'

'Not physically. Merely pride, perhaps. The taxi broke down – or perhaps more accurately, it broke its leg!'

He picked up his wine glass and took a sip.

'What *do* you mean?'

'Come on, Julian, do explain!'

He smiled. 'I'd only been in it for a few minutes. We were driving along Latham Road, but there was a blockage – you know how narrow it is in the evening, with cars parked on both sides. Two cars had met halfway along and neither would give way, apparently, or that's what the taxi driver told me. Anyway, we sat there for ages, and then the taxi driver got impatient – and you can imagine that the meter was ticking away all this time, too! So he decided to turn round and find another route. He reversed to find a wider bit, to turn round. Well, you know what a tight turning circle these taxis have –' Julian looked around and everybody nodded '– we were almost round when there was a ghastly screaming sound, and the whole thing tilted down at the front right corner. And there was the wheel, wobbling in the road!'

'The kingpin must have broken.'

'Quite so. Whatever. So there we were – stuck! Right across the road!'

'The driver must have been pretty upset.'

'You can bet he was! But he just sat there at first, kept saying he couldn't believe it! Then he got out and picked up the wheel, and radioed for help. And for another taxi to come and take me away! I was crumpled up against the window, incidentally, having been attacked by those damn great books when they careered along the seat! I have a bruise to prove it, Moira dear, on my thigh,' Julian added, for the benefit of his ageing but flirtatious hostess.

'Well, you can show me later, darling. We'll send Ted away. But what took so long if the man had ordered another taxi?'

'"Another taxi" didn't come! I sat and waited – and waited. Of course, the radio was crackling away, all those irritatingly one-sided dialogues, you know the sort of thing – "Right, Jimmy, she said she'd be waiting on the corner by The Dog." "Five people and three cats to the airport, can you do it now?" – and I kept wishing that I knew how to work it so that I could shout, "Where the bloody hell is my cab?"'

'Had the taxi driver gone away, then?'

'Oh no. He was outside, leaning on the bonnet and talking to his mates. All these cronies of his seemed to appear out of nowhere, and they were having a fine time – they all thought it was hilarious, by the way. Anyway, I eventually decided I'd waited long enough and would walk back home, phone you, and come by car.'

'Wasn't it a long way? And how did you manage with all those packages? I assume you'd bought the so-called peace offerings in advance!'

'Oh dear, you know me far too well! Serendipity, providence, call it what you will. One of my ardent fans just happened to be walking by as I stepped out of the cab.

Naturally, she rushed to help me, to kiss my feet and to carry my books!'

'I hope she was beautiful. A beautiful damsel saving a knight-in-distress.'

'Well, no, unfortunately. That was rather a disappointment.' He pictured the blonde, lumpy girl, with the red eyes and blotchy face. 'She seemed to be slightly hysterical, couldn't stop giggling at first. She kept muttering that she hoped it wasn't infectious!'

He grinned, looking around at the others and seeing the picture of himself and the taxi through Isobel's eyes.

'What wasn't infectious? Oh! I see!' The girl opposite him started laughing. 'And was it?'

'I offered her a free ticket and an autographed photo of myself playing the fiddle in the nude, and she didn't seem to be having any trouble when she left!'

The others were still looking puzzled as Julian dabbed at a spilt drop of wine, and his hostess seemed to think that something slightly salacious had been hinted at, but one of the guests leapt into the gap, leaning forward earnestly, concentrating on projecting his enthusiasm.

'Really, Julian, you are exactly the person I need. I know we haven't had time to talk yet, but I run an annual festival of the arts for disabled children. I know you won't mind my mentioning this, but I like the way you were not afraid to tell that story against yourself. We have a fortnight in the summer, a mixture of art, drama and music. The kids are great, they come from all over, and—'

'They have all degrees of disability, physical, that is,' the man's wife interjected, 'but they can get involved in whichever of the activities they would like to try.'

'Music's a bit different, of course. Any of them can be involved in music-making at the very basic, percussive level. But we have several who have been learning to play instruments – woodwind, even harpsichord in one case – and we try to get them together to try some ensemble playing.'

Julian listened with a sinking feeling in his stomach and tried to look enthusiastic: they were so enthusiastic themselves, it was such a laudable effort. But what did they want him to do? He couldn't imagine any role for himself in such an enterprise. The idea appalled him.

'And we put on an art exhibition and a concert at the end. You came last year, didn't you, Ted? It's really very impressive what they accomplish and they have a marvellous time. So do we, of course.'

How grotesque, Julian was thinking, a concert of grotesques, twenty children with a complement of functional limbs for only ten; heads lolling, arms spindly, wheelchairs containing frail thin bodies. Thin wasted limbs. No! Not me! I can't! He felt ill with panic.

'How many of you are involved?' someone else was asking. 'I suppose you bring in special tutors?'

'We've got a mixture, really. There are art and drama students, and specialist teachers who are used to helping children with disabilities. We all learn a lot . . .'

'I'm afraid I'm usually terribly busy during the summer, teaching and preparing the new season's concerts,' Julian lied apologetically. 'I'm not sure that I'd be much use.'

'No, Julian, I'm sure you're wrong! I think you are exactly the right person to show our musicians that there is hope ahead. The light at the end of the tunnel. Even fame and fortune!' The earnest impresario raised his glass in salute and smiled.

'A role model,' their hostess suggested helpfully. 'They can aspire to be like you, darling. Perhaps we could even give the boys some gorgeous silk cravats like yours.'

'I was wondering about something along the lines of a masterclass, with you yourself performing something rather special and showing what can be achieved, and then helping them individually . . . something along those lines? If you think you'd be interested. I'm sorry, Moira, I didn't mean to monopolise with my own particular bee in the bonnet.'

But their hostess was waving her hands, excited by a new idea.

'You could extend the idea to the other activities. Think of art – there are those wonderful foot- and mouth-artists, the ones with hardly any limbs at all. Look at what they achieve!'

There was a brief embarrassed silence.

'And there must be a Fat Lady somewhere who could charm the drama students with her ethereal Ariel.' Julian's voice was dry. A freak show, he was thinking, a freak show; pay your penny and see the impossible.

'More wine, anyone?' their host asked, his white hair sticking up like an unsubtle halo. 'There's an interesting antipodean red. I rather go for these Australian reds, don't you? Their quality can be relied on, not like those temperamental Frog wines.'

Isobel was neither drinking Australian wine nor eating venison in green pepper sauce. She was in bed, alone, with a hot-water bottle clutched against her stomach, wishing that the analgesic effect of the paracetamol tablets would have a speedy onset. As she shifted uncomfortably from side to side, drew her knees up towards her chest and then straightened out, she moaned softly and thought what an awful evening it had been.

Even meeting Kersland had been a disaster. Why had that had to happen this evening, when she was looking and feeling awful, and couldn't think of anything interesting to say? He did offer me a free ticket, though. I suppose I could go over some time and collect it. Oh, I don't *care*! Carrying his books for him, like a slave!

And then she had had to walk back here, and drag herself up all those stairs, with aching legs and the waistband of her jeans too tight, and that uncomfortable dampness between her legs. She moaned again and a few tears of self-pity trickled on to the pillow. Damn David and his stupid gel! Damn everything. Damn being a woman and having to work too hard, and damn having her period and feeling pathetic!

She knew she had, probably, been unreasonable. But why had Dave needed to go back to the lab on a Saturday night? It seemed as though she had sat around and waited for Dave all day. There were so many other things she had needed to do, but they had both agreed that they would spend Saturday afternoon and evening together.

She had gone down to the pub to meet him for a late lunch. As she pushed open the door, the warm, beer-laden air rushed out to engulf her, and the grey haze of smoke made everything unfocused and indistinct. She stood for a moment, blinking, trying to find Dave amongst the crowd of lunchtime drinkers.

'Come on in, hen, don't be shy!' A redfaced man with thin greasy hair gestured to her with his cigarette. 'Mick'll move up, won't you, Mick? Plenty of room for a pretty one!'

His mates joined in his throaty laughter, but their laughter was good-humoured and Isobel smiled and shook her head. She squeezed between the tight-packed tables, looking round.

'Iz! Isobel! Over here!'

An arm was waving in the corner, and she waved back, relieved to see faces that she knew. Postgraduates, mainly biochemists, immunologists, geneticists, a couple of other mature students, all with whom she felt relaxed and could talk the same language, were clustered round a rectangular wooden table in the corner. The table was littered with glasses and empty crisp packets, but Dave was not there. Most of the glasses still contained liquid, so she didn't feel guilty when she indicated that she would go to the bar and get herself a drink, and the unspoken, informal means test that operated meant she was rarely expected to buy a round.

A girl came out of the kitchen and yelled, 'Thirty-four! Two pie and chips, one chili potato!' and Isobel stood to one side to let the owner claim his food. Something nudged her arm, and she looked down, then held out her hand.

'Hello, Terry!'

The black-and-white terrier looked up from his master's arms, his dark eyes shiny with hope and love. Isobel knew what was required: Terry and his master, Paddy, a small wizened man without his teeth, who always wore (probably also in bed – if he had a bed) a shiny donkey jacket and a knitted bobble-hat, were regular customers. A packet of cheese and onion crisps lay open on the bar in front of them, and Isobel took one out and held it for the dog. He curled back his lips and delicately ate the crisp, licking crumbs off Paddy's sleeve. She stroked the dog's head and felt his soft, questing nose against her palm.

'Hello, Isobel,' the barman asked. 'What'll it be?'

'Hi, Jim. Half a lemonade shandy, please. And a pint of heavy?' She looked questioningly at Paddy, who clamped his gums together and nodded a toothless smile. 'A pint of heavy for Terry.'

'I thought he was on the wagon, it's Lent,' joked Jim. 'What's he giving up this year, then, Paddy – sex? Where's Dave, then? Don't tell me he's given up drink and sex, too! Changed your mind about working behind the bar, Isobel? We'd give you a better time here.'

'He's given up arriving here on time! He's supposed to be buying me lunch. Can I have one of those cheese salad rolls?'

She counted out coins and watched as Terry stuck his head in the glass of beer and lapped at the thin layer of froth. Bubbles caught on his whiskers and he licked his muzzle with a long pink tongue, watching jealously as Paddy tilted the glass and took his turn. She stroked the little dog's head again, then picked up her lunch and turned to go.

''Bye, Paddy.'

He nodded impassively. She had never heard him speak, indeed it seemed possible that he couldn't speak, and she pushed her way between the tables, her plate and glass held high, to join her friends.

The group shuffled round and made room for her on the bench against the wall. She felt bulky in her coat and jeans and there was scarcely room to move her elbows, but the others had greeted her warmly and made her feel welcome. David, it seemed, was still at the lab; he had recently started writing up his thesis and had seen that there was some tidying up to do, several experiments that should be included for completeness.

'But he said to tell you to wait, he shouldn't be long.'

'Huh! You know Dave!'

Isobel smiled and nodded in resignation, and pushed flakes of grated cheese into a small pile on her plate.

'You OK, Isobel?'

The girl next to her, a second-year postgraduate who worked on mosquito transmission of malaria (she fed the mosquitos on her arm, Isobel remembered, and said she didn't feel a thing), leant back to give Isobel a stare.

'It's so stuffy in here. And this roll is dry. The food's getting worse and worse.'

'Yeah. Hey, look what I got in Barnardo's.' The girl groped under the table and hauled up a crumpled carrier bag that contained a creamy woollen cardigan. 'It was only four pounds. They've always got great pullovers in there, too. You should look.'

'Oxfam's even better. There were some fantastic jackets there last week,' someone else added; and there was a discussion about the relative merits of the local charity shops for buying good, cheap clothes.

Isobel thought of David, and his collection of baggy, nondescript pullovers that were stretched like the mouths of sacks around his hips, and wondered if she could persuade him to spend the afternoon browsing round the shops. Perhaps, though, they would go to his flat and watch the end of the match on television; it would be nice to be lazy and to curl up in a chair.

However, it was nearly three o'clock before David arrived, and the group round the table had thinned out, the table had been cleared of debris, and conversation was desultory. He breezed in, his navy jacket open, his cheeks flushed.

'Iso, I'm sorry. I had to set up a gel.' He dropped his voice and leant across the table. 'Look what I found!' He pulled a five-pound note out of his pocket and waved it at her. 'Caught under the bushes by the main gate. My lucky day!'

'Mine's a pint, then, Dave.'

'Make that two!'

The others were quick to seize the opportunity.

'No chance! This is a bonus. Come on, Iso – we're going to go and get rich. I'll buy you folks a couple of rounds next time I see you.'

'Dave!' Isobel was half laughing, half exasperated. 'Wait! What are you going to do?'

'You'll see. Come on!'

She shrugged at the others, squeezed from behind the table and followed him out of the pub.

'This way!' He took her arm and they slipped quickly, now together, now singly and sideways, through the jostling Saturday shoppers, the pushchairs and the groups of chattering teenagers. David darted into a cobbled back lane, where black refuse sacks leaked their sodden contents and where empty beer cans had been tossed like hand grenades, and Isobel shrieked and skipped to avoid piles of dogshit that were coiled like evil snares. The lane curved, and they came out on another street, that was lined with estate agents' offices and video rental shops. David suddenly grabbed her arm.

'Stop! We're here!'

She looked at the blank plate-glass frontage in amazement. The glass revealed nothing; it was covered in green paper, across which a frieze of horses and their riders galloped and jumped.

'A bookie's! We're going into a bookie's?' She couldn't believe it.

David nodded, beaming at her surprise.

'But do you know what to do?'

'Well – yes, I think so. It can't be difficult. It's all right, you can come in, too.'

But she let him go in first, and she found that she was clutching his jacket for reassurance like a child. Two or three punters turned to give them brief, appraising stares, but then turned back to watch the television screens that hung over the counter that stretched the whole length of the shop. There must have been fifteen or twenty men packed into the open space, either propped against the shelf that ran around the walls, or leaning on the counter itself, but there was little conversation. Apart from the rustle of newspapers and the occasional muttered exchange with the bookmaker or his cashier, the dominating sound was the commentator's voice.

Isobel now saw that David had come prepared, for he took a copy of the newspaper, folded open at the racing pages, from his pocket, and she saw that he had underlined several names. He checked his watch.

'We're just in time for the three thirty-five. Sticks and Stones, that's the one. And then there's the four five at Doncaster, Cut Above.'

'How do you know which ones to choose?' Isobel was bewildered. She had had no inkling that he knew about such things.

David shrugged and smiled. 'Nice names?'

But when she went up to the counter with him and listened to the confident manner in which he queried the odds and placed his bets, she was uneasily sure that he had prior experience.

The television broadcast had switched to football, so they

had to wait for the racing results to come up on the computer screens. Isobel was too uncomfortable to feel involved: not for her the impatient waiting, the thrill, the clammy palms and restlessness. She stood still and tried to look inconspicuous, and glanced at the news pages of the paper that she took from David. She wished she could sit down, but no one here was going to give up a high stool for a lady; here a different brand of equality was the rule.

'Look!' David dug her with his elbow and whispered, 'How about that! Sticks and Stones came in at 13–2. Not bad for starters.'

The man next to them, with slicked-back hair and a dirty grey jacket that had belonged to a suit, looked at David, then cleared his throat roughly. Isobel thought that he would have spat, and she looked down at the floor and imagined the thick white globule splattering noisily on the lino; but he swallowed hard, his Adam's apple bobbing up and down.

'Fuckin' 'ell, mate. You got second sight, or somethin'? That one didn't stand a chance!'

'Beginner's luck. Just luck!'

'How much did you put on the one at five past four?' Isobel whispered. 'Can we leave after that?'

Her back ached and the stale air was pressing in on her so that she felt her lungs were being squeezed.

'A couple of quid. We'll see,' David muttered, absorbed again in the newspaper. He looked up briefly, then put his arm around her shoulders and hugged her to him. 'Hey, cheer up! We'll go out and do something really good tonight with all the winnings.'

She tried to smile, and slipped a hand inside his jacket. 'You could go and buy a new pullover – there's a hole under your arm.'

'Even that. Hold on a minute, though. Look, there's a stool, you grab it while I collect my money.'

He detached himself from her and she was conscious of

covert, and more outright, stares as she hoisted herself up on to the stool against the wall. Why did she sense a prickle of hostility? There was another woman in here, by the counter, but she was smaller, tougher, with tight-permed hair and a strident voice, who could joke with the men around her and laugh hoarsely around her cigarette. She was an unattached woman, an individual, not a pale, droopy blonde who draped herself around her boyfriend and stared round with embarrassed, perhaps judgemental, eyes.

Why didn't I know that David did this? Isobel wondered. I thought I knew everything about him. How could I have been going out with him for so long and not known? What else don't I know? When he arrives late to meet me, has he been down here? But they didn't seem to know him behind the counter. Perhaps that's always the way of it, though, never greet a customer with familiarity, especially when he's accompanied by a stranger. Don't give the game away. All those excuses – gamblers are supposed to be very good at making plausible excuses, aren't they? And perhaps that's why his clothes are rather tatty. But he pays his way, and he pays his rent – he must do or they'd throw him out. He's no richer or poorer than the rest of us. But what if he loses all his grant? A sick feeling of panic was bubbling up inside her as she watched David, elbow on the counter, handing over notes. She wanted to rush over and grab him by the arm, pull him away, and she had actually slipped down off the stool when he turned round and came over towards her.

'Dave! Dave, stop! You'll lose all your money!'

'Sssh!' He glanced at the interested faces that had turned their way. 'It's bad luck to say things like that in here. People get upset.'

'Please stop!' She was whispering, near to tears. 'Please let's go!'

'Everyone's looking. Come outside a moment, come on.' He steered her out of the door, holding it open while she ducked underneath his arm. 'Now – what's the matter? Why are you getting in such a state?'

'I didn't know you gambled. I didn't know, and you'll lose your money and won't be able to pay the rent, and—'

'It's *all right*. I won't lose my money. You don't think I use my own, do you?'

'What do you mean? What *are* you using, then? Where did you get the five pounds?'

'I *found* it, I told you. I'm using that note and some of my winnings. It's all a bonus. I can't bet what I haven't got. You *are* an idiot! Or worse. I don't even want to believe what you seem to have been thinking.' He shook his head, patient explanation ready to veer into anger. 'And it's only the third time in my life that I've ever done this, Isobel. I don't make a habit of it.'

'How did you know what to do? You look so confident, and you understand all that stuff about odds, and "the going's firm" and "dual forecasts", and so on.'

'My grandfather taught me! He was a great one for the horses, used to drive my granny mad!'

'There you are then, you see – it's in your blood!'

'God! And you're a medic, too! You could at least say I had a genetic predisposition or something a bit more scientific. But that's rubbish too. I know what I'm doing, I'm not being reckless or stupid. Look, we have to stay here just a bit longer, OK?'

'I'll stay outside, then – I can't stand the heat. And they don't like me being in there.'

'They couldn't give a damn. The only thing they're interested in is their chance of winning. Now, even if I lose the next—'

'*Lose!*'

'Even if I don't win – even if I don't win the next two, we'll still be eight quid in hand. Relax!' He bent down and kissed her, and smoothed her hot cheeks with his thumbs. 'Patience.

Stay out here for a bit if you want.'

She sighed, and came back inside and read again the scanty tabloid news. Around her, punters were involved in the fate of tons of supple horseflesh, but she sat, detached and un-responsive, and waited until David returned to her and said, 'We can go. You can be happy. Just over twenty pounds, that's what's left after non-winners and commission. I'll treat you to tea and a cream bun and then we'll go out somewhere this evening. I'm starving.'

'Congratulations,' she said. 'I'm impressed. And I'm sorry I was silly.' But she knew that the little knot of anxiety would take time to unravel completely.

And two hours later, as she sat on another stool, this time in the Biochemistry Department, she felt the knot of pain in her abdomen expand and throb, and she knew that she wanted only to go home to bed.

The harsh fluorescent lights shone on the glossy cream walls and reflected off the flat white surfaces of refrigerators and freezers. The lights flickered subliminally over the matt black bench tops and the rows of stoppered bottles and metal racks of polythene tubes on the shelves. It was a familiar environment, comforting in its ordered chaos. David, once more single-minded, emptied a polystyrene bucket of melted ice into the sink, put on his white coat and disposable gloves, and poured reagents into flat glass dishes in the fume cupboard. His movements were unhurried and practised, as he gently tilted the dish back and forth so that the pale sheet of acrylamide gel pulsed and slithered in the liquid like a jellyfish. Isobel watched as he tidied his own few square feet of workbench and dropped pipettes and syringes into boldly coloured containers for disposal, emptying tubes, dunking glassware in buckets of detergent, throwing plastic bottles into plastic bags. He looked at his watch, then glanced at her and smiled.

'Only another half-hour. Do you want a coffee while we wait?'

'David,' she said, 'I think I'll go home.'

'Home? Now? Why? I thought we were going out for a meal. Are you coming back?'

'No. I feel dreadful.' She could feel self-pity welling up inside, and fought it down, crossly. 'I just want to go to bed. I've got such a stomach ache . . . my period's started. I just can't think. I'm really sorry.'

'Oh, Iz. Is it really bad?' He put his arms round her, and cuddled her gently. 'If you can wait, I'll come back with you and tuck you in.'

'No, that's silly. I'll be all right. And I'm such awful company. Just when we were going to have a big celebration, too.'

'The money won't go off. I won't spend it, I promise. Not even on the horses! Look, you go ahead and I'll drop by later. Shall I bring you something to eat?'

'I'm not hungry. And there's not much point, is there? I'll be going to bed with a hot-water bottle.' She put her arms round his waist and hugged him. 'Perhaps we can do something tomorrow, instead? Will you come over in the morning, and we can decide?'

'Izzy, had you forgotten? I'd promised to help Andrew move into his new place tomorrow. I can't back out now. I'll be free in the evening, though.'

Isobel had forgotten, but she found she didn't really care. At the moment, she just felt weak and aching, and she wanted some time to herself.

As she stepped down on to the dimly lit campus road, she looked back. David was locking the door behind her and, as he straightened up, the bright lights of the foyer shone on his face. She caught a puzzled, sad expression, but then he saw her looking, and smiled and blew her a kiss. She turned her face fully towards the light so that he would see her smile, and then she waved, and wandered slowly away between the dark, humming buildings, pressing her hands, inside the pockets of her coat, against her aching stomach.

David's sad face danced in her mind like a flashlit photograph. David's patience accused her; David's unpredictability, his lateness, his absorption in his work, nagged at her. She had waited for him all day. All right, so his grant ran out in a few months, and he didn't yet know about his future – but she, too, worked hard and had important goals. He had hurt her; no, she had hurt him. David's sad face . . . sadness . . . and hurt. Tears started, and she clutched herself and snivelled as she walked, not caring who saw her; but she took a route through the backstreets, where she'd be less likely to meet her friends. She blew her nose and dabbed her eyes. Suddenly she realised that two cars were reversing down the road towards her. The noise of their engines was shrill in protest at their speed, and red rear lights flashed as each car braked, then accelerated forwards in another direction.

She stopped and looked warily up the road. Had some crime been committed? Perhaps these were getaway cars for a murderer or robber. Would she be a valuable witness? Or, worse, a victim? But then she saw that the road was blocked by a taxi, a broken taxi, tilted down at its front corner. The driver was talking to two other men, and they were laughing and looking at the wheel.

As she walked towards them, the taxi's rear door opened and a walking stick appeared. She stopped, intrigued, and then began to giggle. A walking stick! Who was producing a walking stick for the taxi's broken leg? Her laughter made her cry as well, and she dabbed her eyes with the sodden handkerchief. Then the orange streetlamps illuminated Julian Kersland's face as he climbed awkwardly out of the crippled cab; and she was suddenly compelled to speak to him and explain her laughter. He didn't recognise her, of course, although he had seen her at close quarters once before, but he readily agreed that she should help him with his package and his bag. He lived not far away, but the walk had been awkward; physically awkward as she tried to keep out of his way, and mentally awkward as she struggled to think of things to say. He had been amusing, though, and thanked her effusively for her help. He had even offered her a free ticket to a concert. She'd told him that she'd been to one already, the caterwauling one, and he had laughed out loud. She had liked him when he laughed. It had been a spontaneous, genuine laugh and made him, briefly, more approachable.

'How brave! How revolutionary! You certainly deserve a free ticket for that – and for being so delightfully helpful. Do you live close? Drop in sometime, and I'll arrange a ticket for you.'

She wouldn't, of course, and he hadn't meant it; he wouldn't even recognise her again. But it had been interesting to meet him. Isobel clutched the hot-water bottle tighter to her stomach and pushed the image of David's face out of her mind, because it made her feel tearful again. Damn David, and damn her period, and damn and blast that good-looking cripple Kersland! She pulled the duvet cover round her head and sobbed loudly into the pillow then, irritatingly, immediately felt better, as she had known she would. And damn predictability!

Chapter Eight

'**H**is *housekeeper*! You're going to "do" for him? My dear Margaret, what a scream! How wonderfully original of you,' Zoe's voice shrieked out delightedly from the telephone.

'Only occasionally, Zoe. Whenever he feels he needs help.'

'Well, mind he doesn't get it into his head to sack you, lovey, like poor old Mrs K. You'll be having a cosy chat over a cup of coffee one minute, then poof! – you're out!'

'Don't be ridiculous. He's not employing me, I'm helping him as a favour. He does have trouble coping on his own; nobody seems to realise that.'

Margaret's voice was crisp, but she felt the weight of despair settling on her stomach. Now everybody would know and the story would be certain to be embellished in the telling. Iain had warned her that people would gossip. Zoe had such an uncanny persistence. Margaret had told her that she wouldn't be free to help with the temporary charity shop tomorrow, because she would be 'looking after' someone. But Zoe was like a ferret with a rabbit, she wouldn't let go, and Margaret had eventually been forced to mention Julian Kersland's name.

'Julian! Is he ill? I suppose he's caught Robbie's disgusting cold. The boy's snuffling and sneezing his revolting germs all over the place. But surely you don't need to nurse him?'

And thus the information had been dragged out of her and held up for examination, that Kersland was quite well, but that his flat was in need of help. Margaret, of course, had known that Robbie Lutyens had a feverish cold. She had known, and had rejoiced and schemed, because now she knew exactly when Julian would be free. It took her a whole day to make her decision. She had walked past the terrace twice before she finally had the courage to go up the steps. Even then she had nearly changed her mind, but someone came out of the house next door and she felt she would look suspicious if she turned and walked away. When she rang the bell, she thought she was going to faint; her breathing actually seemed to stop. And then he had eventually opened the door, and he was frowning. He was so different from what she had expected that she stepped backwards and nearly fell.

'Be careful!' His reflexes had been surprisingly quick, and he had steadied himself as he had caught her arm. 'Mrs Gillespie! But Robbie's not here today.'

'I know.' She swallowed, trying to think of a different, innocuous, reason why she might be here, but her mind was blank. 'I wonder if I could talk to you for a moment?'

Julian looked briefly at his watch. 'I have a pupil here for another ten or fifteen minutes. Would you like to come inside and wait? Or is that too long?'

Weakly, because she was now committed to a much-rehearsed piece of dialogue, she stepped past him into the hall and then into his flat, listening to his step-thump-slide behind her on the patterned tiles. Naïvely, she had expected that he would be free, that he would not have rearranged his schedule to suit himself. She had not expected that she would have to wait in the kitchen, turning the pages of an old Sunday colour supplement, which was all that Julian could find to occupy her, in his haste to return to his pupil. She had not expected that he would be wearing green cord trousers and a brightly coloured woollen waistcoat, woven with flowers and birds, or that he would look so casual and unconventional – and in command!

A violin started up, then stopped; a passage was explained upon the piano, twice, with emphasis. A girl giggled, and tried again. Did Julian, then, make girls giggle? She heard his voice again, and the girls, and then the crisp snapping of locks. The door of the music room opened, and Julian came out, still smiling, preceding a flushed and smiling girl; a teenager, holding a violin case, and susceptible to laughter shared with a handsome man. They both looked towards the kitchen, and Margaret was sure that they had been laughing at her. Was her mission so obvious?

Julian waited until the girl had left, then came back into the kitchen.

'Well, Mrs Gillespie. Have you decided you'd like to learn the violin?'

Why did he look at her like that? Why did he allow the mockery to show?

'Oh no! I can't even read music! I came to offer my services –' what on earth made her phrase the offer like that? Couldn't she even remember her lines? '– to see if I could help you at all . . . I mean, Zoe – Mrs Lutyens – told me that your housekeeper had left . . . and I was wondering . . .'

'Shall we have a cup of tea? This looks as though it might be quite a serious discussion.'

Julian was taken aback; he didn't know what he had expected when he found Mrs Gillespie on the doorstep, but it certainly wasn't this. He filled the kettle, and busied himself finding cups and saucers, and looking for biscuits. There weren't any.

'Do you mind if we stay in here, in the kitchen? I like to have a break from the music room, it gets a bit claustrophobic in there sometimes. Girls that age are so full of *hormones*, aren't they? She'd be quite a reasonable player if only she'd concentrate.'

He covertly examined his visitor. She was attractive; she knew how to choose her clothes. He liked that. His housekeeper? At the age when many women would be keen to take a lover. Well, well – coming to offer her services. She's sitting there, looking cool and confident, but she's terrified inside. It's not her hormones that have brought her here, Julian laddie, nor the appeal of that thing between your legs. Don't flatter yourself: it's the appeal of your leg that's done it. And I'm not conforming to her preconceived image, am I? – asexual, conservative, and *needy*.

'It was my new waistcoat,' he explained.

'Sorry?' Margaret was startled. What *was* he talking about?

'It made her giggle. She's only half my age and so she thinks I'm almost dead. I have to remind myself that I'm not, occasionally. Milk or lemon?'

The smoky scent of Lapsang was carried upwards in the steam and Julian was thankful that some flavour remained; the packet had been in the cupboard for at least two years.

'Neither, thank you. It's very striking, especially with that shirt.'

Margaret watched as Julian slid sideways on to a chair. Even making the tea looked such an effort; actions such as carrying teapots and jugs without spilling liquid required a balance and precision that one took for granted. Such an effort. It was no wonder that keeping the flat clean was a low priority. Come on, Margaret, don't be intimidated; be brisk and to the point. He's younger than you are and pretends to change his character with his clothes; we all do. Take the initiative, come on!

'As I was saying, Mr Kersland, I heard that you hadn't found another cleaner – I'm sorry, you know how one's business is rarely private around here – and, well, I've plenty of time on my hands these days, so I'd be glad to help out. But you probably feel that this is grossly impertinent and would be a great intrusion on your privacy.' (There! She had said it. Almost word-perfect.)

'I'd rather hoped that I would be able to manage on my

94

own. But I suppose you've noticed that I'm not having much success.' He was self-deprecating, rueful. 'I'm sorry, the music room in particular needs attention, doesn't it?'

Margaret merely smiled.

'But – well, I couldn't really employ you as a cleaner, Mrs Gillespie. I don't think that would be right.'

'Perhaps it's just a question of a title. Perhaps "housekeeper" would be better, although that implies something rather more full time. I'd thought that I could just pop in when you needed me, once or twice a week.'

(Ah, innuendo! When I need you, Mrs Gillespie. How often will that be? But you're not my type. Damn it, man, concentrate!)

'Yes. Not a "daily", not a cleaner. Oh – a "treasure"! That's what my mother's generation called them, didn't they? "I've found such a treasure."'

Margaret's cheeks flushed red.

'No, perhaps not. A housekeeper, it would have to be. But . . . I don't know. It seems an imposition on you, Mrs Gillespie.'

'I think we'd have to try it out. I don't want to intrude or to be in your way, naturally. Perhaps we could try it out for a fortnight or so – if you like.'

Julian stared into his teacup. *Would* he like this? Someone in the house again, prying, spying, probably gossiping. And did she want to be paid, did she need the money? How awkward.

'Zoe Lutyens was looking out for a cleaner for me. Did she suggest this to you?'

'Of course not! It's not her business what I do – and I wouldn't expect to discuss you with her, or for you to discuss this arrangement – if we have an arrangement – with her, either.'

'Well, at least we're in firm agreement on that point.' He smiled, and was relieved to see his visitor smile in return.

'And naturally I don't expect to be – paid. I'll do it for

nothing, I'd just be glad to help. I don't have a lot to occupy my time these days. Although Mrs Lutyens is always trying to inveigle me into helping with her hospice . . .' She stopped, aware that she'd begun to gabble. 'But please take some time and think about it, there's no hurry.'

Aha! A charity case. Home help and meals-on-wheels. But don't bite the hand . . .

'I think it's a wonderful idea. I'm very touched, and tremendously grateful that you think you can spare the time. And please come as often or as little as you like. We'll try it out for a fortnight, as you suggest.'

Margaret couldn't believe that everything had gone so smoothly; that she had proposed something useful, on her own initiative, and that the proposal had been accepted without limitation. She had a *purpose* again, outwith her marriage; something consistent and useful, to fill in the time before Iain came home. The tenseness in her back and neck disappeared and she realised how stiffly she had been sitting. She felt free to look about her and to appreciate the practicality of the kitchen – the oven built in at waist height, the eye-level storage cupboards and plate rack, everything neatly ordered and accessible, an ergonomist's dream, yet curiously characterless, lacking clues – and overlaid by dust and crumbs.

Julian had relaxed, too, his arm dangling over the back of his chair, and he had felt free to study this woman whose ideas seemed to contrast so surprisingly with her appearance. What about her husband, he was a solicitor, wasn't he? God yes, Gillespie Saunders McCaig, quite a big noise. He won't be very pleased that his wife goes out to *clean*!

But that night, Margaret had lain awake for hours, lying still and trying to breathe steadily as though she were asleep. Tomorrow she would phone Julian – no, she'd leave a note, she couldn't bear to hear the amused sarcasm in his voice – to say that it would be impossible, after all, for her to help.

Was Iain pretending to be asleep, too? She couldn't hear him breathing, he was so still. Perhaps the shock had been too great. Perhaps she'd killed him. She poked him with her toe, and he grunted. He grunted in his sleep, too. Perhaps he was asleep after all. Perhaps he didn't really mind.

She had waited for the right moment, waited and waited, tried to turn the conversation; but the evening had passed, and the thing had not been said. Eventually, in desperation, as they were washing cups and locking doors, preparatory to going to bed, she had said, 'Oh, I've found myself a job – unpaid, I'm afraid, but something worthwhile.'

'Have you? I didn't know you even wanted one.'

'I thought I'd wait and surprise you when it was organised. I've arranged to look after that lame musician I told you about – you know, Julian Kersland – perhaps a couple of times a week.'

'I didn't realise he needed looking after. I thought he was fairly mobile. Has his condition deteriorated then, poor chap? I've heard his concerts are rather good.'

'Well no, it's more his flat, actually. He doesn't seem to cope very well these days.'

'In what way, love? How will you look after his flat? I don't quite understand.'

'Oh, generally tidying up, cleaning a bit, things like that.'

Iain had come over to the table where she was putting out cereal and marmalade for breakfast. He was serious, even worried.

'In other words, you're intending to go in and clean this young man's flat – he is young, isn't he? – and wash his clothes for him? I'm sure you've thought seriously about this, darling – you're certainly not a woman who jumps into things feet first and to hell with the consequences – but, well, have you considered how this might be construed by other people?'

Margaret had looked at him, puzzled. 'No, I suppose I've been rather self-centred about it, really. I've only thought of it in terms of something useful to occupy myself – a means of being useful to someone who needs help. What do you mean?'

Iain shrugged slightly, to make light of his unease.

'It might look rather peculiar, the wife of a senior partner of – let's face it, a rather prominent firm of solicitors – popping in and out of a young man's flat, waving a feather duster or a lavatory brush.'

'And with a flowery pinafore and a scarf around my head.' Margaret bit her lip and put down the knife that she was holding. 'Mmm. But it won't be like that. It's just an attitude of mind. People wouldn't find it so strange, would they, if he were old? Or even a small boy? And nobody will know, in any case. It's just a private arrangement.'

'Oh, Meg! You're not so naïve! Within a week, everyone will know. And think of the fun they'll have with it, darling! Think how they'll gossip!'

He regretted that immediately. Margaret's head jerked up, her eyes were blank with shock.

'Fun? Gossip? What could they gossip about?'

Iain merely continued looking at her.

There was a long pause, then she said quietly, 'I've said I'll help him. He was very pleased. I can't let him down. But I'll stop at the end of the fortnight we arranged as a trial period. And that will be the end of it.'

She was fiddling with a spoon, aligning it along the edge of a placemat. Iain caught her hand and held it.

'I'm sorry, darling. It was such a kind idea, but you do see that it might be better to abandon it? I don't want people to laugh.'

'At you – or me?'

'At both of us. We're a unit, aren't we – for better, for worse? But let's ensure that there is no "worse".'

And so she had lain awake worrying, going over and over her interview with Julian, and reinterpreting every nuance, every look and gesture, until she had convinced herself that he had made a fool of her and she had made a fool of herself, in his eyes and the eyes of all their friends.

As for Julian, he veered between feeling flattered and offended that a woman such as Mrs Gillespie should consider him to be a suitable case for care. He was puzzled, yet also amused, and once or twice he thought about telephoning his mother, or even Zoe Lutyens, to discuss this surprising development. Later, when he saw the two cups and saucers sitting unwashed by the sink, their fine gold-patterned rims glinting in the light, he recalled the earnest elegance of his housekeeper-to-be (his 'daily-in-waiting', his incomparable 'treasure'), and he paused, frowning, wondering *why*, why she wanted to have this contact with him. Because he was under no illusion that it was the prospect of cleaning that attracted her.

He tried to see himself through Margaret Gillespie's eyes: Julian with the foot of clay. He knew he was two people, walking in two worlds, each seeing the other from afar and detached, surprised, even, that the other should exist. When he had played that Mozart the other day (when he had had to sack Mrs Knight and had caused Rosemary to cry), the true, *real* Julian had been there in the music – the almost-forgotten Julian, the more-than-half-suppressed Julian. The sublime joy of being that Julian had been there, too, but with the concomitant pain and agony. The joy and fear of being that Julian, with all that entailed, and then the sudden loss. And the escape of sleep, nepenthe.

He'd remembered what it was like to have that Julian dominant, the cost to his other, more basic self, and he had at last acknowledged how he had opted for something lesser, less painful, less consumed. The real Julian, the one who walked in another world and was taken over by the perfect joy of music, was too *alone*. 'But I must find my way back!'

He found he'd spoken out loud. He felt again his old despair. Dreary lunchtime concerts, dreary dinner parties –

there was no point in this denial of self. Yet he wasn't sure that he could bear the struggle. If only there were still someone here to help him – but he was so alone!

Two teacups – and Margaret Gillespie, sitting at the kitchen table. Would *she* help? No, she didn't know, she couldn't know. She saw only his well-spoken, comfortably off, safely middle-class and physically deprived self, a suitable case for self-gratification and treatment. She only saw his earthly powers. She didn't know he could fly. And somehow, fly he must!

Words came to him from the past, long-forgotten words: 'There's a purpose in everything, but sometimes you have to search for the purpose yourself.' Well, this time he wasn't going to bother with a search. He'd have a drink instead, then go to bed.

Nevertheless, on the morning of Margaret's first visit he was unsettled, and when the doorbell rang he jumped, even though he had been expecting her. Under her woollen camel coat she was wearing soft burgundy cord trousers tucked into short navy boots, and the bag she was carrying was not covered in imitation tapestry but was made of plain glossy oilcloth and advertised the name of an expensive department store.

'I've got my duster and my flowery apron in the bag!'

'Oh! Do come in!'

Now that the day had arrived, Margaret felt confident, even happy, because the exhausting anticipation was over. The morning after she had told Iain of her plan, she had felt too tired and defeated to think about contacting Julian to cancel the arrangement, and as the day had progressed she had decided to carry on with the trial period as planned. Three or four visits would restore the flat to a cleaner state and then her obligation would have ended and everyone could feel satisfied.

'I did wonder about dressing up as Mrs Mop! I've brought my own rubber gloves, and I've also brought some biscuits for coffee, if you'd like them. Where would you like me to put my coat? And what would be least disruptive for you?'

She's quite different today, Julian thought; and the familiar resentment of intrusion, the anxiety about where he might escape the searching nozzle of the vacuum cleaner, hovered in his mind. He showed her where the cleaning things were kept and found pretexts to occupy himself in other rooms. Once, he caught sight of himself in the bathroom mirror and he was surprised at his harried appearance; he rubbed his hands over his face and pulled his pullover straight. Should I make us both some coffee? Should I have my coffee with her, sit and talk? And eat her home-made biscuits? Shall I have to do this every time? Although I suppose it could be fun; as long as she doesn't pry.

So he had made coffee and had opened the music room door and signalled to her above the noise, and she had smiled and nodded and turned off the vacuum cleaner to come and join him at the kitchen table. Had it been prying when she asked about the photograph in his bedroom? Perhaps not: they made a striking picture, his grandmother and her three sisters and two brothers, the women in slim white Edwardian dresses, demure yet proud, the men in wing collars and dark grey suits. Anyone would be intrigued by them and their cool confidence: the conductor's baton, the singer's clasped-hand pose, this woman seated by the cello, and these others with right arms raised like swans' necks to hold their bows against the strings. And his grandmother's dark eyes staring out of the picture from a face that was tilted sideways to hold a violin beneath her chin. No, Mrs Gillespie had not been prying to ask about that picture, for the family's talents had been publicly acclaimed in the drawing rooms and private gatherings of the society to which they had belonged. It was a talent which had skipped a generation and had been passed on to him. As he talked to Margaret about the photograph, he saw, in his mind, the adjacent picture on his desk, and regretted that he had not thought of it earlier, and removed it. He hoped she wouldn't question him about that one; he would put it away before she came again. But she hadn't asked, and their conversation had otherwise been brief and not too strained. She had seemed cheerful and more composed today, as though doing things had given her strength; and already the flat looked much improved. Two weeks will be enough, though, Julian thought.

Everything had gone all right, Margaret explained to Iain in the evening. It had not been as awkward as she had feared. She had made good progress and it was satisfying to see an improvement. Another two or three visits would be quite sufficient. She told him about the family photograph, for the mention of Julian's musical forebears could not be classed as gossip. But she wondered, privately, about the photograph that had stood beside it on the desk, of a tall gaunt man wearing a surplice and a clerical collar, whose hand rested on the shoulder of a younger Julian, thin-faced but smiling despite his wheelchair.

Chapter Nine

Julian flicked on the light in the communal hall and put down his violin case and music so that he could lock the door of his flat. At the instant he turned the key his doorbell rang, inside the flat.

'Shit! Who's that?'

Stupidly, he nearly unlocked his own door again, but realised just in time what he was doing. It was still light outside and through the frosted glass of the front door he could see a figure, waiting. That figure would have seen him, too, as a fuzzy shape moving in the bright light of the hall. He would have to answer the door.

For a moment, he didn't recognise the girl who stood there. She was tall and neatly dressed, and the hall light shone on the pale blonde hair that was brushed smoothly back behind her shoulders. But even as she smiled and began to speak, he realised who she was. What a transformation – the dark, tailored jacket and white blouse, the short, dark skirt!

'Hello,' she was saying. 'I don't know if you remember me – Isobel Hutchison. We met the other evening when your taxi broke down . . .' (This is hopeless. He's going out, he's in a rush.)

'Of course! Of course. How could I forget?' (Why did I dismiss her as lumpy and red-nosed?)

'Look, I'll come back another time, I can see you're in a hurry. But . . .'

'But?'

'Well, you remember we were talking about your Sunday concerts, and you offered me a ticket? I was just passing by, and remembered – so I just wondered if I could collect it now. But I can see that it's a bad moment.'

She moved down a step, as though to leave.

'Oh, you *must* come, no doubt about it. But – Isobel, I don't have the tickets myself. Other people deal with the business side of things.'

Julian was thinking quickly, not wanting to abandon this transformed ugly duckling. She could be just what he needed – a new, young groupie, the nucleus for a New Era.

'Look, I'm late already – could you hold this a moment? Take great care now.' He handed Isobel the precious tools of his trade. 'That's a bit more valuable than chocolates or whatever it was you carried for me last time! Now you can say you've carried the great Kersland's fiddle!' He locked the door and then looked down at Isobel and grinned. 'Better still, since I can't arrange a ticket you can come and meet someone who can. I'm on my way to a rehearsal for the next date. Would you like to come along and see how we work?'

Isobel wasn't sure. If she went with him, he'd be distracted and surrounded by other people and that wasn't what she wanted. But it was either that or retreat with no further prospect of renewing his acquaintance. She wouldn't have any other excuses in the future. And he would have to take her there, and bring her back.

'Why not? But only if you don't make me carry your books and walk five paces to the rear.'

'Marvellous! And anyway, I wouldn't be able to see you if you walked behind me!'

(Does he want me to waggle my bum? 'She moves so beautifully, poetry in motion.' What are you *doing* here, Isobel?) But Isobel knew well enough why she was there – curiosity! Curiosity about the limp, and curiosity about the way of life of this almost alien being, a musician. In all probability, if

Kersland hadn't had a limp, she wouldn't have thought any more about him, but finding the link between such an obvious disability and a publicly performing artist could be interesting. And it would make a change, a brief alteration in her highly predictable way of life. This was to be a transient investigation of the life of an older (and yes, all right, good-looking, in a bony sort of way) demonstrably non-scientific male who, unfortunately, had a crooked leg and a smooth line in chat. That was why she was here, getting into his car. That was why she was dressed up in her smartest well-fitting clothes (so she could waggle her bum?) and had taken some trouble with her appearance.

Julian looked across at her and saw that Isobel was smiling to herself. He noticed, too, how the seatbelt pressed against her left breast, pulling her cotton crepe blouse so that the line of buttons was askew. He noticed how her hair fell forwards when she reached down to move her shoulderbag between her feet, and he vividly remembered the blonde girl in the café in the crypt, who had dropped her umbrella at his feet. She had been sitting in the gallery, too, but it was in the café that he remembered her most clearly.

'Who was that boy you were with at that lunchtime do?' he asked abruptly. 'He looked vaguely familiar.'

Isobel looked at him in surprise. So they had not been faceless, after all. The tendrils of the grapevine reached out and curled around the most unsuspecting objects. Each person was an individual polyp in a coral colony that covered the city, all interconnected, each influencing and influenced by the others.

'David? David MacIlvanney. He met you once at a party at Professor Smith's – Smith gave him the concert tickets. That's why I was at the concert, Dave thought I might like to come along. You met him at the Smiths',' she reiterated, remembering Dave's hurt, embarrassed look at the concert lunch, and wanting to ask Julian why he had not acknowledged David then.

'Ah, so that was it.' Julian didn't remember meeting the boy at all. 'Very strange parties, Tony Smith's. Have you been to one with your friend Dave?'

Isobel shook her head.

'Smith's a biochemist or something, isn't he? Anyway, he obviously collects people, the more unusual their métier or their background the better. But he particularly likes to cross the Great Divide.'

'Oh?'

'You know, the Two Cultures, C. P. Snow. Arts v. Science. Surely you've heard of C. P. Snow? Ah Isobel, where have you been all your life?'

'Auchtermuchty,' she replied promptly, and immediately giggled.

'Auchtermuchty?' He was incredulous, delighted. 'You can't mean it. Nobody lives at Auchtermuchty!'

'You're right. But do enlighten me about the Two Cultures, then at least we can be true opponents!'

Julian raised an eyebrow and looked sideways; she wished he would concentrate on the road.

'Now that would be a pity. But you'd better enlighten me first. What do you do, Isobel, since you seem to think that we ought to be adversaries? So far you seem to have been entirely on my side, though only figuratively speaking, unfortunately. The seatbelts are rather a disadvantage.'

'I'm a medic.'

'Are you indeed!' Julian was quiet for a few moments, apparently concentrating on avoiding a suicidal drunkard with a dog.

'Oh, do mind! That's Paddy! And his dog . . . his dog's called Terry.'

'You should tell them to take care or they'll end up in hospital. Friends of yours, are they?'

'Oh, I just *collect* them!'

Julian snorted with amusement. 'Right. So where do you

practise, Dr . . . Hutchison? A smart private clinic on the better side of town?'

'As yet, you're the only one who practises around here, Mr Kersland. Unfortunately, I don't qualify for another three years.' She deliberately avoided the word 'student', with its connotations of youth and irresponsibility. 'And I ought to be at home and working, right now.'

'Instead of which, you chanced to drop in on me as you just passed by. And now you've been abducted to see how the other culture lives – and plays! Wonderful!'

He turned the car into a narrow, dimly lit street, drove up to a pair of tall, bright blue doors and switched off the engine.

'Here we are, right to the door. You can get away with a lot with this useful little sticker.'

'But this isn't the concert hall!'

Just where had he abducted her? What was this place, in this empty, dark backstreet? After all, she didn't really know anything about him. Perhaps all that heavy-handed flirting, those sideways looks . . .

But Julian was undoing his seatbelt, opening his door.

'Of course not!' he was saying. 'We can't afford to hire the concert hall every time we want to rehearse, and anyway, it's in use tonight. We come here instead. It's the Methodist Hall, much cheaper, though it's rather tedious having to bring the stands every time. You can help stack the chairs afterwards, if you like!'

The reality of attending an orchestral rehearsal suddenly caught up with Isobel. Initially, she had thought how unusual, how glamorous, it would be to attend; something to boast about to her friends. But which friends? Dave might not be very pleased. She wouldn't tell Dave, there was no easy way she could begin to explain . . . But now she imagined how she would be stared at and speculated about, and how she would be in the way – when she was not helping to stack the chairs. She shut the door and stood by the car.

'Julian, perhaps I'd better not come in. I'll just be in the way.'

'Of course you won't. Can you hold this again while I lock the boot? Thanks. Now come on, they'll all be waiting for me.'

When he pushed open one of the heavy doors, she saw that the building was not dark and empty at all; light and noise poured out on to the pavement. People were talking, clattering, shuffling music or tuning their instruments. Julian's car stood alone on the street, parked on the double yellow line, but inside the hall, fifteen or twenty people sat or stood in a semicircle, and watched as Isobel and Julian entered. Someone, Isobel couldn't see who, clapped slowly, ironically, and a grey-haired woman with a violin clicked her tongue and said, 'We were about to start without you!'

'*Could* you? I thought I was indispensable. Sorry, everyone, I was unavoidably detained. Can you find yourself a seat?' he asked Isobel. 'It would probably be better if you sat over on that side.'

Isobel's footsteps thudded dully on the scuffed wooden floor as she crossed the room. Christ, poor girl, he thought, seeing how she had flushed scarlet, that was a bit tactless! I can imagine what that randy fool with the viola thinks. She's my doctor, actually. She takes care of me, services my body. Services – that's what my Good Worker offered me, didn't she? What a nasty slip. Your Freudian slip is showing, Mrs Gillespie. Ooh, look at Isobel – medical Isobel isn't wearing a slip, just look at those long slim legs. Don't raise your arms so high, doctor, our concentration's slipping, doctor!

He shook his bow and tightened it, watching while the principal cello helped Isobel lift down a chair from the top of the stack, then placed it at the side of the hall. The other musicians were watching, too, and there were whispered comments and heads bent towards each other. But Rosemary was watching him, and Julian decided that the others had seen enough.

'We'll start with the Telemann,' he called out.

There were sighs and mutters as the musicians lifted music off their stands and sorted through the papers at their feet.

'You said we'd concentrate on the Bach,' an oboist grumbled.

'Sorry, woodwind. This won't take long. But I've been thinking again about that second Allegro – the tempo's wrong.' Pages were turned as everyone found the place. 'We should try it faster, like this.' Julian beat out the time with his bow and hummed the opening bars of melody. 'Since it's the final movement of the concert, I'd like to provide a bit of excitement. I know that's not strictly as it was written, but let's see how it goes.'

Isobel watched from the sideline, thankful that attention was no longer on her, as players fingered the notes according to the new tempo, and tried out short passages.

'Right! Let's try it.'

Julian was sitting now, looking round, and he gave a few beats with his bow. Throughout the piece he occasionally stopped to listen, sometimes reinforcing the beat, now frowning, now nodding.

'That's better. Continuo, you were dragging.'

As Julian conferred briefly with the double bass and cello, one or two musicians carried on, playing a short, rapid phrase over and over again until they had it right, but others nodded or pulled faces at each other.

'Can we try it with the Andante to see how they go together?' the harpsichordist asked.

'Right.' Julian nodded.

This time he paused more often to listen, occasionally gesturing, damping down the sound, pulling it up again in a crescendo; once, he stopped everybody and made them go back a few bars, explaining how he wanted the passage to be played. There was a brief discussion with some of the principals, and agreement was eventually reached. Isobel found it difficult to understand how everyone kept together without a conductor. She remembered again her own difficulties with counting and keeping to the beat when the class had been made to sing and play percussion instruments at school. No one here was obviously counting, there were no moving lips, no rhythmically tapping feet. But as she watched, she became aware that each player occasionally, briefly, lifted his or her eyes from the music and glanced at Julian; they glanced, too, at each other. They obviously heard each other, she thought, and there must be hints and cues in the music. And Julian was far from impassive as he played: his eyebrows lifted, his body moved, and when he wasn't actually playing, however brief the rest, his bow was beating time, his eyes were darting about, his whole body seemed to be giving out signals. She didn't understand the signals, but the players clearly did; he seemed to know what they needed to receive from him as their leader.

She realised that she had been staring at Julian for a long time, so she looked away, searching for a new point of attention, and found that one of the woodwind players was staring at her as he played. She looked down at her hands instead and pushed at the cuticles of her nails, and wished that the annoying blush was not heating her cheeks. The chair was so uncomfortable! The canvas seat was ripped at the front; she fingered the tear and poked the chipped brown paint on the tubular metal frame, then uncrossed and recrossed her legs. How many more pieces will they rehearse? she wondered. I must look a complete idiot sitting here. Why doesn't that oboe player or clarinettist or whatever he is *play* instead of ogling me over his music stand?

The piece ended.

'Sounds a bit over-excited, played at that speed,' someone said. Others disagreed; there was discussion, mostly amicable, accompanied by a few theatrical shrugs and grimaces. Some of the woodwind had included the harpsichord player in their muttered discussion. Isobel kept hearing the word 'temperament', and wondered if they always spoke about Julian like that, so that he could hear. But he paid no attention. 'It'll play,' the grey-haired woman who led the second violins said; and the majority seemed to agree.

'Right. Bach,' Julian called.

At last everyone was involved and the whole atmosphere changed. Even to Isobel's untrained ear it was obvious that some of the movements were dance pieces – courtly dances for women in long, full skirts and men in tight, constricting clothes; no room for free expression but plenty of time for lingering looks and the touch of palms and fingers. The members of the Ensemble were clearly enjoying themselves, to judge by the exchanged glances and smiles. Sometimes Julian stopped them, made them repeat a passage with a different emphasis or different bowing. Isobel was surprised when one of the violinists seated near her stood up and walked out into the hall while the others were playing. Julian was apparently unconcerned. The man faced the orchestra and paced from one side of the hall to the other, then returned to his place and continued to play. Later, one of the viola players did the same, and she supposed that they would otherwise not get a chance to hear how everyone interacted. She should ask Julian; it would be a way of starting a conversation.

The woodwind players were prominent, a distinctive band of sound, and she watched their mobile faces, the long, slow outpouring of breath into their instruments, the snatched replenishments for their lungs. She inhaled and tried to let her own breath leak out in a slow, controlled way, but had soon exhausted her capacity. She fidgeted impatiently on her chair and straightened her jacket and fussed with the hem of her skirt. But her fidgetings had drawn Julian's eyes; she saw him looking towards her as he played, and there was a strange, transient throb inside her, so that she was amazed that she was sitting here, watching him, listening to his

Ensemble rehearse. At the special request of their eponymous leader, Kersland himself! Who cared what the other players thought about her? She had accomplished her aim, in a more surprising way than she could have dreamt. She would be able to talk to him in the car. There would be time then to find out more about him, and perhaps he would even ask her in for coffee.

At the end of the final movement, Julian put down his violin, resting it on its side on the floor, and began a conversation with the violinist next to him. Someone yawned loudly and stood up, and others put down their instruments and moved around. People were passing round biscuits and opening Thermos flasks; the smell of coffee made Isobel's stomach clench with emptiness. The grey-haired woman was coming over, carrying an unopened Thermos and an extra plastic cup.

'Hello,' she said. 'I'm Rosemary, the librarian. That means I look after the music – and keep an eye on Julian. I'm afraid he isn't looking after you at the moment, though.' Julian was now talking to the harpsichord player. 'Would you like some coffee? Milk but no sugar.'

Isobel stood up, smiling, relieved to have someone to talk to.

'Yes please! If you're sure you can spare some.'

'I always bring extra anyway, because Julian always claims he can't manage both coffee and the Ensemble. I hope you won't mind sharing a cup . . .'

Isobel hesitated; she definitely did not like to share cups with people she didn't know. 'Perhaps I could drink out of the other side. My name's Isobel, by the way, Isobel Hutchison. I hope I'm not in your way. It's a bit embarrassing.'

'You must be keen, to want to hear us rehearse. It can seem rather disorganised at times. Are you a student?'

'Yes. Yes, I am, actually. Does it look so obvious?'

'I thought I might have seen you at some of the Sunday

concerts – quite a few of the Academy students come these days. They certainly brighten up the audience. Do you like our Leader's glorious waistcoat? I think he was beginning to feel outshone! Oh, I'm sorry – it's very hot!'

Isobel had burnt her mouth on the coffee. She was slightly bemused, but understood that a mistake had been made.

'I'm not that sort of student. I'm a medical student. Mr Kersland – Julian – asked me if I'd like to come along. He probably thinks it's good for my education, bridging the gulf between the Two Cultures, and all that.'

Rosemary laughed. 'A medic! You must be almost finished, I suppose. My daughter's a GP, she trained here too, and now she's in a country practice up in the north-west. Now, let me introduce you to a few people, they're probably all itching to know the name of their audience! Do you like this sort of music?'

'No, really. Please don't worry.' Isobel's tongue hurt where she had burnt it and her blouse felt wet at her armpits with nervous sweat. 'I'm not really very knowledgeable . . .'

'Fiona! She plays the bassoon, you probably noticed her. Fiona, this is Isobel, who's a medical student. Julian thought she might like to watch us rehearse.'

'A medical student! Goodness! I didn't know Julian knew anyone like that. Are you enjoying it – the rehearsal, I mean? Do you come to the concerts?'

'I came to one a couple of months ago – the one with the cats.'

'Oh dear! Yes—' Fiona looked away for a moment and seemed embarrassed. 'Not one of our best.'

Rosemary was frowning at Fiona. 'Julian merely wanted to provide something a bit different from the usual Bach.'

Fiona was beckoning over a man who was carrying a hipflask with a pewter cup. 'Come and meet Isobel. She's incredibly clever, she's studying medicine. Musicians tend to be rather thick, you know, in general.'

'And some are thicker than others, especially viola players! Yes, I know!' They exchanged glances and Isobel sensed hidden meanings and intimacies. 'Hello, Isobel. Would you like a drop of something to pep up Rosemary's coffee? Or is it Julian's coffee that you're sharing?'

'I think he's too busy talking money to bother about coffee,' Rosemary said. The cellist who had helped Isobel with her chair was standing by his instrument case, showing Julian some papers. 'That's Guy. He's Fiona's husband.'

Isobel looked swiftly at her companions, but they had all turned to look at Guy and Julian, and she guessed that their faces would be quite without expression. Rosemary took the plastic cup and refilled it, and called Julian over. He looked across, his mind elsewhere, but eventually came clopping and weaving through the chairs and abandoned instruments to take the full cup from Isobel's hand. The others had moved away.

'OK? Are you enjoying yourself? Sit somewhere else, move your chair if you want.'

He turned away to talk to another musician before Isobel could say how much she was enjoying things, how good it was of him to bring her, and all the other hopeless platitudes that wanted to jump out of her mouth, so she sat down again and busied herself with the clutter in her bag, turning the pages of her diary with eyes that saw but did not comprehend the endless lists of daily duty. No one came to talk to her; the few yards of empty wooden floor isolated her as completely as if they had contained a bramble patch, and she glanced up only occasionally during the second half of the rehearsal, and not at all when Julian played. His violin teased the orchestra, coaxed them, imitated them, answered them and led them on; but Isobel didn't want to watch, thinking that her interest would imply infatuation, not realising that, instead, she appeared a sulky child.

At the end, uncertain whether or not to help, she stood

quietly to one side and watched as stands were folded and chairs were stacked.

Rosemary recognised and understood the girl's aloofness, and took care to go over and to say goodbye.

'Shall we see you on Sunday week? It's a good programme.'

'Perhaps. Thank you. At least I won't be the only one listening there.'

'I certainly hope not!' Rosemary laughed. 'See you then.'

When Rosemary had gone, Isobel wondered if she should have asked about a ticket, but then she decided that, after all, she no longer really cared whether she went to the concert or not.

Julian's mind was occupied with matters other than driving Isobel home. He saw her waiting and swore to himself because he had promised to drop in on Guy to look through some papers. Now he would have to make a detour and would be late. Perhaps he could ask someone else to take her home? No, nearly everyone had left and he couldn't just hand her over to someone else like an unwanted parcel.

'Isobel!' He gestured towards the door. 'Shall we go?'

'Thank you for inviting me,' she said when they were back in the car; she had to say something. 'It was really interesting. Rosemary was kind, too – she gave me some of her coffee. Did you know she has a daughter who's a doctor?'

'Has she? Mmm, I suppose I may have known. Good.' Julian's hands were busy with the controls, he was scarcely listening.

'I like your waistcoat. Is it Mexican?'

'Peruvian, actually. Do you really?' Julian looked down, even though the waistcoat was now almost covered by his coat. 'I was wondering about buying another. What do you think?'

'And one of those wide-brimmed black hats with the coloured braid. That would look very dashing.'

'Yes!' Julian looked at her with a surprised, assessing smile.

'What an excellent idea! You are clever.'

'That's what the bassoon woman said, too. I got the impression that she thought cleverness was a social stigma. She also said that all musicians were thick.' Isobel deliberately stressed that last word, but kept her voice cool and ironic. 'That's probably a generalisation, don't you think?'

'Oh dear! I would certainly like to think I'm an exception.'

Isobel deliberately did not respond. The silence lengthened, and Julian concentrated on the car. They were not far from her street. She couldn't think of anything now to say, but one of them would have to make some move to apologise. It was Julian who spoke first, as though he had been thinking seriously about what she had said.

'It depends how you define cleverness, doesn't it? And whether you think "thick" is its antithesis. We're very clever with our fingers, and some of us like to think that we're intelligent, too. Are you clever with your fingers, Isobel? Are you going to wield the surgeon's knife?'

Isobel almost smiled in her relief. 'No, I think that's too far down the line for me. I'd rather deal with patients before they reach that stage. Unless I become a pathologist.'

'Not all of us are past it when the surgeon fingers us, you know.' He glanced sideways.

'Oh!' Isobel paused. 'No, that's true. Some are clearly quite avant garde!'

It was Julian's turn to smile. '*Touché*. Will you come and see me wear the hat?'

'At the concert? Surely you wouldn't!'

'Why not? And bring some of your friends – the more the better.'

'You didn't arrange a ticket,' she pointed out drily. 'You seemed to be rather busy.'

'Damn, nor I did! I'll write a note. Where can I drop you? I have to go on and see someone.'

So much for late evening conversation over coffee and

liqueurs, thought Isobel; so much for idle dreams and speculation.

When Julian pulled over to the kerb in front of her house, she said, 'I live right at the top of three flights of stairs, so I won't ask you in for a drink, even if you did have time. Thanks, anyway – and have a nice evening.'

But Julian was searching through the map pocket in the door.

'Here. Let me write a note.' He found a loose-leaf notebook and took out a pen. 'How do you spell your surname? That should get you in – just show it at the door. And bring your friends!'

Isobel took the piece of paper. 'Miss Isobel Hutchison and friends are here at my invitation. Julian Kersland.' It wasn't really a personal invitation – he just wanted bodies to fill the hall.

The pavement was high, and when Isobel bent down low to shut the door and say goodbye, Julian briefly regretted that he had not, after all, been able to take her to his flat. But he raised his hand, then revved the engine and sped away.

Chapter Ten

'It's the insidious cult of personality. "Ensemble" is supposed to indicate togetherness.'

'Oh, come on! Since when have concertos been about togetherness? Whoever heard of . . .'

'It couldn't have been very easy for him to climb up . . .'

'Thank heaven it wasn't *The Four Seasons*, like you-know-who!'

'– was quite exciting . . .'

'– jazz Bach, next! He'll lose half his audience.'

'That lot over there were thumping and cheering.'

'Jeering, more like!'

'What strange clothes! I wonder why they all decided to be so informal?'

'I thought Kersland was an off-duty matador,' Iain smiled, as he picked up a tray. 'If he'd held a red cape over the bow . . . I get the impression that today's performance was atypical, don't you?'

'It certainly wasn't quite what I had expected!'

Margaret, too, had been listening to the conversations. She and Iain were at the tail end of the lunch queue and the tables were filling up fast around them. She liked the look of the food on people's plates – and since nobody was commenting on the food, that at least was presumably the acceptable standard.

She had almost decided not to wait behind upstairs, after all, to introduce Julian to her husband, although that had been

119

her original intention in persuading Iain to come. But Julian was so elated today, so – active! She knew she should be pleased, but she had needed him, perhaps even wanted him, to look awkward and perhaps a little tired or harassed, possibly even to show the odd grimace of pain. She had wanted Iain to see for himself that she had been doing the right thing in volunteering to look after Julian. So she had changed her mind about introducing them, and had been trying to hasten Iain towards the door, when Julian came tap-tapping, almost tap-dancing, out of that back room, ready to greet everyone. He'd obviously loved it when those young people up in the balcony had cheered and stamped their feet after the Vivaldi concerto, *Storm at Sea*.

'He was marvellous,' she said out loud.

'A hint of playing to the gallery, perhaps. But no – he's very impressive. You've chosen well.'

For a moment, Margaret's skin prickled and she was chilled. What did Iain imagine she had chosen Julian *for*? But Iain was smiling and indicating two girls with laden plates of food, who were about to sit down with their friends.

'Things don't change much, do they? We used to share food in restaurants, too, when I was a student. That yellow-haired boy was sitting at the front of the gallery, wasn't he – the lad who came rushing down afterwards?'

Margaret would have liked to have laid her hand on the young man's head. His bright hair stuck up in a short, uniform layer, like the pile of a carpet, and she wanted to feel the texture.

'Yes. He seemed to have enjoyed it, anyway.'

The boy had darted in front of them just as they had been about to greet Julian, and had hastily whispered something and shaken his hand. Julian had looked after him with a puzzled expression, but then he had seen Margaret and was instantly all smiling charm.

'Mrs Gillespie! Mr Gillespie, how nice to meet you. I'm so

pleased you were able to come. Your wife has been so kind to me, Mr Gillespie. I wish you would persuade her to stay on, but I know she has a lot of other commitments. But it's been most kind of you both . . . Are you going down to lunch? I'll see you there.'

Margaret had been about to reply, but one of the violinists, the middle-aged woman with grey hair, had caught hold of Julian's arm and distracted him with a question, and Margaret and Iain had been free to find their way to the crypt. Margaret was unwillingly impressed at the manner in which Julian had openly joined forces with Iain, implying that her husband was in charge of his wife's unusual arrangement. She could have been insulted, but she thought she knew what he had been trying to do: the right degree of familiarity, the implication that Margaret's commitment had now come to an end. She was not insulted, but recognised, as Julian had no doubt intended, the hidden implication of another conspiracy, for neither she nor Julian had made a firm decision about her future. The trial period had ended. She had not been sacked nor had she resigned, and Julian had understood that he should telephone her if he should need her help in the future. He also appeared to have understood that it was not a suitable discussion point in front of preprandial concert-goers, one of whom was his erstwhile housekeeper's husband.

The woman violinist who had interrupted them earlier picked up a tray and joined the queue behind them. She smiled at Margaret and then went over to greet an elderly lady wearing a beret, who was sitting near the door.

'No, Mr Kersland's gone now,' Margaret heard her say. 'But I'll be happy to pass on your message.'

Isobel had hovered near the rear of the hall, hoping to speak to Julian before she left. It had been an extraordinary performance; she hadn't expected to become so caught up in the music, almost, at one stage, overwhelmed. There had been a strange fierce intensity about Julian's playing that had made the skin on her back go cold. She wanted to tell him, not in such words, perhaps, but at least to congratulate him and show him that she had been there in the audience. But he seemed always to be surrounded by admirers, and she didn't want to push in and speak to him in front of all those other people. The note he had given her, his 'invitation', didn't seem to extend to lunch. She had arrived alone and shown the note at the ticket office, trying to look unconcerned while the two women examined the piece of paper and consulted each other in whispers. She didn't have sufficient courage to insist that it also covered her for lunch. There! He'd seen her! He raised a hand, but he was waylaid by a well-dressed couple. He was talking to the man, but now Rosemary had taken him away. Isobel sighed in exasperation. It was hopeless, she might as well leave, and go and sunbathe and watch the ducks in the park.

She had already gone down the steps and was crossing the road when Julian called to her from the door.

'Isobel! Come back!'

He was holding the edge of the door, waving his stick at her, and his face was bright and urgent.

'I want to show you my hat!'

She looked back in amazement, and then returned to the steps, laughing.

'You *didn't* buy a hat!'

'No. But I knew that would make you come back! Why aren't you staying for lunch?'

'Your note didn't mention lunch.'

'What note?'

He had completely forgotten. She took the folded piece of paper out of her bag and showed him.

'Oh, that! Come on, I'm inviting you now. I'll buy you lunch.'

'But you need to talk to all your admirers. I'll just be in the way again. I was going to go and feed the ducks.'

Julian looked out at the sunlit street and the young green leaves on the trees as though he had been unaware of the existence of outdoors. He was so buoyed up that when he had seen Isobel, the idea of lunch with her had suddenly seemed to be the perfect finale to the morning's success. But she was right, if he stayed in here he would be entrapped in tedious conversations.

'What a good idea!' he said. 'Let's have lunch outside. We'll drive out into the country and find a pub. You will come, won't you?'

She nodded, speechless.

'Wait while I collect my fiddle . . .'

The breeze blew her long, flowered skirt against her bare calves, and she crossed back into the sun to wait. She loved surprises and impromptu entertainments. And she didn't want to consider whether what she was about to do was sensible. It would be fun, it would be different; and Julian, anyway, would pay.

They didn't look for a pub. They stopped instead at a supermarket and Isobel carried the wire basket, and thrilled to see it fill with smoked salmon and small brown rolls and early glasshouse strawberries.

'But we'll need a knife,' she said, ever practical, 'and glasses and a corkscrew.'

So Julian bought those too, and cream and small tomatoes and sparkling water, as well as wine. He was elated, showing off. Isobel was elated, too, but there was the underlying worry that she would be seen by David or his friends, and she was more comfortable when they were back in the car and driving out of the city.

There were long silences, then, as they both reflected on the situation into which they had rather hastily thrown themselves, and Isobel, once more, found herself with little to say. She hoped they weren't going far; she ought not to be gone too long. She'd told David she would come round to the flat in the afternoon. How would she explain her absence? She would ask Julian to bring her back soon after lunch.

The thought of food made her stomach contract and gurgle, and she covered the noise by saying, 'Today's concert was very different. There were more people playing, weren't there? The audience was bigger, too.'

Julian wondered why she was twittering on about the concert. He looked at her, and suddenly began to feel more optimistic about the outing. He realised she was probably nervous, and tried to set her at her ease by answering her questions.

'Yes – I pull in more instrumentalists when I need them. It's not always easy because there aren't that many people proficient on baroque instruments. Or the person I want may have got a date somewhere else that week and can't get to our rehearsal. Today I had a couple more desks of violins – and there was the flute, of course. And the trumpets for the Handel. I had to book them up ages ago, they're usually pretty busy. One of them only arrived last night, in time for this morning's rehearsal.'

'Are the baroque instruments very different, then? You play ordinary violin, too, don't you? And you said you gave lessons. Those aren't in baroque violin, surely?'

Julian laughed. 'What a lot of questions! Yes, baroque instruments *are* very different. But I don't suppose you really want a tutorial! Some look different – and the sound is quite different. The woodwind, for example, are very obviously different to look at, with few or no keys, for one thing. And so on. As for teaching, I mostly teach "ordinary" violin, as you call it – but I have a couple of students from the music school who come along for baroque.'

'Which sort do you prefer to play? You were brilliant in the Vivaldi,' she said, a little awkwardly. 'It looked really difficult.'

'It is. Vivaldi was a brilliant fiddle player himself, by the way. I like both styles, they both have their challenges.'

Not least the challenge of finding a teacher for himself, when he was younger. There was, too, the greatest challenge of all, the expression of the Gift. But Julian was still too elated to dwell on that.

'The audience numbers are certainly looking up. More younger people, too.'

'Those students – were they music students? They really seemed to like you.'

'Yes.' Julian grinned, and then remembered the note that the yellow-haired boy had slipped into his hand; he wondered where he had put it. (And wasn't that also the boy with the score who'd come up to him at the end of the Farina concert? Although his hair had possibly been a different colour then.) 'I hope we'll get more of them in future as they spread the word. What about your friends? Did you bring a crowd? I didn't see where you were sitting.'

Isobel intertwined her fingers in her lap and shook her head.

'No, I'm very sorry. Everyone was busy – exams are coming up and we all become rather single-minded.'

Of course, she hadn't asked anyone to come with her: who would she have asked? No one she knew was likely to be interested, apart from Dave. And she would have had to explain to him about the written invitation. She couldn't tell Dave, she didn't want to tell Dave, this interaction with Julian Kersland formed a separate compartment of her life. She hadn't even told Dave about the broken taxi, because that had been an inextricable part of the day on which her uneasiness about their relationship had begun. As a result, she had been unable to tell him that she had attended an orchestral rehearsal and had sat in Kersland's car. And so the thin line of deceit grew and widened into three dimensions until it became a barrier that separated these awkward and unusual incidents from her life with Dave. Attempts to cross this growing barrier would lead to lies, lack of concentration, and mistakes; she had been insane to think of any other outcome. She would have her picnic with Julian, she would make this exploratory link, and then she would place the encounters in a metaphorical box, tick them off as an interesting experience – and return to medicine and what her life was really all about.

The hills rose steeply around them, and they turned off the main road and drove along a narrow lane that led through a winding valley to the side of the loch. Dried leaves and the empty, blackened husks of nuts made a crunchy carpet underneath the bright green of the beech trees and the yellow ochre of aged oaks. Isobel wanted to sit in the sun by the water's edge, but Julian complained that he couldn't walk on shingle, and that the shore was, in any case, too crowded. Isobel looked at the families with their dogs, and the windsurfers and canoeists, and she had to agree, so they took the food and walked slowly up a knoll, to sit within a rocky circle that sheltered them from the breeze. Julian settled himself stiffly on the ground and arranged his leg, then uncorked and poured the wine. He handed Isobel a polystyrene cup.

'Here's to – success!' he said. 'To our success.'

Isobel wondered what successes he wanted for himself but she didn't know him well enough to ask. She knew what success would bring for her, what she had been struggling towards all these years, and so she drank, and then sighed and turned her face to the sun.

'This is nice!'

'Thank you for agreeing to come. I know it must seem rather strange that I asked you since we hardly know each other, but I wanted to share my happiness with someone – and I'm very pleased that you were there, and willing to humour me!'

Julian spoke quietly, rather seriously, but he longed to reach out and touch the bare ankle that showed beneath her skirt, to slide his hands up her smooth legs . . . He had experienced the reality of being again this morning, in the concert hall; he had played and he had been taken over, and he had Given – and the pain had not been too great. Applause had driven the pain away, so that now only the longing remained, the longing to be taken over again. But now there was no music. Now he was all too human again, yet still full of longing, which could only be assuaged in an earthly way. The memory of joy, the need, the wine, the warmth . . . and Isobel was here to help. He looked at her out of the corner of his eye, and he caught his breath, he desired her so strongly. He gulped more wine, and cursed that he had to drive; but there was plenty of time.

'I'm glad, too – that I was there. I never seem to do anything exciting like this any more,' Isobel was saying.

'It sounds as though what you are doing is very dull, in that case.'

'Not at all!' Isobel was almost indignant. 'I'm doing exactly what I want to do, so I'm really very fortunate. The course is hard work, though, and I don't get much free time. But you sound as though you do this all the time.'

'Oh, every week!' he mocked. 'Don't be so serious, Isobel!'

He was leaning back against a rock and his eyes were half closed against the light. For a moment Isobel felt irritated and diminished, but, although he was arrogant, she was not intimidated. So, instead of defending herself, she laughed and stretched. Julian ached.

'Let's have more excitement! Shall I butter these rolls?'

She rummaged through the bags until she found the paper plates, and busied herself sorting out the food. Down on the shore, two children, clutching towels around their taut, juddering bodies, were being handed plastic cups of Thermos tea. Isobel laughed and pointed towards them with the knife.

'I remember that, don't you? Staying in the water until one was blue with cold, then standing shivering and being made to have hot drinks!'

'No, actually,' Julian said lightly. 'I can't say I ever did, really. I didn't go in the water much.'

'Oh. Oh, I see. When – How old were you, then, when you had your accident? I heard – that it was the result of an accident. Prof Smith again. Sorry.'

'Twelve.' He continued looking down at the water so that she wouldn't see the triumph that he felt; he knew she would want to hear the story, but he would keep her waiting. 'But it's pretty boring, really. I don't especially want to talk about it. Where did you used to go to swim?'

Later, though, when they lay together in his bed, he had told her, as she had known he would. When he was relaxed and drowsy, she had stroked his narrow thigh, and had touched the purple, puckered scars. Her hair covered his chest like a shawl and the weight of her head was warm against his ribs, as her fingers ran around his knee and she asked him to tell the tale. For a moment he wondered what to tell her, but although he had begun to know her body he didn't yet know her mind, so he told her the story that Professor Smith had half heard, the abbreviated epic tale of heroism, a drowned friend, and grief. Isobel hugged and caressed him, and kissed him with compassion and mounting lust, until she arose to sit astride him once more and engulfed him with her body and her extravagantly swaying breasts.

She had been smiling to herself as she hurried home through the orange shadows of the streetlights. The smile had disappeared, though, when she saw her name, in David's writing, on a note tucked under her door. 'Isobel, where *are* you? I've called round three times! Phone when you get back. D.'

It was too late to telephone, and what, in any case, could she say? Could she tell him about the effect of hot sun and afternoon wine, and relaxed, drowsy conversations that pushed the time for departure ever away? Could she tell him how Julian's stick caught on a tree root so that he had almost fallen, and she had caught his arm to steady him and had laughed at the reversal of the cliché? Or, how Julian, feeling chilled in his concert-going clothes, had driven them to the Highland Woollen Mill, and had wandered with her amongst the coachloads of senior citizens, encouraging her to help him choose a pullover? And afterwards, how they had waited in a hotel lounge for the slow production of an opulent cream tea? She could not tell David that Julian had driven to a viewpoint and had parked the car, and that they had kissed and touched each other as dusk fell; or how she had reached back between the seats to retrieve her cardigan, so that the proximity of what Julian so obviously desired, the invitation of the open top buttons, had been too much for Julian's hands. She could not tell David that for the first time in many years she had gloried in the uninhibited use of her body as a sexual snare and means of gratification. Because Julian had been ensnared – and she was exultant and intrigued.

Julian could tell no one, either, about the day of extraordinary, unimagined success. There was no one to tell, and he was too restless and astonished to sleep. When he lay naked in his bed, he closed his eyes to recapture the image of Isobel's pale torso, caught like a snapshot in the flash of headlights from a turning car.

Chapter Eleven

'I saw something strange in the Sunday paper recently, a review of a concert by a young Chinese pianist – "an incandescent talent snatched from the gods". What do you think that means?'

'That he or she is likely to reach white heat and burn out, presumably.'

'But why "snatched"? And by whom? What gods, even?' Margaret was persistent. 'Did the audience snatch him before he was destroyed? Or his agent?'

'Why are you asking me all this?'

'The pianist existed to please the gods by playing to them, presumably using the talent that they had given him. By snatching him, the snatcher would incur heavenly – assuming these gods are in the heavens – displeasure.'

Margaret stopped and examined Julian's blank stare.

'I'm sorry! It was just that the wording caught my attention. Do you get any unusual reviews yourself?'

Julian ignored her last question and stopped watching the surface of his coffee slanting as he tipped his cup.

'It depends where you think the talent comes from. In my case, it probably results from some genetic input from my grandmother.'

'And where did she get it from? Do you think there are genes for musical ability – or acting ability? I wish I knew about that sort of thing.'

'Or genes for a talent in medical research. I know a

scientist – of sorts! – who could tell me.'

'Possibly some of those homeless people sleeping down by the river have a talent for music, but they have never been aware of it. There must be the possibility to recognise the ability, mustn't there, and to explore and expand it. There must be the *opportunity*. You have, I suppose, always had the opportunity.'

'There were quite a few years when I didn't have the opportunity. Or rather, I had the opportunity but didn't exercise it. Chose not to, in fact.'

There was a silence between them. Then Margaret stood up and collected together the cups and took them to the sink. She wondered if she could push Julian further; she wasn't certain why she wanted to know more about him, her motive certainly was not to obtain fuel for gossip, not even so that she could discuss him with Iain. She felt she needed some insight into Julian's character, perhaps so she could better justify (to herself?) why she wanted to look after him. She leant against the sink and stared out of the window.

'Do you mind if I ask why you chose not to explore your particular talent? I know it's impertinent of me.'

Julian looked at Margaret's back; although her face was turned in profile, he could see her puzzled frown, the wrinkles at the edges of her eyes. He was not used to talking about his feelings, especially not to a woman; yet this woman was unusual in that she seemed thoughtful, almost self-effacing. He had never discussed this question of . . . opportunity, with anyone except . . . except . . . It might be a relief to talk about it with her; perhaps that was what he needed, an outpouring, catharsis. Could he even tell her about Isobel? At the thought of Isobel there was a strange lurch in his stomach. What was there to tell about Isobel except that she had not phoned? His agitation made him answer Margaret sharply.

'I chose not to because it was irrelevant and a waste of time!'

Margaret pressed the soil beneath a pot plant on the

windowsill and decided that it was already damp enough.

Finally she said, 'I'm sorry, Julian, I shouldn't have asked you. But I'm very glad – for the rest of us – that you decided at some stage to change your mind. Perhaps you still feel your talent is irrelevant – to you yourself – but it's certainly not a waste of time for other people. For those who listen to you.'

She smiled briefly, anxiously, at him. 'I should start to do some housework. Tell me what you'd like me to do.'

'No. I didn't intend to be so brusque – I'm sorry. I'm a bit unsettled today. What you said was interesting. It was what Canon Bothwell said, too. The one in the photograph.'

Margaret looked at him enquiringly. They had not discussed that photo, and Julian had put it away after her first visit.

The photograph was so clear in Julian's mind that when he swung round in his chair to go and fetch it, he was momentarily surprised that the chair did not swing with him and roll across the floor.

Someone had made him smile, Margaret thought, when she looked at the photo that he had fetched; he had been able to smile despite the wheelchair and the gaunt, thin-lipped man who stood behind him and rested a (comforting? possessive?) hand on his shoulder.

'Canon Bothwell convinced me that my ability – or my talent, however you like to refer to it – was a gift.' Julian swallowed, and paused. 'And that my disability was a gift, too.'

'A remarkable man.'

Then the enormity of the clergyman's suggestion slowly overwhelmed her, so that she held her breath and dared not speak.

'Yes. You see, the resultant isolation – my inability to *join in* – was bestowed on me for a specific reason, in order to provide me with time and space in which to practise and excel at the violin. I had talent, but I needed mental and physical discipline.'

'Could you believe that?' The idea frightened and horrified her.

'Not at first, no. But later, I believed that he was right. He was a very committed, caring man. And if he hadn't helped me at that time, I probably would have given up my music, serious music-making, anyway, permanently. I'd probably have ended up in a mental institution!' Julian gave a short, barking laugh.

It had not been the pain, the interminable pain, the pain that never entirely faded and was then renewed after each operation, that had nearly driven him mad, but fear. And guilt. Without the clergyman's gently persistent probing he would still be thinking (if he could still think rationally at all) that the pain had been a punishment. But the man's quiet conviction had finally convinced him, too, that he had also been prized as well as punished. Yet he could never explain that to Margaret Gillespie, it was too dangerously personal. Now that he looked carefully at the photograph, and examined the face that seemed lined by inner conflicts and yet, paradoxically, to embody spiritual certainty, Julian wanted to tell Margaret something about the man and his beliefs. Perhaps then his own disquiet would be slightly eased.

Margaret watched Julian looking at the photograph and waited for him to tell her more. She dared not question him while he talked, but merely prompted him occasionally with a nod or murmured sound. Julian told her that Canon Bothwell had been the school chaplain and had visited him in hospital, presumably out of a sense of duty, shortly after the accident that broke his knee. At first Julian had been embarrassed, even angry, that the chaplain had come to see him and to sit by his bed in a public place as though he, Julian, needed spiritual guidance and consolation. But the chaplain had not talked about God or even about religion. He had brought magazines and news of outside matters and school, and he had not been visibly upset, nor had he been driven away, when Julian ignored him or was deliberately rude.

'I'm afraid I was rather arrogant, even then,' Julian acknowledged, and Margaret smiled.

But Julian still found it almost impossible to acknowledge, even to himself (and certainly not to Margaret Gillespie) how badly he must have treated his parents at that time, particularly his mother. Fear and misery had been brought into the open as bitterness and fury at his immobility and dependence, and had made him scream and throw objects and abuse, or sulk and refuse to be distracted or comforted. His mother had told him later, without condemning, that it had been at least a year before they had all been able to find some form of peace.

Canon Bothwell had arrived one day with some music that Julian's violin teacher had sent. It was easy stuff, simplified versions of popular tunes, thought likely to be sufficiently simple and melodic to lift Julian's low spirits. He had eventually agreed to play it, and the instrument had been unpacked for him, the music stand arranged to suit his chair.

'But I hadn't played for six or eight months,' Julian explained to Margaret. 'I couldn't play the damned thing, the notes were all over the place. It was terrible. I don't think I'd realised – before the accident – what fiddle-playing had meant to me. It was just something that I did – went to music lessons, grumbled about them, went to orchestra, practised – or not! But now, when suddenly it seemed I wouldn't be able to do it any more, I was completely shattered. Even that had gone!' He paused: he could still remember the despair and anger. 'I remember I was gripping the fiddle by the neck, and I lifted it up in the air – I was actually crying – and I was going to slam it down against the corner of the table. I wanted to break it into bits and be done with it for ever!' And to die, to go to bed and cry, and wake up dead! 'But Canon Bothwell caught hold of it in time and stopped me.'

'What did he say?'

'Nothing. He just put the fiddle on the table, and then sat and held my hand. It was the strangest thing. He didn't even look at me.'

Margaret looked at the photograph again and tried to imagine Julian in his chair (an ordinary chair, or that same wheelchair?) with his head bowed, while the stern, quiet man sat beside him and looked into infinity, and asked God to flow from his mind, through his hand, to the hand and mind of the troubled, wounded child.

There had been so many times, Julian thought, when Canon Bothwell had held his hand to transfer to him strength and comfort; but it had been the power and conviction of the man that he had felt, and not the love of God. Julian had pretended, though, had acquiesced, for the chaplain's sake. Or had it been for his own? Throughout those chair-bound months the chaplain had encouraged him and assured him of the Gift of his talent.

The violin teacher used to come to the house, Julian explained to Margaret, and often Canon Bothwell came too.

'It was a hard struggle at first. For one thing, I had always preferred to stand up to play, or perhaps that was what I decided I had preferred, in retrospect, and at first nothing would go right. I had gone backwards in ability. I hated it! I would think of all kinds of reasons for cancelling the lessons – but the adults wouldn't give in. Gradually I began to improve, and suddenly, not long after, I was breaking new ground, then beginning to race ahead. When I went back to school, I couldn't do any sports so I spent a lot of my free time playing in the music cells. I reached Grade VIII violin two years before I was due to leave school, and then I was free to try to play anything I wanted.'

'Did Canon Bothwell maintain his interest in you?'

Julian thought about that, looking out of the window. 'Yes. But I'm afraid I rather abandoned him. Once I'd found my feet again – so to speak – I was terribly tied up in my own affairs. He must have had lots of other concerns, anyway. I'm sure he was very busy. He still used to come to the house occasionally, and he always came to the concerts in which I was playing. I made him cry once! I played for him at home, and it made him cry.' And I pretended that I hadn't seen, and didn't help. I made Rosemary cry, too. 'Music has that power, sometimes. It isn't abstract, but the circumstances must be right. The power has to come from within the player, and has to be transferred – but the listener must be receptive, too, or in a certain state of mind. He told me then that I had repaid the Gift, I remember.'

'The Gift, again. Was the debt thus cancelled out? Did he imply that was the end? I'm not sure I understand, really.'

'No, it didn't make sense, did it? But I don't remember being concerned about his meaning at the time. I was probably too embarrassed by all that emotion! You see, according to Canon Bothwell, my musical talent was a Gift from God – and therefore nothing to do with genes, by the way! But it wasn't a gift purely for my self-gratification – though it had a very beneficial effect on me personally in helping my mental and physical recovery. It was a gift that must be nurtured, I imagine that was his word, for the pleasure of other people.'

'You were a – what is it called? – a "vessel"?'

'I suppose that was the idea, although he didn't ever say so explicitly, because I imagine a teenage boy would not care in the least to hear that he and his damaged leg were merely set on earth for the gratification of others. But I did come to believe that what I had, what I had been *given*, was very special, and that it was noble, it would make me feel good, if I could pass on the products of that gift for other people's enjoyment.' Yet it was, it is, such a burden, too.

Margaret pushed biscuit crumbs into a small, square pile on the table. She tried to imagine someone convincing her, as a teenager, that a particular skill (she had none, so it was even more difficult to imagine) was given to her as a sign of God's love for her, to be used for the good of humankind. What an extraordinary responsibility for a child to bear. How had the man persuaded Julian, to such success? But *was* it success? Did Julian feel himself successful? How far does one's fame have to spread before one is deemed successful by others?

In her bewilderment and need to understand, she blurted out, 'But do you believe that now? Do you think of public performances as a means of giving? Surely not!'

Julian slumped in his chair, then turned the framed photograph over so that the picture lay face-down on the table.

'I suppose I do,' he said eventually, 'if I allow myself to think about it. It's not an issue that I've thought about for a very long time. Canon Bothwell died when I was a student. Perhaps I should have given the belief a little more consideration along the way, but I've rather avoided it.'

'Perhaps you will think about it again now. It sounds as though it's quite important, although I'm sorry if I've made you remember things that you'd prefer to have forgotten. Anyway, you make me feel very envious, because I can't do anything very well.'

'You're a very good listener. And you didn't *make* me discuss this. I don't think I've ever talked about Canon Bothwell before – and you won't discuss what I told you with anyone else, will you? Not even your husband, please.'

'Of course not! I'm honoured that you told me. I think it's a question that I would like to think about by myself, though – the idea of a "gift", I mean. The "incandescent talent" idea is another matter entirely!' She looked at her watch. 'Julian, is there something particular that you would like me to do? I need to go home fairly soon. I can do a quick vacuum round now, if you like, or I can come another day and stay longer.'

He looked at her in surprise for a moment, and then remembered that she was here because he had telephoned her to ask if she had time to help. He couldn't tell her that he had really only wanted to talk to someone, that his thoughts of Isobel and the uncertainties about his own future had suddenly threatened to take him over, so that he needed to escape. Not that he had intended to discuss *those* matters with Margaret; he scarcely knew her, but he had needed to talk about something, about the weather or even beeswax polish, if need be. He had telephoned her, and she had come at once, claiming to be unexpectedly free; she had come expecting to 'help', as she euphemistically called her cleaning. She had helped already, but nevertheless he asked her if she could tidy the music room.

Naturally, Margaret agreed, and as she dragged the vacuum cleaner between the chairs she thought about the extraordinary things she had heard, and wondered how she would tell Iain (if, indeed, she would tell Iain) that she had, once again, been to Julian Kersland's house.

Julian took the photograph back into his bedroom and restored it to its original place on the desk. He wondered if Mrs Gillespie would have liked Canon Bothwell. His mother hadn't. Julian realised later, through remarks that she made and through his own better, but imperfect, understanding of the adult mind, that she had probably worried about the influence that the clergyman appeared to have upon her son. Julian would not have become a musician, a professional musician, without the clergyman's encouragement. His mother could not have understood or even communicated with that deeply serious man, who sometimes wore his fanaticism like a halo. Margaret Gillespie would have had the ability, though. Underneath the nervousness and the sudden swings to apparently confident briskness was a woman who worried over meanings, and attitudes, and reasons. At times this morning she had been so still and quiet that he had thought she was bored and had switched off her attention, but he realised that she had been puzzling over the implications of what he was saying. She was a strange woman; she probably had too much time available for worrying. She wasn't intrusive, either, in the way that Mrs Knight had been; there wasn't the stream of questions and unasked-for comments, there wasn't so much *noise*. I wonder how Mrs Gillespie will square it with her husband, he thought, if she intends to keep on coming here. I won't give her a key, though, not like Mrs Knight.

And a picture came into his mind, of Mrs Knight opening the front door as Isobel (naked, bare-breasted Isobel) swayed across the hall between bathroom and bedroom, trailing a swathe of golden hair. He shuddered strangely with desire (or was it fear?) as he remembered Isobel, and he groaned, slapping the desk top with his palms. Three days! And she hadn't even phoned! He couldn't find her, he couldn't even reach her in her eyrie. Fear that he had been found wanting, that she was even now laughing at him (but not, surely, with her friends?) nudged at him. Had she spent the day with him, unbuttoned herself to him, merely out of transient lust – or even curiosity? Medical curiosity! His hands were cold as he gripped his leg. That was all it had been! She had looked at his leg, she had touched it (ahh! she had touched all of him, he could feel the weight of her in his mind) and, curiosity assuaged, she had gone home to write him up as an unusual case – as a warning. But she didn't know, she *couldn't* know! Julian's throat was tight, he felt he couldn't breathe. He would be a laughing stock, not an object of desire, a star. He hobbled round his bedroom in agitation. Seeing his spare walking stick propped against the wardrobe door, he picked it up and, holding it in both hands, repeatedly raised it and thwacked it down hard on the bed. The soft, gargling cry that he made drowned Margaret's timid knock, and she stopped in amazement then softly pulled the door closed again and tiptoed down the hall into the kitchen.

Isobel, too, would have been amazed: not at what Julian was doing (she would have laughed) but at the reasoning behind his action. But at that moment she was daydreaming and doodling in the margins of her pad of filepaper. She sighed, and looked down the steeply raked tier of seats at the lecturer, and realised that many more words – names of drugs and receptors – had been written on the board. She must concentrate! This was all new, a special lecture; she wouldn't be able to look it up in textbooks later.

She would have to have lunch with Dave – they always had lunch together on Wednesdays. She had lied to him about Sunday. She had told him that she had gone home to see her family for the day, she saw them so rarely and there had been the surprise offer of a lift from an uncle. She had almost believed the story herself and Dave, although hurt, had been unworried. Anyway, for the past two nights he had been booked on to a departmental word processor, typing the first draft of his thesis. If only she could concentrate; she shouldn't allow herself to be distracted, but her body felt so good – and sexy. It was odd that Julian should have this effect, because with Dave she felt almost shy.

Julian had left her a note, too. 'Isobel Hutchison,' the envelope said: 'By hand.' It had been lying amongst the pile of circulars and mail on Monday night. 'I came to see you. Please call. J.' But she hadn't. She had been swithering, balancing David against Julian, but feeling the heaviness of work pressing down over all. She went over the advantages and disadvantages, Julian versus David, over and over again, sometimes concluding that she would be better off with neither, that she should lock herself away in her room or in the library. Because often she was in love with studying itself, with the thrill of acquiring new knowledge and the delight in organising her notes and augmenting them with extra information. Yet it was frustrating, too: there was no room for originality, she was tied to learning facts, to soaking them up like a sponge and then to squeezing them out again in precisely ordered droplets at the precisely ordained time. Julian was originality: he was not constrained, and the precisely ordered black notes of his music seemed to be only a basic framework for his own interpretation.

'I can't imagine what it's like,' she'd said to him, 'earning a living from playing music. It seems sort of – insubstantial, somehow.'

'How do you mean, insubstantial? Unreal, nebulous? Not a proper occupation, perhaps?'

Isobel had laughed, slightly awkwardly. 'I don't know, really. I suppose my idea of musicians, professional musicians, that is – not that I've thought about them before – is that most of the time they're not doing anything very much. A bit of practising on their own, a few rehearsals, but nothing very much in the daytime – apart from the Sunday lunchtime concerts in your case, of course! And then, on concert nights, they pick up their instruments and play whatever's written down for them. A bit like reading aloud.' She was beginning to enjoy this. 'And as long as they can read the words – that's where the practising comes in, because remember how that bassoonist told me that musicians were thick – they'll be OK. Oh, and of course they each have to learn to read a different part in time with the others. That's probably quite tricky.'

'A little,' Julian had agreed drily, refusing to be goaded.

'And another thing, why is playing music supposed to be creative when all you do is read aloud a line of notes that someone else has written? I can see that an artist creates, and that a composer creates – but are *you* creative?'

For a moment, she had wondered if her impudence had pushed him too far. His expression had tightened, and he'd seemed to hide away within himself, had been on the point of rolling over and turning away. But then he'd smiled.

'Oh yes, I can create. I can interpret, I can play you as I play the music, I can make you laugh or cry. Or I can leave myself, and you, unmoved. Cold. And how about you, Dr Isobel? What do *you* create, other than mischief with my blood pressure?'

She had had to admit that there was nothing creative in her character, or her work. 'Not even in my previous job in the hospital lab. It was all routine, following recipes and set methods. I wouldn't really consider myself a scientist, in the proper sense – but research scientists, well, they're very different. You remember my friend David, the one I was at that concert with?' David! How can I even dare to think about him, here? 'He's in research, and he has to be creative, it's not just an "arts" thing. He says a lot of biochemistry is what he calls "cooking", but he has to design his own experiments, which is a sort of creativity, I suppose. And then he has to interpret the results – which might be the same as you having to interpret the written music, except with him there are probably only one or two possible interpretations – and to juggle everything in his head to create a hypothesis. Some of the friends that I meet up with in the pub – they were having a conversation the other day about the excitement of science, and they all seemed to agree that if your hoped-for result turned up, or if something unexpected and exciting turned up, the thrill was fantastic. Never to be forgotten!'

'So scientists aren't all as dry and boring as the rest of us imagine?'

'No.'

'Well, it's good to hear that artists, in the broad sense of the word, and scientists are all fighting on the same side in one respect, anyway. All terribly creative.' Julian had smiled lazily, clearly unimpressed. 'I'd rather like you to be on my side, you know, even though you say you're not very creative.'

Isobel, daydreaming in the lecture theatre, smiled to herself as she remembered the bad puns, 'playing second fiddle', 'an extra string to your bow', that they had exchanged. Julian might have a double bed, but he led a single life. He had laughed at her tentative enquiry about his girlfriend, the one that she had supposed he visited after the rehearsal.

'You're cuckolding no one,' he had said, 'but I was visiting a cuckold – on a purely business matter! I'm an eligible bachelor, Isabella, my beautiful Bella, belladonna. I was nearly married once, but my fiancée left me for her double bass. A five-string bass, at that!'

'You were engaged?'

'Ah yes! Eight years ago, now. Engaged, on course for a marriage of convenience, perhaps. An instant duet. But unfortunately, our roles were reversed, soprano and bass, and when wheelchairs and walking sticks also threatened to play a role, I'm afraid she became otherwise engaged – and left me vacant!'

Isobel had laughed. It sounded a well-practised speech, although she doubted that he had often used it in public.

'But I thought you hurt yourself when you were twelve. So you would have had the walking sticks and so on at the start of your relationship, surely? They can't have been new to her!'

'Of course. But I had to have another operation, the final one as it turned out, when I was twenty-five. And that set things back a bit. It was very difficult for her to handle a wheelchair and a double bass at the same time.'

Isobel thought about the unknown young woman, struggling through swing doors, pushing a recalcitrant wheelchair and towing a hard-cased bass. The lecturer was talking about beta-blockers, nothing new, but she wondered instead about the boy who had jumped out of a tree to save a drowning friend, and whose reward had been a permanently damaged knee and, later, a half-vacant double bed.

She would have lunch with David, and then she would phone Julian. The situation would sort itself out somehow.

Chapter Twelve

Margaret brought in the last two carrier bags from the car and dumped them on the kitchen table. When she opened the window, the sound of a blackbird singing to his broody mate streamed in. She couldn't be bothered to unpack the shopping just yet, so she poured out a glass of cold apple juice, collected a small paper bag from her handbag and went out into the garden to sit on the stone bench beneath the wall. A light breeze stirred her hair, and she pushed off her shoes and stretched her feet.

The paper bag contained a music cassette; she would look at it in a moment but, as yet, she was still enjoying the anticipation. Buying cassettes was almost as enjoyable as buying new books. The sequence in which they appealed to the senses was different, though: with books, the feel came first, the feel of the glossy clean cover, and then the smell of the smooth pages. To enjoy the words, however, you needed uninterrupted time. With a music cassette, first you had to spend time examining it, looking at the cover picture, reading the details of the musicians and the composer; only then should you listen to the music, perhaps while you did some practical task, something mechanical, that would allow you to hear the sound with your thinking brain. I can listen while I unpack the shopping, Margaret thought. But I can look now.

The members of the Ensemble were posed, holding their instruments 'at ease', on the steps of the converted church. There was Rosemary, her grey hair neatly waved for the photograph, and there was the girl with the bassoon. Margaret recognised several other faces: the man without an instrument was the harpsichordist, and there was the viola player who pulled agonised faces as he played. The musicians formed a squat triangle on the steps, and a young man with an oboe stood, rather importantly, just below the apex; he must be the soloist in the oboe and violin concerto, Margaret decided. Julian leant casually against the curved balustrade; his violin was tucked beneath his arm and his lower body was hidden by the oboist. It was a good picture of the group, informal and cheerful. They looked as though they enjoyed their music-making.

There was a certain thrill in knowing that she knew that apical figure; she had heard him play (so had many others) but who else, looking at that photograph, would know that Julian Kersland's favourite bath towel was thick and deep red, that he kept an outdated packet of Lapsang Souchong in the kitchen cupboard – and that he had learnt to consider that his musical talent was a gift. Nobody! Nobody else could possibly know such a combination of facts about Julian! Margaret smiled to herself and watched a bluetit searching for greenfly on the rose bushes. She was proud of this secret knowledge. There was power in a shared secret. She also wanted to find out more. If I could understand him better, she rationalised, perhaps I could help him more. But, in fact, the notion that she would be able to help almost made her laugh. She knew, really, that she had no means of helping at all, and that the reason why she wanted to know more about Julian was probably so that she could think about the information privately and know that she had access to someone's possible *raison d'être*. Or, at the very least, someone's *concept* of their *raison d'être*; for who knew the true reason for an individual's existence?

She sensed quite strongly, though, that Julian had somehow lost his way. One needed a driving force to make oneself successful. Personal ambition was the obvious force, but was predominantly selfish, whereas the concept of responsibility to others could be an equally strong force, in the right person. Julian apparently no longer had faith in the latter, and it wasn't clear to her what had taken its place. It must be good to be a success, however limited, at something, she thought. Iain was obviously successful. Zoe Lutyens was successful, at fundraising and energising other people to support her projects. I'm not unsuccessful, though, Margaret thought; I'm not a hopeless failure at everything I do. It was odd how, pondering over Julian's reason for existence, she was also starting to think about her own. It was unsettling, and she wasn't very good at analysing motives and reasons. It would be better to go and listen to Julian's music now, before she read the details on the sleeve.

The kitchen was cool and dim, and she turned up the volume on the cassette player and tried to imagine Julian as he played. But the music failed to move her, suddenly she was no longer receptive. Would Iain mind that she had bought the cassette? It was possible that he worried lest she was becoming 'involved' with Julian. Well, she probably was, but not in the way Iain might imagine. She would have to tell him that she was going to continue to keep house for Julian, she couldn't deceive Iain. And no harm had come of it so far, surely?

There was Zoe, of course; ever-prying Zoe. She had telephoned yesterday.

'Robbie tells me that Mr Kersland's flat looks very neat and clean – even fresh flowers, I hear!'

'What an observant boy he is! Is this supposed to have something to do with me, Zoe?'

'You are still going there, aren't you, lovey? I'm sure I couldn't bear to stop, if it were me!'

'Why? I don't understand.'

'Tell me, have you found out anything interesting? You must

have discovered a few skeletons in his cupboard during the course of your tidying round! I'm longing to hear all about it. Do you sit and have cosy chats over the coffee cups? I gather from poor Mrs Knight that he's terribly sensitive to the sound of the vacuum cleaner. It's out of key or something dreadful.'

'Zoe, you are impossible! And there's nothing to tell. It's all terribly boring – *clean* and boring!'

'No secret women? Or men? What about men?'

Margaret remembered the chaplain's hand and taut-skinned, skull-like head, but she pushed the thought away quickly in case it was picked up and transmitted down the wire.

'I haven't the faintest idea about Julian's private life – if indeed he has any. He's probably immersed in music . . .'

'Well, I'm sure he doesn't go drinking on his own. And what about that woman who's often around there or else leaving notes, Robbie tells me?'

'What woman?' Margaret was aware that her voice sounded more shocked than she'd intended.

'Oh – Rosemary something-or-other, I don't know.'

'Rosemary? Oh, Zoe! She's old enough to be his mother – she even *knows* his mother slightly, apparently! She's the orchestral librarian. I met her the other day.'

'Did you? I hope you got a good look at her. These motherly types are often more than they seem, you know!'

'Well, she seemed quite straightforward when we were introduced to her at the concert. Did you know that it's possible to get lunch at the church? It's very—'

'So Iain approves, does he?' Zoe was quick to seize that piece of information. 'I thought you might have had a little bit of trouble there! Dear old Mrs Knight, she was terribly shocked to hear you were taking her old job. She's such a scream! "Poor Mr Gillespie," she kept saying. "What can he feel like, with his wife going out to scrub?" To scrub, Margaret dear! I could hardly keep a straight face, the poor old dear obviously didn't realise what she was saying!'

Margaret couldn't think of a reply. She held the telephone away from her ear and waited. Zoe's voice continued to flow out of the earpiece, and she imagined the words spilling down on to the floor to form a little heap. She reached out her foot and squashed them with the toe of her shoe, grinding them into the hall floor.

'Margaret? Are you still there?'

'Yes. I'm here.'

'*Can* you come, then, tomorrow morning?'

To what? Margaret didn't know, but she would not, in any case, be free.

'No, I'm sorry, I'm busy tomorrow.'

'What about Friday, then?'

'Oh no, sorry—'

'Margaret! You can't be going to your beloved violinist's every day!'

'Of course not! And he's *not*— Oh, honestly, Zoe! It's just that . . . Zoe, I've a lot of other commitments at the moment, I'm not sure . . .' (I want to be here in case Julian calls.)

'I see.' Zoe was clearly affronted. 'Well, do let me know, won't you, lovey, when you get things sorted out? We do need you, you know. But perhaps, anyway, you could spare some time to look out something for the sale. Something for the bric-a-brac would be just fine, then you won't have to worry about making anything. Do phone, Margaret dear. 'Bye!'

Oh lord! Margaret thought. How on earth could I have been so stupid? What's the matter with me, this sudden urge to hold myself in readiness for . . . what? For a once-weekly, once-fortnightly, request that I should go to Julian's flat and dust! It's insane! I'd better go and help Zoe tomorrow with whatever it was. But no, I won't be able to endure the questions. I'll have to find something for the sale, instead; some *objets*, fine *objets*, conscience-salving things.

She wandered aimlessly from room to room, restless and irritated with herself. She looked through the drawers of the sideboard, but there was nothing suitable for the sale in there. She went upstairs to the drawing room and opened the walnut writing desk. There was a heart-shaped Wedgwood box, an unused present from one of Iain's clients. She didn't like the shape, and the blue was wrong for the room – perhaps she could send that?

There was nothing in the kitchen that she didn't either like or need, but then she thought of the darkroom, and Iain's photographs. There were prints in there, hung up to dry by coloured plastic pegs. Margaret switched on the bright light and saw that they were pictures of the gannet's skull and seaweed, driftwood and pebbles. The black-and-white images were stark and natural. Is this Iain's gift? she wondered. Is it a gift, or a talent, or just a learnt skill that anyone can do? She opened the filing cabinet and took out the front folder of prints; tucked behind it was a newspaper, folded open at page three. The girl flaunted herself in a most inviting manner, and Margaret looked at her in surprise.

'What are *you* doing in my husband's darkroom?' she asked. 'He's not *that* kind of photographer, you know!'

She frowned a moment, trying to imagine what it would feel like to pose like that, and to know that thousands of men (and women) would soon be staring at the photograph of your body. Then she turned to the other open page and saw that there was a small, sensationalist article about new misdemeanours of the titled owner of the land adjacent to their cottage: someone must have shown it to Iain at the office, and somehow the paper had become mixed in with these prints. The photographs in his file were of mountains and lochs, and one or two of them, framed, would be sure to fetch a good price at the sale. She would have to ask Iain about them, casually, and persuade him to give them to her . . . Margaret put the folder away. She would also, casually, tell

Iain that she was still working at Julian's flat – but first she ought to tell Julian.

She telephoned him at once, before her brief spurt of courage drained away. He was brusque, she had interrupted a lesson, and she regretted her haste; but there had been sufficient time to confirm that she would be there tomorrow.

That evening, she and Iain took an after-dinner stroll around the Botanic Gardens. The afternoon sun had drawn the scent out of the blossoms, and the air was humid and perfumed. Blue spikes of irises stuck up amongst the lush, varied greens of the sprouting herbaceous borders, and big orange poppies trailed black-throated petals like handkerchiefs. Other people, too, were enjoying the evening calm, and it was easy to interpose serious questions amongst lazy observations about the plants and trees and passers-by. Iain thus found that he had agreed to look out a couple of landscape prints for the hospice sale; and he had also acquiesced without too much anxiety to Margaret's continuing wish to help out, occasionally, at Julian's flat.

There were bats flittering around the trees as they walked home, arm in arm, and a late blackbird sang as though he didn't want the day to end. Margaret, relieved, and at peace with herself, suddenly looked forward to the future.

Julian had been teaching his lunchtime girl when Margaret phoned. He hated being interrupted – and when the phone rang he practically snarled, then stumped off into the hall. His pupil grinned to herself and took a quick bite of a caramel wafer that was in her pocket, but had to gulp it hastily because Julian returned so quickly. Last week she had been unable to eat most of her lunch because he had driven up beside her as she was coming up the hill, and had offered her a lift. She'd had to wait while his girlfriend got out of the car. Perhaps if she used camomile on her hair, that would make it blonder, like that girl; and if she stood up straighter, and pushed out her chest . . .

'Elizabeth! I said to go back to the double bar! And you've got chocolate on your chin . . .'

All these damnable interruptions! Telephone ringing, Elizabeth snacking on chocolate biscuits – and last week he hadn't been able to concentrate at all! He'd never get this girl up to exam standard in time. He'd have to fit in an extra lesson for her soon. He'd tried to persuade Isobel to meet him for an early lunch again today, but it was probably as well for his peace of mind that she couldn't come. And his piece of body! He almost sniggered, but a discordant chord, where all should have been harmonious, distracted him briefly, and he had to reprimand his pupil. It had been exactly a week ago that Isobel had telephoned him, from a callbox that must have been in a corridor, judging by the noise. She'd wanted to see him that evening, but he'd had to explain that there were music lessons arranged until ten o'clock.

'But I'll see you now!' he'd said. 'I'll come and fetch you.'

She'd been flustered. 'No! Not here! And I've got to be back at one – there's no time!'

'Isobel! I must see you. I can't wait until ten o'clock tonight. Why haven't you been in touch? Don't tell me you're not interested any more?'

'Julian, I can't talk here, there are too many people. I've just come out of a lecture. Look, meet me in the car park by the traffic lights. I'll walk down there now – can you be there in ten minutes?'

Isobel had bundled her files and her rucksack into her locker and dashed to the cloakroom to check that her hair and make-up was all right. She'd miss the next lecture and she wouldn't be able to have lunch with David. What a mess! Oh God! She must be quick! She dodged along the corridor, not bothering to answer her friends' greetings, and ran out of the gates and down the road. Her heart was pounding, not just from exertion, and she slowed down, aware that her face would be red and shiny and that her skirt was flapping.

She was rushing to meet him, Julian saw. She looked pink and anguished, and he knew that she had come to tell him that she didn't want to see him any more. He reached across and unlocked the door, and waited while she climbed in. She was wearing another of her long Indian skirts, and it caught around her calves. He waited while her breathing settled down.

'Glad you were in such a rush to see me,' Julian finally said, drily.

Isobel's mouth was dry and her chest ached. 'I'm supposed to be revising. I have a test this afternoon.'

'I have a lunchtime lesson – I only remembered it after I put the phone down.'

They were both silent. Isobel saw several of her classmates walk past, but they didn't look into the car.

'So . . . ?'

'So you had better hurry up and say what you have to say.'

'What do you mean?'

'The fact that you've waited three days – and that you look embarrassed, and haven't rushed into my waiting arms – suggests that—'

'They weren't! Waiting! Your hands have hardly moved.'

'– suggests that you're going to tell me that what we did on Sunday was merely an amusing contrivance to pass the time. And that I'm deluding myself if I expect you to spend more time with me.' Go on! Lay it on! Ah, the self-inflicted pain, the self-pity.

Isobel was aghast. 'You can't really believe that I would behave like that, can you? *Can* you? Look at me, Julian, for God's sake!'

She grabbed his arm and shook it, prising it away from the steering wheel, and then, surprising even herself, she twisted it and pulled his hand against her breast.

'I wanted to see you.'

His hand was warm, she pressed against it. Julian shifted uncomfortably.

'At least let me use my right hand,' he said, 'the angle's wrong. And this is rather public. Are those your friends staring in?'

They weren't, but Isobel moved away.

'Put on your seatbelt. There's no time to go home, but I know somewhere quiet where we can talk.'

Isobel kept her head down, frightened that she would see David or his friends. After only a few minutes Julian pulled in and stopped the car next to a side entrance to the Botanic Gardens.

'Here? But it'll be crowded, it's almost lunchtime.'

'We'll see!'

Isobel waited until Julian levered himself out of the car, and then trailed passively after him as he hobbled towards the banana house. One or two people glanced at them, and she thought what a strange pair they must make, grim-faced and unspeaking, an untidy fair-haired girl and an older, limping man. Someone held open the outer door to the glasshouse for them and when Isobel pushed open the inner door, the steamy air made her gasp. But Julian was already hobbling anticlockwise round the pond, his right foot scuffing lines in the thin white layer of gravel. Huge fish, repulsive in their paleness, gulped lazily at the surface of the water, their eyes swivelling as they looked for food. Isobel wanted to scatter gravel on their heads, to dislodge their insolent stares, but the attendant was watching her. There were benches around the pond, and statuary – smooth, hairless figures with unblemished, unintelligent faces. People sat at the statues' feet and ate sandwiches, and watched other strange and imperfect people passing by. There were feathery ferns, and palms, and creepers, and livid splashes of scent and colour; there was an empty bench –

But Julian shook his head. 'No. There's a better place further round.'

They reached the far end of the glasshouse, where the vegetation was dark and lush. There was a single bench, and on it sat a Sikh. Julian stopped. The old man's eyes were closed and his hands were folded in his lap on top of his long white beard. Behind the seat were broad, glossy fronds of plants that Isobel couldn't recognise. Creepers hung like curtains from the ornamental ironwork overhead. A banana palm pressed against the curved glass roof and blocked out the daylight.

'Sssh!' Julian looked at Isobel and held up a finger. His face was suddenly bright with amusement as he started to walk cautiously towards the bench.

'No! You mustn't!' Isobel was horrified, and grabbed the back of his jacket.

But Julian grinned and shook his head, and pointed to one side of the bench. There was a small red-and-white metal barrier and, beneath it, the hint of a brick path, now overgrown. He beckoned her to come.

'Can you get round the end of the barrier?' he whispered. 'Quickly! No one's coming. Just follow the path.'

She looked round quickly; there was nobody in sight except the sleeping Sikh.

'You go first. I'll follow – I promise!'

She grinned delightedly; this was crazy, this was fun! She watched as Julian bent double beneath the leaves and, holding the end of the barrier, squeezed past and shuffled himself in amongst the plants.

'Keep going! I'm coming!' she called, and laughed as he gestured at her to be quiet. She could hear people approaching, and she pushed hastily, noisily, into the undergrowth.

'Hush! You'll wake him!' Julian was quite cross in his agitation.

She giggled. 'We won't disturb him – he's deaf! I know

him, or at least I've seen him around. He can't hear a thing! Where are we going?'

They were both bent over, faces close together.

'It can only be a few yards away. There should be a bench.' Julian parted the vegetation with his stick. 'There! You can see the back of it.'

'You should have brought a machete.'

Isobel giggled again, but then they were both quiet as they heard people passing on the gravel, no more than ten feet away.

The bench, when they reached it, was fragile and damp. Ferns and trailing leaves pushed in at them to create a green, humid box, and Julian scraped dead leaves – compost – off the seat.

'How did you know this was here? Did you come here with your fiancée?'

Julian looked at her in surprise. 'No. I didn't know about it then. But anyway, it would have been almost impossible, wouldn't it?'

Isobel frowned, then remembered, and half-laughed. She looked back where they had come and thought of the wheelchair sticking in the soft loam, slipping on the liverwort; and the double bass tangled in the vines.

'I wasn't even sure if I'd find it. Rosemary told me about it – do you remember Rosemary, who gave you coffee? – she said she did her courting here. Do you think we dare sit down?'

'What are we doing here, Julian? Why *here*?'

'L'après-midi d'un faune,' he muttered, obscurely. 'Come and sit by me – we haven't got long. Why didn't you telephone me sooner?'

Isobel sighed and brushed at the bench, then sat down carefully. 'I wish you hadn't said that about my amusing myself with you on Sunday. Yes, it was fun – *this* is fun – amusing, but not in the derogatory way that you meant in the car. Why do you have to be so dramatic, Julian? You know you didn't really mean that.'

'I'm not a telepath, Isobel. Three days!'

'Listen! I've spent the last three days worrying what to do. Mid-term tests started yesterday, I have to do well, and this is a *bloody* stupid time to get in an emotional muddle like this.'

'Thanks.'

'Don't be silly, you know what I mean. I can't concentrate on my work. I've got to sort things out, about my work – and with Dave, the boy you saw me with at the concert.'

'You've been very evasive about him. What are you going to do?'

'He's probably leaving in a few months anyway because his grant runs out.'

'That's no answer.'

'I know. I'd been intending to see him this lunchtime.'

'But now you're seeing me instead. Hmm.' Julian gave her his deep, steadfast look, and then glanced quickly at his watch. 'Forget about Dave. We didn't hack our way into the jungle in order to discuss him, Bella.'

Almost unwillingly, even though this was what she wanted, Isobel leant towards him to kiss him and when, after a few moments, he started to undo the buttons on her cardigan and then the buttons on her blouse, she helped him.

'Now you're seeing *me*!' she whispered.

'Were you dressed – undressed – like this because you were going to see Dave at lunchtime? I hope not.'

'Hardly – we were going to meet in the refectory. I was going to come to you later.'

The soft buzz of voices and the grating of feet on gravel seemed far away; the novelty and danger excited her. She undid Julian's shirt, too, and they pressed their bare chests together. It was difficult on the bench and the tension was almost unbearable. She slipped her clothes off her shoulders and leant backwards, curving her arms above her head, catching at the creepers with her hands.

'Isobel! You're so uninhibited!' Julian's excitement at the confrontation almost died of nervousness.

'I'm a *medic*!' she whispered into his ear.

Julian saw a flash of white behind her shoulder. He was sure the leaves had shaken; there were fingers holding back the leaves, there peered a dark brown eye. For a moment he was still with horror; but then he saw that there was nothing there.

Isobel moaned and caught at his hands. 'What's wrong?'

'Don't look over your shoulder, or you may turn to stone.'

'That's how they collect the statues around here. They haven't yet collected a couple *in flagrante.* Will this bench cope?'

But the bench plainly was too weak and the impracticalities too great. The situation was too dangerous and too frustrating. Too inconclusive, Isobel thought, and she pushed Julian upright and began to struggle back into her crumpled clothes. None the less, there was a tiny glow of triumph inside her.

Wouldn't Kersland's audience be surprised to know that Julian, half-naked, had held her gloriously naked *tits* amongst the glasshouse greenery, just a few yards from where people walked! Once these exams were over . . .

Julian was uncomfortable, and much unsettled. He prodded his stick into the ground.

'Will you come round tonight after ten o'clock? Will you come and stay with me tonight? You're not going to keep your boyfriend floating in attendance, are you? We're all too old to play games like this, Isobel – me especially.'

Reality came back, and all its problems.

'I'll see David today. But I can't come round that late – can I come on Friday?'

'Friday! I can't wait until then!'

'Now I've got to be getting back.'

Isobel held Julian's hand and they began to creep towards the gravel path.

'What if he's awake?'

'We'll just have to walk out coolly, and ignore him.'

Julian crept out first, stopping to check that no one was around. The Sikh still sat, head back, eyes closed, on the bench. Isobel came out; crumpled, her lips full and flushed; there were green stains on her skirt and on Julian's trousers. They looked at each other then tidied their clothes, straight-faced.

At that moment, another Sikh, a few years younger, came round the corner. He sat down on the bench and tapped the old man on the knee; the old man was, indeed, deaf. His young friend started to talk to him in sign language, his brown, bony hands flying through the air with rapid strokes and flutters.

As he and Isobel walked away, Julian turned once to look back. The old man was watching him impassively, but when he saw Julian turn, his wrinkled old face split into a grin and he stretched backwards and lifted his arms above his head in a parody of Isobel's statuesque pose. Julian's stick slipped on the gravel and gouged a small, dark furrow as he hobbled after his pale wood nymph.

Chapter Thirteen

'Sssh! I'm in the middle of a meeting, but they'll be gone soon. Make yourself a cup of coffee. There's a radio in the bedroom, you can wait in there if you want.'

Julian ushered Isobel along the hall and then returned to the music room.

'Sorry – somebody to see me. It can wait until we've finished, though.'

He carried on searching for some papers in the filing cabinet; various members of the Ensemble sat around the room, and talked while they waited. Rosemary gathered up the coffee cups and loaded them on to the tray; Julian, busy hunting, didn't realise she had left the room until he heard her voice in the hall.

'Oh, hello. Are you all right in there? We've nearly finished.'

'I think the letter's in there.'

Julian handed Guy a file and went hurriedly into the hall. Rosemary was standing by the bedroom door talking to Isobel, who was sprawled on the bed, barefoot, her hair shining brightly in the light.

'Oh, you've already met, I think . . .' Julian was embarrassed. Isobel's proprietorial position on the bed was rather too revealing.

'Yes indeed. I'm afraid you always seem to be abandoning the poor girl for Ensemble business! It's all right, Julian dear, you go and finish whatever you were doing. We can look after ourselves.' Rosemary smiled teasingly at him.

When the business was finished, Julian was able to shepherd everyone fairly quickly down the hall, managing, by the positioning of his body and his stick, to dissuade anyone from last-minute urges to use the bathroom, opposite the open bedroom door. Rosemary remained for a few minutes to pick up some music, and as she was putting on her coat in the hall, Isobel emerged from the bedroom.

Julian looked at her and then at Rosemary, and suddenly grinned. 'Oh, by the way, we were in the banana house a few weeks ago and we found that bench you told me about. I was telling Isobel that it used to be your secret place for courting!'

'*Did* you?' Rosemary looked from one to the other; Isobel's cheeks were rather pink. 'But surely you can't get to it any more?'

'No – the undergrowth's too thick. I expect the gardeners have forgotten it's there!'

He walked with her to the outer door, and as she started down the steps, she said, 'You're looking very pleased with yourself. You not only seem to be getting your way about changing our style, but now you seem to have all these women in your life, too!'

'All? Isobel's only one – not a harem.'

'What about that nice woman Mrs Gillespie, that I met not long ago – when she dropped in to tidy your flat and bring you smoked salmon pâté?' She pushed his arm, teasing again. 'You needn't think I'm going to run around after you any more, young man. And I bet those home-made biscuits tonight were made in Mrs Gillespie's kitchen.'

'She's a kind woman.' He dropped his voice. 'She likes to have something to do – I'm her Good Cause.'

'Well, you're looking very well on it.'

'Margaret – Mrs Gillespie – thought I was looking rather pale, actually. I'm to spend a weekend at her country cottage.'

'Oh! And what does your Isobel think about that?'

Julian pulled the outer door partly closed behind him.

'She doesn't know yet, but there's nothing for her to "think about" anyway. For goodness' sake, Rosemary, I'm not going for a dirty weekend. The woman's years older than me – and her husband's going to be there. They've both invited me.'

'I'm sure you will be very well looked after – and it will do you good.'

'Yes. I suppose so . . .'

'Don't sound so doubtful. You and Isobel will appreciate each other all the more when you get back!'

'Rosemary! You are becoming quite an agony aunt!' Julian was quite annoyed.

'Sorry, my dear!' She patted his arm again, and smiled. 'I've out-stayed my welcome, I can see!'

Isobel had gone back to the bedroom and was sitting on the bed.

'What were you and Rosemary talking about for so long, on the steps?'

'Nothing important – orchestra business. I'm negotiating a contract for a recording.'

'Did she say anything about me being here?'

'No – why should she?'

'No reason.' Isobel looked a bit crestfallen; part of the fun was hearing what other people had to say. 'I suppose she might think that I'm too young for you.'

'If she thinks about you at all, which I doubt,' Julian sat down beside her and ran his hand along her leg, 'she will be pleased that I have found someone who is beautiful, and outrageously sexy – and intelligent.'

'Certainly intelligent enough to appreciate what a schemer and conniver you are!'

Julian stretched out on the bed beside her, his right hand hanging down on to the floor. 'That comes with age, along with charm and good looks. I like your outfit – new clothes?'

'Yes, I went out shopping after work.'

'What a pity! I bought you something today, too – but you won't need it now.'

'Let me guess. Underclothes! I bet you bought me something black and lacy. And if you did I shall wrap it around your neck and strangle you! And if it's a garter I shall wrap it around *your* leg!' She gave a deep chuckle.

'Now that would have some interesting psychosexual connotations, wouldn't it? A garter! Why didn't I think of that? No, something potentially more superficial.'

He sat up and pushed himself off the bed. There was a coloured paper bag on his desk and he peered in and took out three folded squares of material, then shook them out and let the long scarves drift down gently over Isobel's face.

She puffed at them so that they billowed upwards, and gathered them up to look at them, one with mingled deep rainbow colours, one sewn with tiny sequins, another glittering dully with gold and silver thread. She wrapped them round her head and arms.

'They're beautiful. Thank you!'

'Now, wait – I want to play you something. Wait there.'

Isobel sat on the bed and waited, slightly embarrassed. Julian returned with a violin and bow and leant his back against the wall. He tested a few notes, and then played a long, high note, that turned into a falling, bubbling sequence, which climbed again and soared.

'Scheherazade's tune,' he explained. 'Do you know about her – "A Thousand and One Nights"? She told the Sultan a different story each night, often very erotic, beautiful stories. And she was beautiful, too. Dressed in gauzy materials, she danced for the Sultan. Listen, the music's incredibly erotic, too.'

He played more and Isobel, despite her embarrassment, was impressed and stirred; but she thought about the gauzy scarves wrapped around herself, and was uncomfortable.

Julian stopped playing and looked at her. 'You do look very

. . . desirable,' he said. He put his violin on the desk and went to the cupboard and took out a black silk dressing gown. 'I had this idea, that you might be my Scheherazade, dressed in those scarves. I would very much like to play for you. And then we could, er, play together . . . ? We could be *creative*. It would be rather exciting, don't you think?'

Isobel held up the rainbow-coloured material to the light and passed her hand behind it; every detail of her skin was revealed. She imagined her naked body swathed in transparent glittering folds, and her skin tingled . . . but, to *dance*?

'I think I might need to be drunk, Julian,' she said uneasily. 'Besides, it would be rather like doing a strip-show. You would be cold sober, watching, not really participating because you'd be playing the music. I don't think I could do that.'

She got up and put her arm round his neck and kissed him.

'I'm not sure I can behave like that.'

He was unyielding and sulky. 'If I can perform for you, can't you perform for me?'

'You'd be exercising a skill, though, in your performance. There'd be no skill in what I would be doing, or at least not unless I practised. Or went to belly-dancing classes. And I don't want to practise that, Julian. I don't want to be an experienced belly-dancer or tassel-spinner, even in private!'

She was still holding the rainbow scarf and she wrapped it around his neck and hers, so that they stood tied together.

'Do you see?'

Eventually, Julian sighed and smiled. 'OK. I take your point. You'll have to forgive me.' He put his arms round her and held her. 'I can't help dreaming, though, and that evening in the car – and in the jungle – you seemed happy enough . . .'

'Oh well, we'll see.' Suddenly she was impatient with the discussion. 'Maybe one day I'll surprise you – Christmas, or sometime like that!'

She pulled the scarf away from him and twined it around

herself, then followed him through to the music room and wandered around, picking up pieces of music, pressing keys on the piano.

'What other instruments do you play apart from piano and violins?'

'I'm not very good at piano. Viola, cello. Recorders. Did you play the descant recorder at school?'

'No. Not even that. There was a teacher in the children's ward today. She was making the children sing along with her recorder – nursery rhymes and things. I was supposed to be doing the geriatrics, but I stopped to watch for a bit. It was really nice.'

Julian lowered himself into an armchair and held out his hand towards her.

'I haven't asked you about your job. Come and sit here and tell me about it.'

But Isobel shook her head and chose the armchair opposite. 'I can see you better from here. It's hard work, but I get my first pay cheque tomorrow. It's such a relief to be able to keep my room on over the summer and not have to flat-hunt again in the autumn. And to be able to have some extra money for clothes and so on. It's good to be able to see a different side of hospital life, too. Perhaps seeing what the cleaners do and how they're treated will make me a bit more compassionate when I'm doing my residency.'

'Maybe it should be compulsory for all medics to take turns as cleaners and bedmakers.'

'Normally the hospital isn't too keen to employ us. My tutor put in a good word, though – and I went to my old department and asked the Prof there if he could help. My tutor's really helpful. She thinks the fact that I'm older and an Easton Scholar, and partly self-supporting, shows my dedication. Being female helps, too.'

'The women stick together, then, do they?'

'Not really. You'd expect that to happen, but the senior

women have got where they are by their own hard work and determination – so they reckon, anyway – so they don't see why they should hand out any favours. You have to show your worth to them just as much as you have to show it to the men. They're more likely to notice, though! The men seem to focus on other attributes first, before they admit to recognising intelligence!'

'Oh, come on, Isobel! I can't believe that's true any more. It's such a cliché!'

'Well, I bet appearance influences you when you audition orchestral players. I can't believe that you'd choose a plain-looking female violinist in preference to a gorgeous one, especially if the pretty one had big boobs!'

'Of course appearance comes into it, everyone is influenced by appearance – and if a group of players look pleasant and happy, of course they're going to create a stronger bond with the audience. But you're wrong, though, about the beauty with the – boobs, as you so crudely call them. I'm surprised you don't refer to them as mammary glands. With concert musicians, it's immediately apparent to everyone listening – and what else are musicians for, if not to be *heard*? – whether or not they are any good. You don't go to a concert to look at the soloist's tits.'

'Especially not if he's male!'

'The trouble with many professions, medicine included, is that it is not immediately apparent whether or not the person has any skill or intelligence. You may have to speak to the person, or observe him for quite some time. And so appearance may well play quite a part in your initial judgement about that person. I don't know why you personally are worrying, anyway.'

'Because I've got beauty and brains, you mean! Don't you dare pretend to me that it's my intelligence and not my body that you're after!'

'If you'd been plain and flat-chested, I wouldn't have given you another look,' Julian grinned, and remembered, briefly, the untidy, blotchy girl who had helped him from the taxi all those weeks ago.

Isobel gave him a considering glance, and then shook her head with a wry laugh. 'Do you want another cup of coffee?'

He nodded. 'There are probably some biscuits on the kitchen table – if the others have left any.'

Isobel frequently visited the flat these days, and she knew where everything was kept; but she almost never stayed the night, preferring to keep her independence. In any case, at present she had to start work early each morning, and she also had some studying and catching up to do. Intelligent! It had not been intelligent to let her private life interfere with her work. She would have to resit two of her examinations at the end of the summer; the Easton Trust would not be terribly impressed at her commitment when they heard about that. Her exam results might have been even worse, but her tutor had, presumably, argued in her favour at the examiners' meeting. Isobel had taken the precaution of going to see her tutor before the examinations started, because she knew that her concentration had been eroded at that critical time. Her tutor was a bright, quick-thinking woman, who perhaps should not have been appointed as an adviser and tutor because she had little time for 'fools', but she admired Isobel for 'doing things the hard way', as she called it, and she was invariably helpful and supportive.

'What a time to mess up your love life,' she had said, when Isobel, apparently shame-faced, had come to talk to her. 'Life never works out according to a proper timetable, does it? It probably won't seem very important in a few years' time, but it's no good me telling you that now. Just try to minimise the damage, and do the best you can – I can't say more.'

Privately, Isobel had been realistic enough to acknowledge the likely future unimportance of her present turmoil, but at that moment she had wanted official recognition (and backing, in a crisis) of her personal difficulties. She hoped that her tutor's voice would be strong enough against an old, male establishment, when they all came to adjudicate on borderline results.

The net result was that she had lost David, failed two exams, and gained Julian. She had also gained a summer job, and time, and some, limited, financial freedom.

The loss of Dave had been accomplished unexpectedly easily. After their sojourn in the jungle, Isobel and Julian had strolled around the Botanic Gardens. At first, she had felt awkward, rather shocked at her wanton behaviour. ('Flaunting herself' – her mother's phrase came to mind; but this had been more than flaunting, which implied at least a flimsy pretence at cover-up!) But their slow, considered walking had provided the rhythm for some necessary talking. They had talked quietly, sometimes whispering, sometimes laughing, and with long, intimate looks. If anyone is watching us, Isobel thought – and many people were: the benches were crowded with lunchtime sun-seekers, all with free time to stare and speculate about passers-by – they would know at once, even though we do not touch, that we are lovers. Do they admire me for partnering a cripple? Do they wonder if he's any good in bed? Do they wonder how we fuck?

Julian realised he would be late. He offered to drive Isobel partway, but as they drove towards the university he saw his pupil wandering towards his house, drinking from a can. He stopped the car, and Isobel thrust her arms around his neck and kissed him on the mouth, then wriggled out and waved gaily to the girl before hurrying along the road.

There was time, after all, for her to talk to Dave. She had found him in the refectory, and she sat quietly and waited while he ploughed through a mound of pie and chips. Afterwards, they sat on the sloping lawn and stared down over the city. Isobel tried to pick out the spire of the converted church where the Ensemble played, and she plucked short blades of grass and piled them in a stack beside her skirt. David lay on his back with his hands behind his head, and closed his eyes.

'How's your thesis going?'

'OK. I've typed in the chapters on experimental work. And the Prof's given back the first draft of the introduction.'

'All right?'

'Not bad – some change of emphasis.' David turned his head to look at her. 'Iz?'

'Mmm?'

'There's a possibility that I can work in Goldstein's lab in New York.'

'Oh. When?'

'Whenever my thesis has been examined. Sometime in the autumn, I suppose. I've been wanting to tell you for ages, but there hasn't been much opportunity, has there? Would you mind? I know we haven't really talked about this very much.'

Isobel felt sick. She'd come here to talk to David, to tell him that she didn't want to go out with him any more – but the scene had all been rather vague in her mind, rather too abstract, almost as though she'd been visualising it as happening to someone else. But this was real. Dave was real, and he was about to leave her, to leave her out of his life and to go to America. Dave was going to go away; he wouldn't still be there, 'just in case . . .'

'Oh, Dave.' She looked at his tense expression, and tears welled up. 'Dave, I'm really sorry . . .'

She reached out and held his hand. They stayed like that for a while, silently, neither knowing what to say, but knowing this to be the end.

Eventually, Isobel said, 'It will be a fantastic opportunity. I'm really pleased for you. We didn't really imagine spending our – lives together, did we? I mean – it was never very likely that you'd get a job here.'

'And you've still got three years to go . . .'

'I suppose we've just bumbled along, not really thinking...'

'And we don't seem to have had much time for each other, lately, do we?' David held her knuckles against his lips. 'It's my fault, isn't it – ever since that afternoon at the bookie's? I wish I'd never gone there.'

There were tears in Isobel's eyes, and she and Dave hugged each other tightly. She opened her bag to find a handkerchief, and then remembered what else the bag contained. She should just leave it, forget about it; the solution had already been handed to her. But that would be dishonest. She rummaged in her bag.

'Here. Your toothbrush.'

'Why? Why was it in your bag?'

'Dave – I was going to talk to you today. I brought the toothbrush so I could give it back.'

David stared at the symbol of their intimacy, and then hurled it towards a rhododendron bush; the toothbrush landed on the lawn and stuck there, conspicuously red. They both stared at it for a while.

'I suppose there are other bits and pieces of mine, too. Do you want me to come and collect them?'

'Whenever is convenient for you, yes.'

There was a terrible grey dullness about everything, the air, the city, the trees, even the noise of traffic and the crying gulls. It was as though she and Dave were caught and submerged by the mediocrity, the lack of contrast, around them. Or perhaps it emanated from them, they were the dull nucleus from which the greyness radiated. She pressed her face against her knees so that red and silver stars burst behind her eyelids.

When she finally looked up, David had gone.

Gradually the colours and sounds returned, and her tears dried and crusted her eyelashes. A wood pigeon clapped its wings and flung itself vertically into the air, before dropping heavily among the branches of a tree. The toothbrush was shockingly red against the green of the lawn, and Isobel stood up and flung it deep within the trees, so that a startled blackbird exploded, squawking, from a bush.

Chapter Fourteen

There was opera on the radio, *Idomeneo*, but the reception was variable because of the hills and Iain occasionally fiddled with the tuning as he drove. That annoyed Margaret intensely, and she was tempted to reach out and turn the radio off, but she kept quiet because Iain was already irritated.

'We could have been there by now,' he said for the second time in the past half-hour.

'I know. It really was very thoughtless of him. But it's done, now – and we must try not to show our irritation when he arrives tomorrow.'

'If he were a teenager or in his early twenties, it might be excusable – just. One comes to accept irresponsibility from that age group. But he's in his thirties, dammit, and he's obviously been brought up properly. Why can't these people organise their lives sensibly, everything's so *last minute!*'

'I suppose it must have been something important.' Although I can't imagine what it could have been that would make Julian telephone at the last minute, only half an hour before we were due to pick him up, to tell us that he had unexpectedly to stay behind and that he'd drive up tomorrow.

As it was, Iain and Margaret had delayed their normal time of departure to the cottage in order to accommodate Julian; it had seemed so much more sensible for them all to travel in one car. Now Margaret wished she had not invited Julian. The weekend was sure to be a disaster: Iain was angry, and Julian presumably didn't really want to come, for whatever reason. She'd planned everything to be so pleasant for him, too, so relaxing. She had even organised the food in advance – the cool-box was completely full – so that she wouldn't have to spend too much time in the kitchen but would have time for strolling on the shore, or sitting and talking. It would have been so good for Julian to get away from the city: and now he wouldn't even have one full day at the cottage, if he didn't arrive until coffee-time tomorrow. She was hurt and frustrated, and the tenor, crackling in and out of focus, annoyed her so much that she clicked the radio off.

'Sorry. It's driving me mad!'

Iain grunted, and accelerated rapidly round a corner so that bottles clanked together in the boot. They drove for the next twenty minutes in silence, each busy with his or her own uncharitable thoughts.

It was nearly nine o'clock when they went through the village. The row of whitewashed houses gleamed palely in the evening light and there was a smell of seaweed. A small boy trundled his plastic tricycle along the road, struggling to catch his brother on his grown-up bike. A notice in the window of the shop caught Margaret's eye.

'Oh! Stop a minute! I want to see what that says.'

She scrambled out of the car, and waved at the children, who were watching her suspiciously.

'There's a ceilidh tomorrow in the village hall,' she explained as she slid on to her seat. 'We haven't been to one for years, have we? It would give us something to do if things got sticky,' she added, seeing Iain's dubious expression. 'I bet you Julian's never been to a genuine ceilidh before. I bet you – oh, a bottle of Islay malt!'

At that, Iain raised his eyebrows and laughed, as Margaret had hoped he would. 'Good lord, that's a heavy bet, Meg!'

'Well, I'm feeling guilty about inflicting one of my enthusiasms on you for a precious weekend. Especially since already it isn't looking very promising. That's what you think about Julian, isn't it – that he's one of my *enthusiasms*?'

'Well, isn't he? Yes, I suppose I do, my love, although I'm glad, because you don't seem to have found much to be enthusiastic about for quite a long while.'

Margaret could sense his enquiring glance, but she didn't want to have to answer. Fortunately, a black-faced ewe, trailing its old grey wool like a dirty blanket, chose that moment to amble across the road, and Iain had to slow down to avoid its distraught lamb. After that, Margaret was able to divert him with an account she had read somewhere of sheep-shearing in the Outer Isles, and quite soon they reached the cottage.

In the morning, however, her anxiety returned. To make matters worse, grey cloud formed a low, flat layer that hid the hills, and the loch was dark and sulky. Margaret wondered what picture Julian had formed of the cottage, and hoped that he wouldn't be too disappointed. Why couldn't the sun shine so that everything would look its welcoming best? Would he find the entrance to the track, had her instructions been adequate on the telephone? For the fifth or sixth time she checked the spare room, straightened the towels on the triple wooden rail, and adjusted the amount the window was open. Iain was pottering around the garden, patching and tightening the wire fence (subconsciously checking the defences? she wondered). He had already tied back the pink rambler rose that was their only concession to cultivated garden flowers. It was nearly eleven o'clock and Margaret, after a final look to make sure that the bedroom was tidy, went downstairs to organise the coffee. She was surprisingly nervous. Julian hadn't been to their home in the city; he really didn't know anything about the Gillespies' likes and dislikes, or their tastes in furniture and food. He was so young, too, in comparison, and they were so set in their ways. It wasn't often that friends were invited to stay at the cottage either. People dropped in for coffee en route to somewhere else, and occasionally friends visited for a day. But for someone, a single man at that, to stay overnight was most unusual; in retrospect, it was surprising that Iain had agreed. Fifteen minutes had passed: the coffee was ready, there was no sign of Julian. She couldn't even see his car on the track when she went upstairs to check.

'Am I allowed to have some coffee, or must we wait for our absent friend?' Iain toed off his boots in the back porch and stuck his head into the kitchen. 'We can give him a cup of instant when he arrives – although at this rate it will probably be time for sherry!'

It was midday when Julian finally appeared. Margaret made herself wait inside while he clambered awkwardly out of the car. When the car door slammed, she went out to greet him.

'Julian! I'm sorry – were my instructions awful?'

He looked surprised for a moment, then gave his charming smile.

'No, they were perfect, right down to the fallen tree and the stack of old tyres. What are they for, by the way?'

'For covering the silage clamp. But there always seem to be more than the farmer needs. Here's Iain. Let us help you in with your bags and then we can have a drink.'

Julian sat down on the bed and looked around. He could just see out of the front window from where he sat; he supposed there were probably hills somewhere in that thick cloud. Margaret was very keen on the hills, he recalled; she'd mentioned them two or three times when she had been persuading him to come and stay. There was a window that looked out to the back, too, but there was nothing much to see there except rough grass on the hill that rose up behind the house, and sheep. The house – cottage, they called it – looked all right. This room was comfortable enough, a good carpet and thick curtains to keep out the draughts. The Gillespies hadn't made the mistake of cluttering the place with cosy cottage furniture, either, and he liked the polished floor and rugs downstairs. Sensible, practical. He yawned, and stretched out on the bed, and tried to imagine himself here with Isobel, just the two of them. On a dismal grey afternoon like this they could stay in bed, there'd be no reason to get up at all. She'd still been in bed when he left home this morning. She'd been very scathing about his weekend away with his smart friends, and wanted him to ask if she could come, too! He had tried to tell her that she would find it boring, that Iain Gillespie was twice her age, for example, and that she would have to be on her best behaviour and sit around and make polite conversation. Then, predictably, she'd accused him of snobbery and sexism and ageism, and Christ knows what else. But she wouldn't have fitted in here – even if he could have spoken to Margaret about her. He was certain that Margaret didn't know that he had a girlfriend; she would probably stop coming round to look after him if she thought there was someone else who could do the job. He had to be rather careful that there were no obvious traces of Isobel in the flat on the days that Margaret was due. From that point of view, it was probably just as well that Bella preferred to keep her independence, and didn't leave a trail of talc and tights. Or textbooks!

He hadn't wanted to leave her this morning. She'd teased him and tempted him back into bed as it was, so that he was late in leaving. He'd arrived only an hour late – well, probably eighteen hours, if you counted the fact that he'd pulled out of driving up last night. That had obviously caused a bit of friction with his hosts. Not surprising. Socially unacceptable. Although I bet if Iain Gillespie knew why I was late, he thought, he would have sympathised! Gillespie wouldn't have expected him to turn down the opportunity of an evening with bella Isabella. If it rained tomorrow he'd use the weather as an excuse and go home early. And now they were all supposed to be going out for a walk. A walk! In the mud and mist! But they probably wouldn't go far, Margaret would see to that, she'd be aware of the difficulties. She was a thoughtful woman, and the situation was probably a little awkward for her, too . . .

He sat up carefully to avoid hitting his head on the sloping ceiling, and went to the bedroom door to try to determine what his hosts were doing. He could hear music downstairs, opera, Verdi, and he sighed and clumped down the narrow, polished stairs, holding tightly to the single rail.

'Ah, Julian! Come in!' Iain lowered the newspaper he was reading. 'It was good of you to bring papers, that's something we always miss when we come here. Are you feeling rested?'

'Fine, thank you. The room's very comfortable.'

'I think the weather's brightening,' Margaret said. 'Would you like to come out for a short stroll along the shore? Have you got boots?'

He hadn't, of course (why should he?) so they found a spare pair that almost fitted from the collection in the back porch, and then they all put on waterproofs and went outside. It was true: the cloud was lifting, and there was a luminous whiteness where there had formerly been dark grey. The wind had dropped, too, and the surface of the loch was smooth and only slightly dimpled by occasional light rain.

'What's that smell – rather sweet, like herbs?' Julian sniffed.

'Bog myrtle. It always smells especially good after rain,' Margaret smiled. 'Over there, do you see, those low greyish-green plants?'

'The girls always used to pick it and dry it when they were young,' Iain said, 'then sew it into little bags for Christmas presents. The problem was, the leaves often weren't properly dry – the girls were in too much of a rush – and the bags would turn mildewed. Not very pleasant, really!'

'I didn't know you had children.'

'Oh – not ours, jointly. They're Iain's. They're both grown up now and have families. But they sometimes come here for holidays. The cottage is a fairly recent acquisition so the novelty hasn't worn off! That's why there were spare wellies, they always seem to leave things behind!'

'They're keen on sailing, and hillwalking,' Iain added.

'Your famous hills might be going to show themselves at last,' Julian pointed with his stick. 'I was beginning to think they might be a myth.'

'No, that's what they've been covered in all morning.'

Margaret and Julian looked puzzled.

'The hillth,' Iain explained, and was pleased when they both groaned.

After that, the mood lightened, and Julian soon found that he was beginning to appreciate his surroundings a little more. At one point Margaret, who was walking behind him along the narrow path, grabbed his arm.

'Stop! Don't move!'

'What's wrong?'

'Look at your feet – you nearly squashed it!'

Julian swayed to one side as Margaret bent down to cup her hands around a young frog, only an inch long, that was hopping and crawling towards the undergrowth. They found several more frogs after that, and huge black slugs that lay, like evil omens, across the path. A heron, previously so still that they hadn't noticed it, finally lost its nerve and pushed itself into the air, lumbering off across the loch. The wind had dropped entirely, and the air was warm and damp. Margaret and Julian sat on a treetrunk that was bleached and furry from immersion in the sea, and watched while Iain poked along the strand line.

'Are you managing all right? We needn't go any further if it's too difficult.'

'I'm fine. I'm not a cripple.' He laughed at her uncertain expression. 'Well, not entirely, anyway. This is very different, isn't it? It's so peaceful. It must be strange for you, always shifting between the city and this. Dislocating.'

Margaret smiled. 'Did you do this sort of thing when you were young? Go to the hills or to the beach?'

'Not really, no. My mother always hated the British coast. She says it's cold and uncivilised. We sometimes went to a friend's farm, though, particularly when I was young. But I stopped going.' He paused for a moment. 'And I seem to have spent the rest of my life in cities. I should do this more often, I suppose. One's viewpoint tends to become rather limited in the city, doesn't it? I feel I ought to be sitting on top of a hill – if I could – and taking advantage of the wider perspective. Assuming there *was* a view!'

'Well, you'd be welcome to come again.' Margaret said that automatically, as a good hostess might, and then was surprised to find that she probably, almost, meant it. The difficulties and disappointments of last night and this morning had, apparently, been overcome. 'On a clear day you can see for miles and miles, as the song has it, even from the top of that little hill at the back of the cottage – right out to sea and some of the islands. The hills across the loch rather block the view south, but you can see inland, mountain tops and ridges, one after the other. The landscape looks very empty, I suppose because you can't see into the valleys where humans live. I wonder, if it's a clear morning tomorrow, whether you could get up there?'

She touched the walking stick that was propped between them against the treetrunk, and lifted it slightly as though to test its strength.

'If Iain came too . . . if you'd like to . . . I'm sure we could both help . . .'

But even as she made the suggestion, she saw that it couldn't work. She saw herself anxiously fluttering around, holding out a hand; Iain, impatient, grabbing Julian's elbow, and Julian himself, irritated, waving away assistance and yet struggling and sliding, out of breath. And, if they ever reached the top, the prospect of the slippery downward journey would destroy any hope of peaceful meditation. The air would buzz, she thought, it would vibrate and prickle, and would not lie flat and smooth. The thought made her smile fleetingly.

'It would be too difficult, wouldn't it?' she said, still smiling, before Julian could reply. 'But, if you wanted, we could go out in the boat. If you would like to. And if the weather's good.'

Julian, too, had imagined the scene of humiliation and (an aspect that Margaret, unknowing, had not considered) pain. He knew he could not, in the presence of others, climb that hill. Alone, and given strong incentives, he might have tried. But what incentive could there possibly be? If fame were offered him (by whom?), would he climb? But fame itself would need to be specifically described; it was too unfocused. He wouldn't want to be the famous half-cripple who had climbed a hill. There was no fame in that when disabled people climbed up Everest. Yet if he were to be offered fame as a violinist . . . ? Well, then he would try, and would succeed. If someone said to him, 'Julian, climb to the mountain top unaided. Crawl, if you must. In reward for your labour, your violin-playing will be universally acclaimed. You will be famous,' he would go.

'No, Julian, fame is merely an incidental acquisition. Fame is superficial,' Canon Bothwell had said. 'Remember what we agreed. It is the talent, your Gift, that is the root from which all else will grow.'

Julian had sighed and nodded. He had heard the arguments before. He was tired, and the pain dominated his body. It crept upwards, spreading, forcing its jagged nails towards his head. There was no escape.

'You must nurture the talent. Expand it, allow it to engulf your soul so that it cannot help but spill out, to touch your audience. You have to *become* the music, allow it to take you over. Feel the Truth within you. You will forget the pain, Julian, the pain will no longer be important. Submit to the music, not the pain. And when you are filled with the music it will overflow to your audience so that they, too, will be able to understand. You will be famous then, dear Julian. But the fame itself will be unimportant, because you, and those who hear you, will be fulfilled. *That* is what will sustain you, not the fame.'

'I can't do it! I keep trying – I am trying – but it hurts too much!'

Julian had gripped his leg and rocked backwards and forwards, squeezing his eyelids against his tears.

'I'll help you, you know I can help you.' Canon Bothwell's hand was on his arm. Julian could feel its weight and warmth, and his arm tingled. 'Open your eyes, Julian. Hold my hand, and we'll pray together. God will help us. It's a difficult path and we will both need extra strength. Take my hand, Julian.'

The man's voice was strong and low, and his eyes, in their dark hollows, were compelling.

'Take my hand, and let us ask for strength. Remember, if you reach the top of that mountain, you will be no longer lame. You will be whole – and free!'

'NO! You're mistaken!'

'Julian, are you all right?'

Julian focused on Margaret's face, and then on her hand resting on his arm. His voice was high-pitched when he spoke, and he stopped, bewildered, and cleared his throat.

'Canon Bothwell said . . . he said I'd no longer . . .' No, he didn't! Canon Bothwell could not have said such a dangerous thing! He *needed* to be lame; the lameness was the whole point, wasn't it? Canon Bothwell's entire thesis had been founded on the disability.

Margaret watched Julian in consternation. His face had become quite pale and his teeth were chattering. She gripped his cold hand.

'Is there something I can do?' Perhaps he needed special medication, perhaps his disability was deeper than she had realised. 'Shall we go back to the cottage? Julian?'

She shook his hand slightly to get his attention, and Julian blinked and looked at his hand in hers.

'No. Oh no, I'm fine. Sorry – I had a very vivid memory, then, of Canon Bothwell.'

'The one in the photo. Yes, you told me about him.'

She saw again the wheelchair-bound boy, and that possessive hand. Poor boy, poor Julian! Her throat tightened in compassion; but there was also a warmth and happiness inside her because it was clear, now, that he needed help. She was nearly overwhelmed with pity for him, and with thankfulness. Julian released his hand.

'Your husband seems to have found something interesting.' He nodded in Iain's direction. Iain was waving and calling.

'Do come and look at this.'

Margaret jumped up, then looked down at Julian.

'It's all right – I'll just stay here. I'm quite happy looking at the view.'

'If you're sure you'll be all right? I won't be long. Here, you take the glasses.'

She pulled the strap of the binoculars over her head, tugging when it caught against her hood. 'See if you can see the salmon jumping in the pens.'

Julian watched as she hurried across the loose shingle. He focused the binoculars on her and Iain, wondering if she would tell her husband about his strange attack; but he could see her smiling and talking as she bent over the object that Iain had found in the weed, and neither of them looked his way. He was still shaken by the intensity of his dream (his daydream, he hadn't been asleep). If only Canon Bothwell were here to explain. He could still feel the touch of the chaplain's hand and the power of confidence that seemed to flow from it. But it was the abrupt betrayal that Julian felt most: to alter the original credo that the disability was imposed in order to nurture and succour the Gift, to claim now that the disability was an irrelevance and could be removed . . . It could not be removed; nothing short of magic or a miracle would restore his knee. He must have misunderstood, or the Devil had been speaking in the chaplain's voice and tempting him. Julian shook his head, as though to shake out the jumbled thoughts. It was all meaningless mumbo jumbo, noises in the head, a cacophony of noises; the water, the wind and the calls of seabirds, a conspiracy. God! There were so many noises out here, all clashing and jangling together. How could Margaret stand it? But she wouldn't hear the music, she couldn't hear the music. Unless it poured out through him. That was his own great strength.

The cloudbase had dropped again, to a few hundred feet above the loch. Iain lit a log fire in the sitting room, even though it was midsummer, and the interior of the cottage was warm and comfortable. Margaret was pleased to see that Julian appeared more at ease. He had spent some time before dinner examining the various framed photographs on the wall, and asking Iain about his hobby. As a result, the two men had talked easily at dinner about a variety of topics, so that Margaret felt that she had become a bystander, the bringer of meats and victuals to feed their careless intellect. But this, after all, was ostensibly the reason for inviting Julian – conversation, relaxation, and a complete change of scene. That strange episode this afternoon seemed only to have been a brief disturbance, and Julian now appeared quite normal. Margaret carried the pudding bowls out to the small kitchen and prepared to make the coffee. It was pleasant to look forward to an evening around the fire, with music, a dram or two, and casual conversation.

'Meg? I thought you wanted to go to that ceilidh. Did you say it started at nine?'

She had forgotten all about it, and she wasn't sure that she could be bothered, now.

'I don't know. What do you think? There's a ceilidh, Julian, in the village hall. I'd wondered if we should look in, but perhaps we're all feeling too lazy now . . . ?'

'I've never been to a real ceilidh. It's not just dancing, is it?'

'Not at all! There'll be a real mixture, I should imagine. And one is allowed to sit and enjoy the entertainment!'

'It sounds an excellent idea.' Julian pushed back his chair. 'Let me come and help you with the washing-up. It's nearly nine o'clock now, isn't it?'

Margaret was still doubtful, but Julian was boyishly enthusiastic about an unusual evening out, and teased Iain that he should wear a kilt. Iain admitted to possessing a kilt that had been his grandfather's, but said that he refused to wear it because it was too short and didn't hide his bony knees.

Julian laughed. 'Well, can you imagine me wearing one? I'd need one that was mid-calf length or else I'd have to sit with a tartan rug around my legs in case I scared the girls away!'

'I imagine either of those options would be more likely to scare them away – to see you dressed either as a girl or as a geriatric,' Iain grinned. 'Talking of geriatrics, we'd better go before we change our minds and sink into sloth in front of the fire. Have you got the glasses, Meg?'

The hall was at the edge of the village, a small cement-rendered building with a slate roof and peeling, brown-painted windows. Fir trees had been planted on one side and at the back to provide some protection from the wind, but rubbish had blown about and chewed scraps of food wrappers and milk cartons were pressed into the surrounding gravel and caught around the wire litterbin. Two ewes and their lambs nestled against one wall of the building and eyed Iain's car nervously as it pulled into the car park. A red pick-up truck and a motorbike were already parked. The hall door was open and the interior lit, but only the sound of voices talking drifted out.

'Perhaps it's been cancelled.' Margaret was hopeful.

'No, we're just a bit early yet. We'll wait in the car for a few minutes until someone else comes.'

A man looked out of the hall door. 'Evening. Thought I heard a car. Are you coming in?'

'Er . . . yes, if this is the ceilidh.' We're such outsiders, Margaret thought. Nobody will want to talk to us, we're going to look silly and be in the way.

'Aye. It's the ceilidh right enough. Come away in, we'll be starting in a wee while.'

Margaret let Julian go in first.

'All right?' she whispered, but he just shrugged and raised his eyebrows. There were a dozen or fifteen people clustered round inside the door, and they all turned to look briefly at the newcomers and then politely turned back to their own conversations.

'Ach, it's Mr Gillespie. And Missus.'

The village's shopkeeper and postmaster came across and shook Iain's hand.

'Welcome to you – and your guest.'

Iain introduced Julian, and Margaret began to recognise a few faces that she knew, and nodded and smiled. A space had been cleared in the centre of the hall and the chairs were set around the edges, facing inwards. There was an old bruised upright piano against the end wall, and milk, a tea urn and plastic cups on a table. The ages of the people already present seemed to range from fifty upwards, and Margaret wondered if this was, in fact, the Senior Citizens' evening out. But even as she was worrying how she and Iain might extricate themselves from what promised to be an awkward evening, a couple in their thirties entered, carrying guitars, and were followed by a young, bearded man with a variety of flat and tubular instrument cases. There was much joking, back-slapping and shouted comment, and then suddenly everyone was moving towards the seats. Other folk had been drifting in and soon there was a great deal of discussion about who should go first. Finally Duncan, the shopkeeper, and his wife stood up amid whistles and hand-clapping. Duncan, it turned out, had a fine strong tenor voice, and his wife pummelled tunes out of the old piano with great determination and enthusiasm. The songs were of the type that Margaret thought of as the Scots music-hall variety and reminded her of Hogmanay entertainments on television, but she tried to look as though she were loving every minute, even when the listeners were cajoled into joining in the fifth song. Iain was droning tunelessly next to her, occasionally hitting the right word or note, but Julian couldn't, or wouldn't join in. More likely the latter – he was looking very uncomfortable.

Duncan and his wife finished, to great applause and offers of drink from their friends, and now the young bearded man offered to play. Margaret wondered what he did for a living, his face and arms were so pale compared to most of the local men, but he and his music were obviously well known in the community. He took a flute out of a rectangular black case and slotted it together; then, after a few warming up runs and trills on the instrument, he walked into the central area and began to play. It was a light, lilting tune that soon had feet tapping, and that slid almost without one noticing into a complex, ballad-type melody.

Julian was greatly relieved. He was also intrigued and impressed and, at the end of the ballad, he caught the flautist's eye and raised his glass in salute. There were calls from the floor for favourite tunes when the young man exchanged the flute for a whistle, and one or two people began to clap when they recognised the music. The room was filling up and was as full of activity as a Brueghel painting, albeit discreet. Now the girl with the guitar began to sing to the whistle music and there was general encouragement for her to join in properly.

The guitarists and the flautist had clearly played together before; this was a well-established routine. Somebody dragged out two chairs into the central space, the musicians conferred, and the bearded man gulped whisky and licked his lips. It was so informal, Julian thought; people were coming and going, handing round bottles, there was continual banter and laughter, and this very communal music-making. He looked around the hall. Margaret and Iain had turned round and were talking with a couple sitting behind them, children were chasing each other round the table that held the tea urn and were crawling underneath and giggling, and an old woman one seat along from him was knitting and murmuring to her neighbour. But despite all the activity, attention was always focused on the music, and the applause and comments were loud and appreciative.

Now there was a call for dancing, and a short man with a huge beer gut, over which was stretched a striped and not-too-clean T-shirt, came forward with a can of beer in one hand and an accordion supported by the other. Julian looked at Margaret out of the corner of his eye, and she saw his look and grimaced slightly.

'I hate accordion music,' she whispered, 'don't you? Perhaps we should push our chairs back a bit? Or shall we go and stand by the door and get some fresh air?'

'I think I'd rather stand by the door. We're likely to get trampled here if things get wild!'

Margaret explained to Iain what they were doing, and he nodded and carried on talking to the man behind.

The accordion player started off with one of the more energetic group dances, to get as many people as possible on to the floor. There were good-humoured jeers and whistles from amongst the teenagers as they chose their partners, and soon there were about twenty people dancing, all ages, shouting instructions and shrieking with laughter as they tangled with each other or missed their cues. A can of beer that had been tucked underneath a chair went flying, and so did its owner's subsequent oaths, to the accompaniment of admonishments from the older women that he should 'hush, and mind his tongue'.

The hall was hot and sticky, and smelt of dust and beer. Julian leant back against the open door and enjoyed the smell and feel of the night breeze against his face.

'A bit different from a Kersland Ensemble concert.' Margaret almost had to shout to make herself heard.

'Mmm. I was just thinking the same myself.' He smiled at her, amused to see that her face was pink and slightly shiny. 'Perhaps we, too, should dole out whisky and get everybody dancing to warm things up.'

'In their Sunday best? Felt hats flying, pearls tinkling on to the floor?'

'It's not *that* bad, surely? Not everybody – aaagh! *Hell!*' Julian's stick clattered to the floor.

'Oh, sorry, mate! I wasn't looking.' In consternation, the man bent down to pick up the stick. 'Are you OK? Fuckin' fiddle's always in the way. Leads me a merry dance.'

He slapped the case as though to reprove it for butting Julian's leg. He was slightly older than Julian; his dark hair was pulled back into a ponytail, and he wore jeans and a leather waistcoat over a short-sleeved shirt.

'Aw, shit! Bob's on his fuckin' accordion again! No point going in there for a bit. Want a top-up?' He took a half-bottle out of his pocket and waved it towards Julian's glass.

'Thanks, yes.'

'How about your friend?' He gestured towards Margaret, ready to slop whisky into her glass, but she smiled and shook her head.

'I'm Tom, by the way. My mate Chris's just on his way.'

'I'm Julian,' Julian said, conscious of how he sounded, and the hidden connotations of background in such a name. 'This is Mrs Gillespie – Margaret. Her husband, Iain, is over there,' he added, not wanting Tom to make mistaken assumptions about his relationship with his 'friend'.

'Hi, Julian. Hi, Margaret. Julian . . . if you're going to drink my whisky we'd better call you Jools.' Tom grinned. 'Your leg OK now? Where d'you come from then, you and your friends?'

'We have a cottage across the loch, down the track opposite the silage clamp,' Margaret explained.

'Oh aye.' It was obvious that Tom neither knew nor cared about the cottage. 'Have you come to experience the ethnic music in its true, primitive environmental setting, then? Connoisseurs of the art form, are you? Or have you come to *play*?' He lowered his voice on the last word, making it sound rough and sensuous.

Julian rubbed the hand containing his glass across his face; he didn't know whether to be amused or threatened by this man. He certainly felt at a disadvantage.

'I'm the Gillespies' guest. They heard that this was on, and brought me.'

'Julian is a violinist, too,' said Margaret clearly. There was a challenge in her voice, and she chinked her glass against his.

'That's incidental,' he said. 'I'm a classical violinist – concerts, and all that stuff.' He shrugged, trying to look self-deprecating.

'Solos, concertos?' Tom whistled. 'Hey, Chris love. Come here! This is Jools – he's a famous violinist, not like us. *Are* you famous, Jools? What's your last name?'

'Not really. Kersland. I run a small orchestra – the Kersland Ensemble – in the city. Mainly baroque music, nothing like this, I'm afraid.' Afraid? Why the hell was he afraid?

Chris and Tom exchanged glances and grinned.

'Aye well,' Chris said, 'we can't all be perfect. Look, there's Euan.' He waved at the flautist. 'We'll see you later, Jools!'

'Why did you have to tell them that?'

Julian, irritated at being made to feel inferior, turned round to accuse Margaret, but found that she had gone. The dancing had just ended, and she had taken the opportunity to return to her husband. He was out of his depth here among all these noisy exuberant people. He felt that he was in danger. Red-faced, sweating dancers were pushing towards the door for cool air and Julian had to press himself against the wall until the crush had passed. Now women were handing out plastic cups of tea, and plates of plain biscuits were being circulated. Margaret handed him a biscuit when he returned to his seat, and then clutched Iain's arm.

'I told the fiddlers that Julian played.'

'Meg! You didn't!' Iain was concerned, although also (for which he was slightly ashamed) secretly rather entertained. 'You shouldn't have done that!'

'No,' Julian agreed, and then looked at the biscuit that Margaret had given him, and handed it back. 'Perhaps we should go, now. It's quite late, isn't it?'

But even as he looked at his watch, Duncan called for quiet and indicated that they should all sit down and rest because Mary was going to sing.

Mary was small and wiry, of an indefinably old age; her blue cardigan was buttoned over a shapeless blue-and-white patterned dress, and she wore thick tights and stout black shoes, but her sallow, wrinkled face was full of mirth. There was clapping, but also muted groans, hastily hushed, from the younger listeners. She came into the middle of the floor and opened her almost toothless mouth. A powerful wail streamed out and filled the corners of the hall. It slipped and twisted through unidentifiable words, sliding from one note to the next in unfamiliar cadences, and the terrifying starkness of the sound made Julian rigid. His scalp prickled and he gripped his stick. There was no other sound in the hall until she finished. Then there was clapping, and, 'That was a good one, Mary,' and, 'Give us another,' but she shook her head

191

and beamed round at everyone, then sat down, accepting her friends' praise with pleased nods.

'That was a bit weird, wasn't it?' Margaret whispered. 'I don't really care for mouth music.'

But Julian noticed that Tom was looking across at him, so he kept his expression neutral.

'It looks as though our two fiddlers are going to have a go now. Oh, is the skinny guitarist going to play with them, too? She does get around, doesn't she?'

The whisky was having a very relaxing effect on Margaret, Julian thought; he hoped she wouldn't volunteer to sing.

Cheering and clapping interrupted the chatter and chinking of glasses, and Tom, Chris and Euan came out on to the floor.

'Good evening, everyone,' Tom said. 'It's good to be back. Chris and I met up with Euan a few weeks ago, across in Aberdeen, and we spent a few hours – probably too many hours, if you'd seen the pile of empty cans at the end – working up a couple of new tunes for you. To kick off, then, we've got "Lachlan's Lazy-beds". Chris heard this one over in Stornoway last year, but – you all know Chris! – his head was too full of booze to remember it properly –' laughter and catcalls interrupted him '– so it was up to Euan here – you all know him too, doesn't get pissed until the alcohol level reaches his neck – to put us right. OK then . . .'

He tucked the fiddle under his chin, tapped his foot to give the beat, and the three of them swung into a rapid, bubbling tune, Euan's fingers flicking up and down the whistle, the fiddlers' bows rocking rapidly over the strings, feet tapping, bodies swaying. At once, people were tapping with their shoes and fingers or whistling soundlessly; Julian was caught up, too, his body responded on its own, and the Gillespies were equally ensnared. Tom and Chris were laughing and shouting to each other as they played and Euan's eyes, in his pale, serious face, were bright with enjoyment. Julian marvelled at the number of variations on the tune and how the musicians slid from one to the next and back again. Then suddenly, without warning, they stopped. Tom held up his hand to end the applause and the mood changed again in accord with the sweet, lilting sadness of the second tune. Julian found himself watching Tom, who was now very still and serious, his eyes unseeing, as he played. There was no play-acting about the man, though, he had instantly turned inwards, into the music, and it was impossible for the listener not to be moved. For a moment, Julian closed his eyes as he listened, and he felt that strangely intense thrill stirring inside his body, hinting at the onset of weightlessness, and pain. A single sharp spasm from his knee caused him to wince, and when he opened his eyes he saw that Tom's eyes were wide open, too, and were looking at him. He was confused, not only because of the eye contact but because, briefly, he had switched into his *alter ego*, he had *been* switched, and not by music of his own making. Automatically, he banged his stick enthusiastically on the floor when the others clapped.

'More whisky?' Iain leant across with the bottle, and Julian didn't notice when Tom looked over at Margaret and winked.

'And now,' Tom said, 'we can't let you all sit around and do nothing. Some of the rest of you should be working – or playing. We have a real violinist here among us, from the Big City, no less, and I'm going to ask him to play something for us before we carry on.'

Julian stared in disbelief as Tom came across to him.

'Oh no!' he said. 'Not here!'

But Tom held out his hand. 'Come on, Jools. It's a ceilidh, man, don't be shy!'

'No. I can't play that sort of music.' Julian looked at Margaret and Iain for help but, although Iain looked uncomfortable, Margaret was smiling and nodding in a proprietorial way.

'Go on!' she said. 'You can think of something.'

'Aye, lad, give us a tune. We'll no' eat you,' someone called, and everybody laughed.

Tom was standing in front of him and held out his fiddle. He dropped his voice. 'Come on, man, you must be able to think of something light – Russian dances or something. Come on.'

There was no escape. Julian handed Margaret his glass and looked round at the curious faces.

'I'll need a chair.'

'Yeah, sorry. Will you be OK? Sorry about knackering your leg. Don't beat hell out of the fiddle in revenge, will you? She's the best I've got!'

Julian took the fiddle and tested the strings with the bow: the tone was rough and vibrant, and the bow was short of hairs. He retuned it, holding it on his knee because the pegs were stiff. Conversations had resumed; there was a crash and an oath from near the door as someone dropped a glass, and he took advantage of the small commotion to stand up and limp across to the seat.

'This is an unexpected pleasure,' he said, and was encouraged when a few people laughed. 'And it's obviously a plot hatched up by my hosts, Margaret and Iain, to make me earn my keep. Not another drop, Margaret said, until you go out there and play. She's very strict.' He pulled a woebegone face and raised his shoulders, and then grinned at Margaret's pink face. 'Sorry I can't play like the lads here. The only bit of music that I can think of, on the spur of the moment, is a Hungarian dance. But, like Chris, my memory isn't too good when I've had a dram or two! Here goes, anyway.'

He tried out the first few bars to remind himself, and then burst into the powerful opening chords, and the changes of tempo. He was too much taken by surprise to put his soul into his playing but his well-lubricated audience, even the youngsters, were enjoying the novelty of having an outsider (and a lame one, at that!) play. At the end, Tom put an arm across his shoulder.

'Great, Jools! I knew you'd do it. That's where you and I went wrong, Chris, not sticking with the classical stuff. Do you give lessons? We'll come and visit, won't we, Chris? Now look, then . . .' He pulled a roll of music from his waistcoat pocket. 'You take Chris's fiddle and give me mine, and I'll teach you to play some real music.'

This plan obviously took Chris by surprise, and he was clearly about to remonstrate, but Tom told Euan to give him a drink, and that this was the least they could do for one who hadn't yet seen the light. He grabbed a child who was sidling past.

'Here! Stand here and hold the music so Jools can see. I'll give you a drink from my bottle if you promise not to tell your mammy. Right? Sit down then, and hold it above your head. That's it. OK, Jools. Can you see?'

Julian looked across at the Gillespies and shook his head in disbelief. Margaret appeared delighted. Iain had slumped back in his chair, apparently in resignation. Tom, though, had started to play the first few bars, a typical skipping, dotted crotchet-quaver pattern.

'Now you!'

Julian copied, but he was too smooth, too fluent.

'No, you need to attack more. Accent the difference.'

This time Julian was more successful. They went back to the beginning and played in unison, carrying on. Tom caught his eye.

'Yeah! That's *it*!'

Then the music became more complicated, spiky chords, and Julian had to concentrate. Tom got ahead and grimaced, so they stopped and tried again.

'Come on, everyone – it's "sing along with Jools and Tom" time!'

It turned out that most people knew the words, or at least

the tune, and everyone joined in, in one way or another; even the boy holding the music began to swing the pages from side to side.

Julian was dazed with the enthusiasm and attention. It was wonderful to feel part of the group, to be accepted and to entertain. This was what he should be doing, making music live! They were made to play again, and again, and then when they finally ended, Julian pushed himself to his feet and shook Tom's hand.

'Thank you, mate. You've really given me something good to work on. You'll have to come and visit and teach me your technique.'

'My *technique*?' Tom gripped his hand and gave him a quizzical look. 'You'll have to ask Chris about that. He can tell you what it's all about! You need to relax, man, think a bit about yourself. Here – take the music as a memento. I'll look you up next time I'm in the city.' He looked round at the noisy audience. 'Jools is going to practise hard and then he's going to join us with his fiddle. We'll expand the band. Hey – we'll call ourselves MacDonald's Ensemble! OK, Chris, Euan – let's go! Thanks, Jools. See you around!'

Julian limped back to his chair, holding the music that Tom had given him. He took back his glass and drained it, smiling at the Gillespies' enthusiastic remarks, then sat in a daze, applauding when everyone else applauded, as the performers went through their repertoires.

It was long past midnight when the Gillespies decided that they should leave. The dancing had started again and it looked as though the ceilidh would go on for hours. Iain took Julian's arm, and Margaret's, and steered them through the bodies and bottles towards the door, so that when Julian heard Tom shout goodbye, he didn't have a free hand to wave. He wanted to go back and clasp Tom's hand, but he could only look back and shout 'Thanks!' before he was guided towards the car.

Chapter Fifteen

The high-pitched purr of the little outboard motor bounced back at them from the hollows and inlets on the shore, and the wash slapped against the shore. Julian groaned inwardly and cursed himself for not taking up Iain's offer of an old donkey jacket. Although the air was thick and humid, even the slow puttering of the boat created a breeze that winkled its way through his pullover. And the damn island looked like a bloody jungle. Look at it! Brambles trailing over the rocks at the edges, waist-high bracken, and a tangle of bushes and trees! Nothing could live in there. Any animal would get worn out just trying to move. It was all right for Margaret: she looked very comfortable, completely at home in the boat, wrapped up in that canvas smock thing. She and Iain had practically bundled him into the dinghy after lunch. He hadn't been given time to think of a good excuse to go home to Isobel. If only he'd got up earlier instead of lying in bed and thinking about her – and thinking about fiddles, and last night, and too much to drink! Then he could have been on his way home to Bella, instead of in this bloody draughty boat. He could have left his hosts to their bloody outdoor pursuits, Iain probably steaming up that hillside with his cameras and stout leather boots, Margaret wandering around and daydreaming about the view from the top of that *fucking* hill. His head still hurt. And he'd had to eat his bloody breakfast grapefruit at lunchtime. He hated grapefruit, he could still taste its acid sharpness. Julian shivered and hunched down lower in the bow.

'Are you all right? You do look a bit cold. But it'll be warmer once we get ashore. We can land just round the corner.' Margaret waved her arm, pointing vaguely somewhere in the distance.

She's enjoying this, Julian grumbled to himself. I thought she wanted to look after me! She's a sadist, not a Good Worker. Next thing she'll tell me it's all for my own good. He glowered at her from inside his upturned shirt collar, but she smiled happily.

'You know, I really think that being able to go out on the loch is one of my greatest pleasures. And I've wanted to explore the island for years, but somehow we never seem to get around to it . . .'

So you keep saying, Julian thought. Why me? Why does it have to be me?

'The vegetation does look a bit thick, doesn't it? Perhaps we should have brought a machete or something to hack our way through the undergrowth!'

'Only if there's a coffee shop at the centre!'

'Poor Julian! I'm sorry, I should have brought a Thermos. Look, though, we should be able to land by those rocks, I think. I've seen them from the shore, with the binoculars, and it might be a good way in.'

The island seemed to rise straight out of the loch, for there was no sloping shore on which to beach the boat. Bands of black and yellow lichen and glistening brown kelp marked the levels like Plimsoll lines. Margaret steered for a gap between two huge grey rocks that projected from the shore, round and sleek as basking porpoises. She cut the engine and allowed the boat to drift slowly in. The wind of progress dropped and Julian felt the still silence; even the ripples scarcely made a sound and the water was dark and smooth. Margaret bent down and lifted an object like a soft plastic spindle attached to a short rope, dropping it over the side where it hung, grazing the surface of the water.

'Could you drop out that other fender at the bow?'

She pointed to a similar object behind Julian, and he raised an eyebrow and did as he was asked. The boat, protected by its fenders, nudged gently against a porpoise-rock's flank, and Margaret reached out and grasped the slightly roughened surface, pulling the boat along until she could find a firm grip to hold it steady. The rock made a perfect natural jetty, leading up on to a grassy spit of land, and Julian suddenly felt more hopeful. After all, it would be quite an amusing adventure to recount, intrepid explorer of untrodden soil and so on. But he frowned slightly at the rock.

'Now what?' he asked. 'No steps!'

'If you can keep holding us in close, I'll get ashore and help you out.'

'Not likely! I don't want to be left in charge! What if it starts to drift away? I'll be left drifting around on the ocean and you'll be marooned on a desert island. Not a Bible in sight, either, even though it's Sunday. I'll get out first.'

Margaret looked dubious, but she held the boat steady as Julian shuffled his bottom across and reached out to grasp the rock. The boat tipped alarmingly and he gave a strange, whooping yell, but she knew they were quite safe. Because the tide was almost high, the rocks were only slightly taller than the side of the boat. Julian stood up, looking alarmed when the boat rocked, and then he bent his lame leg and rested it on the seat. The problem was, of course, that the weak leg, straightened, would not be able to support him, either inside the boat or out on the rock. Margaret gripped the rock more tightly.

'I do think you should let me get out first.'

'I'll manage,' he said curtly, and by a seemingly impossible contortion he stretched his undamaged leg over the side and on to the rock. He leant forward and grabbed for a new handhold, but the force of his lunge pushed the boat violently so that it swung away, pivoting on Margaret's arm. For a moment, it appeared that Julian's centre of gravity was above the rock and that he would be able to fall forward and save himself. He wobbled, and his bent leg flailed like a counterweight. He threw himself forwards, and slid down the rock into the dark water, pushing the boat further away with his submerging body.

'Shit! Christ! Help!' Hair was plastered over his eyes, he was gasping with shock, lunging for the side of the boat.

'No!' Margaret stood, and shouted at him. 'Don't! Let go! You'll capsize it!'

She almost beat at his clutching fingers with her fist.

'Grab the rock! Can you swim? Hold the rock – I'll get you out!'

For a moment she felt quite helpless. Then she seized one of the oars that was tucked in the bottom of the boat and used it to paddle the boat closer to the side. Julian's thrashing created waves that wanted to push the boat away. But she found a handhold, caught up the mooring rope, and heaved herself ashore. Julian was splashing furiously but in silence, and she hovered helplessly above him as he reached a hand towards her.

She didn't think she would have the single-handed strength to pull him ashore.

'Mind! Get out of the *fucking* way!'

Did he really say 'fucking'? But she moved back to give him room. It was apparent, then, how strong his arms were, because he was able to flatten himself against the rock and pull. His legs kicked uselessly, showering her with icy water, but he pulled himself ashore by the strength of his arms alone, and then collapsed in a gasping, sodden heap.

'Are you hurt? Julian! Oh lord, we must get you home! Please – stand up! Take my pullover. Quick! Oh lord!'

Water poured off him; he was breathing in great moaning gasps. For a moment he had thought he would drown! He'd thought the cold had stopped his heart! Now his teeth were beginning to chatter, and he felt again the water sucking at his head, pushing at his nose and mouth. Trying to suffocate him. Shutting out the air . . . a cold hand smothering his face. Showing him what it had been like . . . face down . . . in the water . . .

He started shuddering with cold and fear. He slowly got to his feet, pulling himself up against Margaret's arm. She was shaking, too, and she put her arms around him to comfort him, and also to reassure herself, but the mooring rope was still in one hand and intruded. She put it down and stood on it; the boat tugged gently as it rocked in the disturbed water.

'Oh Julian! Here, try and dry your face.' She handed him a handkerchief, and began to pull the canvas smock over her head. Her voice was muffled. 'Take off your pullover and shirt, or else you'll freeze.'

Why didn't he speak? What did one do for patients in shock? She helped him tug off his sodden clothes, dropping them with a soggy thud on to the rock. His bare chest was already bluish-pink from the cold. He looked so pathetic. Poor boy! What had she done! She wanted to hug him again, to rub him warm and dry, but instead she took off her own thick pullover.

'It'll be a bit tight, but just get it on. Quickly!'

The rough wool stuck and dragged against his wet flesh and he might, under other circumstances, have laughed at the absurd situation, but now he was being pushed into the too-tight smock, and Margaret was pulling the boat closer, and throwing his sodden clothes on to the bottom boards.

'Sit down on the rock, slide down on your bottom until your feet are right inside. I've got it – just go slowly. Huddle down in the bow.'

Margaret was amazed at how calm she suddenly felt; he'd be all right now. His teeth still chattered, he still hadn't spoken, but they would soon be home and have hot baths . . .

Julian cowered down in the bottom of the boat, his trousers

and shoes squelching slightly as he bent his legs. He peered up over the side; he could see the cottage clearly, it wasn't far to go. He felt numb, and closed his eyes, trying to contract his senses into a warm core in the centre of his body, trying to forget his freezing skin, and the grazes and bruises on his arms and thighs.

The boat grated on the shingle; Margaret climbed out and pulled it further up the shore. As she watched the difficulty he had in clambering over the side she realised how stupid she had been in expecting him to be able to climb up on to the rock. She just hadn't appreciated how great was his disability: apart from yesterday on the shingle, she'd always seen him in the city, on his home territory. Even on stairs, although he struggled, it always seemed manageable. How much she had to learn! What a fool she'd been!

She tied the rope to a boulder, and she and Julian walked silently and carefully back to the house. Iain wasn't there, thank God! Explanations could wait awhile. Margaret's teeth were chattering now, but she indicated that Julian should use the bathroom first.

Julian looked at her worried face and dark, wind-tangled hair, almost in bewilderment. He felt safer now, out of sight of the untamed water, but he didn't want to speak. Was the punishment never to end? To be teased like this, nearly drowned . . . He couldn't unravel the conundrum: had the leg caused the drowning, or the drowning caused the leg? He felt again the cold water grasping at his face, sucking at his fingers and clothes, and heard the roaring of the water diminish to an insidious hiss, insinuating its threat: 'Play, Julian! Play, and Give me music! You're not working hard enough at your playing! Promise me you will Give, and I'll release you.' And he had cried out underwater, his mouth filled with bitter salt, 'I promise! Just help me, please!' So that now, the mention of warm clothes and hot baths seemed an irrelevance.

While Julian was in the bath, Margaret busied herself rinsing the brackish water from his clothes. Her own, too, were splashed and damp, and she wrapped herself in Iain's thick dressing gown to wait her turn for the bath. She was still cold and slightly dazed. What if Julian hadn't been strong enough? Would she have found the strength to pull him out? Iain would be so annoyed with her. And he wouldn't be pleased at having to lend his clothes. There was a pullover, and a shirt, and there were some tracksuit bottoms, too – Iain's trousers would be too big, too . . . old. She saw again Julian's half-bared body, a young man's body, not too hairy and still dark-haired, his young man's waist. There had been broad scratches on his arms, his arms would hurt. Pity and guilt overcame her. And suddenly she wanted to touch those arms, to feel his young man's skin and, without quite knowing what she was doing, she picked up the spare clothes and went to the bathroom door.

'Julian! I've brought the clothes.'

He opened the door at once. Steam drifted out past him and his face was pink and slightly damp. His long, black silk dressing gown was pulled tightly around him.

'Thank you.'

Margaret stood still and looked at him, holding the clothes in front of her; she wondered why she seemed to be shaking.

'Are your arms badly grazed? And what about your hands? You'll still be able to play all right, won't you?' Her voice sounded odd.

Julian stretched up his arms so that the sleeves of the dressing gown fell back. There were small raw patches near his wrists and elbows. Margaret touched the inner surface of his left arm. And then she reached up and put her arm around his neck and pressed her cheek against his face.

'I'm so sorry.'

The bundle of clothes was in the way, so she dropped it

and put her other arm around him, too, in an awkward embrace.

'I should have taken better care of you.'

Margaret's hair was in Julian's eyes. He noticed that there were quite a few grey ones. He stared past them and out of the landing window; the mountain tops were clear of cloud, he saw. Those clothes on the floor were in the way, he and Margaret were tilted towards each other like the sides of a triangle. It was uncomfortable. And he was astonished.

'I'm all right,' he muttered into her hair. 'Really, I'm fine.' He put an arm round her and patted her back. 'You've looked after me very well.' Her back was bony and rigid beneath the towelling dressing gown.

Margaret gave a small, embarrassed laugh, and kicked at the pullover on the floor so that she could move closer and hug him more tightly. They remained still like that for what seemed, to Julian, like minutes; neither of them seemed to know what to do. His arm was still around her, her face was still tight against his cheek and neck, her body now was leaning against his and he thought that he might overbalance. Oh no! he thought. Not this! What now? And then again, a few seconds later, oh *no*! He stepped back, flustered, so that their bodies were no longer in contact. He looked at her to see if she had noticed. Margaret wouldn't look at him – she seemed to be embarrassed – and then she hastily kissed him on the mouth and touched his cheek with her hand.

'Oh no!' Julian exclaimed out loud, and retreated quickly into the bathroom, staring out of the window. 'Look!'

Margaret turned, suddenly afraid. It must be Iain! He must have seen them! But a car was driving cautiously along the stony track.

'It's Rosemary.'

'*Rosemary?* From the orchestra? But why?'

'Quick! She'll see us!' Julian caught Margaret's sleeve and pulled her into the bathroom.

'No, into my bedroom, or we'll be trapped. Why is she here?'

'She was driving up to see her daughter for a few days. She told me she often drives back this way. Don't you remember, you met her once at the flat and you were talking about this place, she knew where it was?'

'Yes. But I scarcely know her!'

'She knew I was coming for the weekend, so perhaps she thought she'd come and look, perhaps she needs a pee, or something. I don't know.'

Julian did know: he had just remembered that he had suggested to Rosemary that she should drop in – the Gillespies would love to see her, he'd said, they're very hospitable – because he'd privately thought that he might need a lift home early if the weekend was proving too awful. He hadn't known then that he would arrive here late, in his own car.

'But look at us!' Margaret's voice was rather shrill. She started untying her dressing gown to take it off, but then remembered Julian and knotted it again. 'What will she think if she sees us like this? No, I *know* what she will think! Quick, get dressed. You'll have to crawl along the landing or she may see. Hurry!'

'I can't crawl. It's too late. We'll just have to pretend that we're not in.'

The car had already drawn up in front of the gate.

'But what if she waits? What if Iain comes back while she's waiting and brings her in for a cup of tea?'

Julian looked at her. 'He won't, will he?' But it was very probable that that could happen. They looked at each other helplessly.

The car door slammed.

'It'll take me far too long to get dressed now, and then she'll wonder what we've been doing . . . We can't stay here!'

Margaret rushed to the partly open window that looked out on to the hill at the back. She pushed and tugged at it.

'Oh, the *ruddy* thing! It's always getting jammed! I keep asking Iain to fix it.'

'This is hardly his fault! What are you doing? Don't!'

Julian had a vision of Margaret flying out of the window, dressing gown spread wide like wings, and leaping and dodging across the hill and into the trees.

'We'll have to get dressed and climb out. We can't—'

Rap, rap, rap. They both jumped. No one had used the door knocker in years. Margaret scarcely recognised the sound.

'Oh my gosh! Julian, come on!'

Julian helped her push, and the lower half of the window slid up, squeaking loudly.

'Margaret, I cannot climb out of that window.'

'Sssh! Look, the roof of the back porch – it's easy. The ground slopes up, look yourself and see. It's no distance. You *could*, I'm sure.'

'You thought I could climb out on to those rocks, too.'

'*I* didn't – you did. Oh, never mind!' (And if you hadn't tried, we wouldn't be in this appalling situation now!)

'*You* climb out. I'll go to bed and pretend I was asleep. I had a late night last night, remember. I can let her in once you've got away.'

'She won't believe that. Why should you be asleep here, while Iain and I are out?'

'She knows I sometimes sleep in the daytime. And you've gone out to give me some peace, or to walk off your hangover – or whatever.'

Margaret looked out of the back window again; she hoped she could do this. She looked back at Julian. He was clearly excited by the intrigue and, briefly, the excitement thrilled her too.

'Go on, then. You'll have to get to your bedroom quietly. Oh dear, I wonder what she's doing?'

'I ought to make certain that you've got down safely, first.'

'Turn your back, then. I need to dress.'

Margaret dragged on a pullover and trousers – no time to button a shirt. Socks, quickly, a scarf . . . Shoes! She couldn't go barefoot! Then she remembered that her walking boots were in the back porch. Rosemary was knocking on the door again.

'Hurry, Margaret. Are you ready?' Julian didn't wait for her to reply. 'I'll help you out.'

It was true; the relative heights were not too great. Margaret sat on the windowsill and swung one leg out, then gripped the frame and lowered her head and shoulders until she was outside the window. She looked back at him through the glass, ever anxious, and he grinned and blew her an ironical kiss.

'Good luck!'

It took her only a few seconds to drop the small distance on to the porch roof, lower herself into a sitting position on its slope and then, using feet and hands as brakes, to wriggle to the edge and jump down. She caught her shoulder on the gutter as she dropped, but managed not to cry out loud, and ducked into the porch to find her boots.

Julian didn't wait any longer. He dragged down the bedroom window and opened the bedroom door cautiously, then, snorting quietly with laughter, sat down and shuffled on his backside into his own bedroom, and shut the door.

From his window he could see Rosemary's car, but the angle was too steep to allow him to see the front door. He could hear Rosemary, though; he could hear her footsteps pacing on the path. He ducked back behind the curtain. She was going back to her car. He heard the car door open, and he waited for it to slam and for her to drive away. But there was silence. At last he couldn't bear not knowing what she was doing, and he peered round the edge of the curtain. Rosemary was standing by her car, with her back to the cottage, staring across the loch to the fish pens and the hills. Her handbag was on the car bonnet, and she opened it and took out a mirror and applied lipstick. With a quick glance at the house – she nearly caught him! – she adjusted her petticoat, lifting her skirt and wriggling slightly as she did so.

It looked as though she would be quite prepared to wait. Julian moved away from the window and yawned and groaned; he was getting cold again, and he felt battered and wearied, and full of a deep unease. He wanted to sleep, to forget about it all, and wake up safely in his own bed, so he took off his dressing gown and climbed into bed, and rolled himself tightly in the duvet. He would like Rosemary to come and hold his hand and tuck him in, but Rosemary was outside. Margaret could sort it out; she seemed to have been the agent of his misfortune rather than his angel of mercy, this weekend. Had she really been after him all this time, though? Had the cleaning and casseroles merely been displacement activities? He tried to imagine what a sexual relationship with her would be like, tried to escape the other thoughts that wanted to make themselves heard. He pulled the duvet over his head and prepared to doze. But his mind slowly filled up with images of drowning; gift-wrapped parcels rose past him through the water, to bob above him on the surface, and he heard shrieks, perhaps of laughter, and tearing paper, and the liquid notes of a chromatic scale, descending, falling . . . falling . . .

Margaret heard Julian close the window; surely Rosemary would also have heard him? She remained where she was, crouched in the back porch, wondering if Rosemary would try the back door, too. When, after a minute or so, nothing happened, she crept out into the back garden. She was about to climb over the wall on to the hillside when she remembered Iain. What if he were up there and saw her skulking in this peculiar manner? Anxiously she scanned the hillside, but she couldn't see him anywhere. Of course, there were a thousand rocks and hollows where he might be hiding. (Hiding? Why should he be hiding? Come on, Margaret, you're the guilty party! Aren't you? But I've done nothing wrong – a quick kiss, that's all it was.) Was Julian watching her from his window?

If Rosemary hadn't arrived . . . Oh, Julian, Julian! Margaret felt that she couldn't breathe. She looked up at the window at the back of Julian's room, certain that he was there, but there was no one, and she realised that he might already have gone downstairs to let Rosemary in. She climbed over the wire fence, muttering at a lamb that bounded off in eloquent surprise, and sat down to wait with her back against the wall. So much had happened in the past twenty-four hours; it had not been a relaxing weekend at all. She rested her head on her knees and closed her eyes and tried to let her mind go blank.

It was difficult to guess how much time had passed since she had climbed out of the window – perhaps ten minutes. Rosemary ought to be sitting comfortably inside the cottage by now, being entertained by her Leader. A cup of tea would be so very welcome; she wondered if Julian had put the kettle on. Iain would surely be back soon, and Rosemary wouldn't stay long. Margaret stood up and stretched, and realised that she was chilled and stiff. She strolled round to the side of the cottage and squelched through the rushes and soggy sphagnum to reach the track. At once, the door of the car opened and Rosemary climbed out, smiling.

'Rosemary!' Margaret was completely – and genuinely – shocked. 'What are you doing here?'

'Mrs Gillespie! I do hope you don't mind. Didn't Julian tell you I might look in?' Rosemary pulled a face. 'Oh dear, I'm so sorry – you must think me very rude. He asked me to drop by in case he needed a lift home . . . in case you wanted to stay an extra night,' she added hastily, aware that she had been tactless. 'And of course, as soon as I got here I saw his car. I was just about to leave again since no one was around.'

'Oh! What a muddle!' Margaret was confused about what she shouldn't and didn't know. And why was Rosemary still sitting in the car? 'Er – have you been here long? Did you knock? I'm terribly sorry, I've been out walking – and my husband is off somewhere taking photos . . .'

'Oh, only a minute or two. When I realised the place was empty . . .' Rosemary tailed off.

'But Julian's in. He decided to have a snooze. We had a very late night—'

'Rosemary, hi!' Julian was leaning out of the window, bare-chested. Margaret's heart lurched. 'I'll be right down.'

Just as Margaret was pouring water into the teapot, Iain returned, kicking off his boots in the back porch. 'I smelt the tea from half a mile away,' he grinned. 'And I see we have a visitor.'

He glanced through the door. Margaret reminded him quietly that he'd met Rosemary before, at a Sunday concert.

'I see Kersland's wearing my clothes! He looks a bit worse for wear. What on earth have you been doing to him, darling?'

Margaret smiled wryly and shrugged. 'I'm afraid we both got a wee bit wet. But no harm's done. I'll tell you about it later.'

Tea-time chat intervened, and first Rosemary left, then Julian. Later, after she and Iain had secured the boat and sorted out what was to be taken home, Margaret sank into the comfortable seat in the car and guiltily looked forward to a journey of dreams and speculations.

'It's lucky he wasn't swaddled in bombazine and whalebone.'

'*What!*' Margaret's face went hot with shock. How could Iain have known what she was thinking?'

'There you were, the local boatperson, rowing the intrepid explorer past hazardous whirlpools to search for hidden temples – and he fell in! But on the other hand, I can't quite imagine young Kersland striding through the Highlands dressed in an Indian cotton shirt and boxer shorts, can you?'

Margaret, who almost could – although the striding was clearly a major problem – spluttered with relieved laughter.

'You'd have had to lend him a few more pullovers, I think!'

The Fiddler's Leg

* * *

Rosemary, too, was thinking about Julian as she drove back to Glasgow, but she was thinking about his sudden daytime interludes of deep sleep. Right enough, he probably had been tired, if they'd been out late last night – and he'd probably not got much sleep the night before, either, because he'd presumably stayed behind to be with Isobel. Rude, that, and inconsiderate, but that was the trouble with sex, neither partner thought of anything but need. She was glad to have all that nonsense behind her now! But late nights didn't explain the various other occasions on which she'd found him asleep.

She didn't think he was ill, anaemic or underfed, or anything physical like that. She supposed it was a sort of escape reaction, really. A funny lad, a funny, mixed-up young man. Too complicated for her. She thanked the lord that her own two grown-up children had been relatively straightforward to deal with. But she was fond of Julian, and she thought he was probably quite fond of her, in his own way, insofar as he was fairly relaxed with her, and she probably saw most sides of him, warts and all.

Rosemary smiled to herself. Sometimes Julian was like a little boy, seeking a hug of approval. And then, alternately petulant, sarcastic or charming – look at the way all the dear old groupies doted on him. And Margaret Gillespie – what was going on there? And the luscious Isobel! *She* ought to be getting on with her studying, if she had any sense, but obviously the dear boy's equipment functioned all right, because it could only be sex that kept those two together. Well, *that* wouldn't last!

She braked and pulled over as an idiot with a windsurfer on his roof rack overtook her on the twisting road that led down from the pass. Silly fool! And what's the point of it all? If only the dear boy would decide who he wanted to be. He'd had such promise, such extraordinary talent when he was younger. Look at the way he can play if he wants to – but he hardly ever does it any more, he's just coasting, not wanting to exert himself, not wanting to *touch* anyone. That's probably why he goes to sleep all over the place. If only dear old Canon Bothwell were still alive to encourage him, or whatever it was he used to do. Or at least to remind Julian what he could do if he really tried. Instead of which, the silly boy gets himself bogged down with administration, and needy women – and silly clothes.

Rosemary caught up with the tail end of a slow-moving queue of cars that was trailing its way down the lochside, and she was distracted by the sight of water-skiers, and then memories of her weekend with her daughter's family. But just as she reached the first set of traffic lights on the outskirts of the city, the idea suddenly came into her mind that perhaps Julian was not at all self-sufficient, but was perhaps, mentally, very alone, and frightened – and she felt very sad.

Chapter Sixteen

'What's wrong?'

Isobel switched off the vacuum cleaner and went over to the bed. The little girl had twisted on to her side and pulled up her blanket so that her bandaged ankle was completely uncovered within the tubular cage.

'Shall I put your bedclothes straight? Your leg must be getting cold.'

The little girl shook her head; her dark hair was tangled and damp beneath her cheek.

'It's so *noisy*,' she muttered into her fist. Isobel bent down to hear what she was saying. 'Everything's so noisy – I can't sleep.'

'Someone should invent a completely silent vacuum cleaner, shouldn't they?' Isobel agreed. 'But I've got to clean up all the dust and germs or you might get sick, as well. Is your ankle sore?'

The girl nodded. 'It makes my head hurt.' Then she rolled over and stared up at Isobel. 'My mummy's coming with my baby brother. He's only six months old. I hope he doesn't yell, or my head will hurt again. And I hope he doesn't smell.'

Isobel smiled. 'Shall I ask one of the nurses to come and help you sit up? Do you want to draw a picture for your brother – something for him to look at when he comes?'

'Nah. He'll eat it. He's too little, he just sucks things.' Nevertheless, the girl's face had brightened a little at the idea. 'I could do a picture for my mum.'

Isobel pushed the cleaner under the bed so that no one would fall over it and walked down the ward. It was a bright, cheerful room, full of warm colours, and with toys and books on a carpet in the play corner. There was a television, and floor cushions, and the small rooms along the corridor had two beds, to allow a parent to stay. The children in the ward that she had been cleaning were all surgical cases. The boy in the corner had had his appendix out yesterday and was already fidgeting and chattering and wanting to be out of bed. She waved to him as she passed. She wasn't sure about that older boy, though. He'd had something done to his ear; she would have to find out more about it.

There were two nurses standing by the desk in the corridor and she explained about the little girl who would like to draw. As she accompanied one of the nurses back to the ward she asked about the boy with the ear problem. Even though Isobel had only been moved to this ward a couple of weeks ago, the nurses already knew that she was a student and, to her relief, were willing to talk to her about medical matters. Perhaps because she was older than the other students, and female, and was being seen to work to pay her way, and because her position was thus such an anomaly in the normally rigid hierarchy, the nursing staff were prepared to talk more freely. She scribbled a few notes in the little book that she kept in her top pocket, and went back to her cleaning.

This bed held a mischievous little boy, the type with a battered, freckled face and bright red hair. He pointed out to her that he had spilt his juice underneath his bed, and he grinned when she shook her head at him for his carelessness. On hands and knees underneath the bed, rubbing at the floor with a wet cloth, she was all too aware of her tight, ill-fitting grey uniform, and she could hear the little lad whispering and sniggering with his neighbour. Then, whack! on her bottom, and the mattress above her shook and bounced with laughter. In her rage she got up too quickly and banged her head, and she was about to stuff the sticky floorcloth under the bedclothes and into the boy's hidden face, when she remembered just where and who she was, and took three deep breaths.

'Nurse!' she called. 'I think this boy needs an injection in his buttocks – with a very large needle. Don't you?'

The nurse, who had seen Isobel leap up and could easily imagine the cause, nodded seriously.

'We keep a great big needle especially for that reason.'

She walked along with Isobel as she went to fetch the vacuum cleaner. 'I'm sorry. There are always one or two who get bored and get up to mischief. Little monkey! The instant you turn your back . . .'

'Or your bum!' They both snorted.

'There's plenty for them to do, if they want to, but of course some of them want to be quiet, or don't want to read or play games. We've been getting in a few folk from outside to entertain, recently – puppeteers a few weeks ago. They were really good.'

'What a great idea! Do the entertainers go round each ward, or what?'

'That would take too long. No – we have it in the dayroom, and carry or wheel through the ones that can't get there on their own.'

'That's such a nice idea.' Isobel was impressed. 'You know, I have a friend who plays the violin – fiddle, really. Would they like music, do you think? Folk, dance music, that sort of thing? There are two or three fiddlers, actually,' she added recklessly. (Julian could learn to play the stuff, couldn't he? And the Tom person that Julian had met at the ceilidh could probably be persuaded to come along.) 'They're all well known.'

The nurse smiled and shrugged. 'It sounds fun. It's worth a try. You'd have to ask one of the high-ups, though. I don't know who, but Sister will. That lot take ages to make up their minds, though!'

Isobel finished off in the ward, keeping well clear of the bottom-slapper. She was irritated with herself for feeling so angry with the boy; she could see that some of the children couldn't concentrate on anything because they were uncomfortable, and so they soon got bored. She wished she felt a little more sympathetic; she had no maternal feelings about the children at all even though the words 'sick children' were supposed to be so emotive. At present, the children were merely just 'interesting cases' for her to learn from. But didn't doctors have to have a warm, caring approach to be successful? Perhaps that would develop with time. Perhaps when she was a qualified doctor, no longer having to worry about her finances and exams and absorbing information, she would have time to find the necessary sympathy and understanding. She must care a little, though, to have suggested a means of entertaining the children. Or was her real motive the need to be noticed by the authorities, the 'high-ups', as the student with bright ideas for care of the community? The it-will-look-good-on-my-c.v. approach to care? She wasn't sure that she wanted to explore that idea any further. And anyway, Julian probably wouldn't agree. Or Tom, the mysterious Tom. 'Who is Thomas, what is he?'

While she swept the corridors, she thought back to the conversation about Tom. She and Julian had been sitting at a table in an Italian restaurant, a table that was anachronistically complete with red-and-white checked cloth and a wax-encrusted bottle that acted as a candle holder. The flame had flickered between them at eye level, so that they had to push the bottle to one side in order to see each other's faces. It was the night after Julian had returned from the Gillespies' cottage, and Julian was telling her about his weekend, sporadically, in uncoordinated bursts, because the conversation kept straying.

She *was* pleased to see him again, she thought. Now that they were here, on neutral ground, their relationship seemed quite straightforward and uncomplicated. She was proud to be seen with him; she noticed how the woman at the next table looked at him surreptitiously. It was early evening and the restaurant was almost empty, but the few diners had all been seated near to each other at one end. A thin band of cigarette smoke drifted across from a nearby table and distracted Isobel, so that she blew at it and flapped her hand.

'– it was Margaret's fault. She let slip – no, she *prompted* them, she told them *blatantly* – that I was a fiddle player. Well, no – that I was a *violinist*, actually. It was fortunate that I was able to think of something suitable. Bella! You're not listening!'

'No! When you look at me like that, I want— Shall we go home now?' She reached across and ran a finger along his wrist, and then fluttered her eyelashes at him in a parody of star-struck love. 'And don't leer at me like that, you'll put me off my food. Although I'm not hungry for food – just for passion!' She hissed the final word loudly, so that the woman with the annoying cigarette looked askance and raised an eyebrow.

'Ssh! Don't be childish. I was telling you about the ceilidh.'

'Sorry. Yes. You played your fiddle at a ceilidh. Not whatshisname's cats, I hope.'

'They were all so pissed that they probably wouldn't have noticed if I had! No, of course not – and it was not my fiddle, either. I hadn't taken it with me, I was supposed to be going there for a relaxing weekend, remember? I played Tom's fiddle. He and his friend were fiddlers, and he was the one who made me play.'

'What? What did you play?'

'A Hungarian dance, I told you.'

'That must have gone down well.' Isobel took a sip of red wine.

'It was all right.' Julian was defensive. 'And then Tom showed me a few fiddle techniques.'

'How embarrassing.'

'Not at all, I think everyone was quite interested – shades of Menuhin and Ravi Shankar.'

'Oh. Was he nice? Tom, not those other blokes.'

Julian was silent for a moment. 'I don't know, really. I think so. Perhaps not "nice", though. Men don't see each other as "nice". He had a ponytail and he called me Jools.'

Isobel snorted. 'What did your dear hostess think about all this?'

'Well, she was the one who dropped me in it. I haven't yet enquired about her reason. She also dropped me in it literally yesterday – into the loch! And then took me home, and was all prepared to scrub my back and towel me dry. And to put me to bed – with a cup of hot cocoa.'

'No!' Isobel's eyes gleamed with shocked delight. 'Tell me! Come on! Oh – you're teasing me.'

Julian looked mysterious and forked up a mouthful of pasta. 'That made you listen properly, didn't it? Are you jealous? Did you miss me? I lay in bed for hours yesterday morning and thought about you.'

'Huh. I suppose you couldn't get up because you had a hangover. But did you really fall in the water?'

'I'm afraid so. We were out in her bloody boat, supposed to be exploring an island, but I disembarked rather incompetently, as you might imagine. No great damage done, just a few grazes. Look, doctor, shall I show you? And I had to come home in the solicitor's clothes. *Very* smart!'

He paused, looking inward for a moment, and then sighed.

'What makes you sigh like that? The water, the clothes, or your fiddling friend, who seems to have you puzzled?'

'The fiddler, I suppose. You know, he'd trained in classical violin. He threatened that he'd come to the Big City and find me, so that he could take some lessons, and teach me, too. I don't know how he'll do that – I purposely didn't give him my address.'

'The famous Kersland won't be that difficult to find, surely?

There can't be too many one-legged violinists around, who lead a baroque orchestra at Sunday lunchtime. And certainly none who has a beautiful blonde medic as girlfriend. Although I don't suppose you told him about me!'

Isobel was pleased to see that she had judged his mood correctly and the description had made him smile.

She pushes her luck, sometimes, Julian thought. Though he had smiled, her words had produced a sharp, cold sting inside him. Was that really how people saw him? Was that the only impression he had made on the world in all this time? He thought he meant more than that now to Isobel, although he could see that, at first, it had been his unusualness that had attracted her. He felt he was becoming obsessed by her, and it worried him because he knew it was detrimental. This continual lusting was using energy that should be used elsewhere. But then, why not? What else was there? (But that was heresy.) She danced about out of reach, alternately naïve then brazen, thoughtful then outspoken, socially inept and then confident in her own knowledge and intelligence. God, but he did lust after her! The smooth wholeness of her, Venus de Milo, intact! And her lack of shame – that was it, her enjoyment of her nakedness and willingness to share it with him! His one-time fiancée hadn't been like that. Nor had the woman he'd had a brief affair with last year. She'd been embarrassed, she couldn't bear to look at him naked, his scrawny thigh and the puckered scars. She'd wanted the lights off, in fact she had much preferred to *talk*. He and Isobel talked, too, but she wasn't always seeking after deeper meanings. What *did* she seek after? His hands wanted to touch her, so he could reassure himself of her smooth perfection. But even as he felt for her leg under the table, and began to gather up the fabric of her skirt, 'one-legged violinist' stabbed again at his mind. He pulled himself back to his previous train of thought. The one-legged violinist. Canon Bothwell had seen him differently, so did Margaret Gillespie: but wasn't it the very one-leggedness that had captured their attention and led them onwards to their different conceptions and ideals? And now Margaret's perceptions had apparently suffered a sea change.

The near-farcical nature of the Great Escape had almost pushed that other incident – or incipient incident – out of his mind. He hoped that Margaret would diplomatically forget about it. After all, it had been an indiscretion brought about by her pity and her maternal attitude. (He had been very close to committing the extraordinary indiscretion of telling Isobel the truth, or at least the truth as he perceived it.) He had been very foolish to post that letter this morning. He'd written to thank the Gillespies for their hospitality, and for the interesting and varied weekend 'that has also given me plenty to think about with respect to my future.' Some demon had taunted him to include those words, teasing him with the picture of Margaret reading them over and over again, seeking every possible meaning. Yes, he had been very foolish. Pity slipped too easily towards tenderness, and tenderness could easily be mistaken for love – and all its attendant subterfuges. Had Margaret *really* climbed out of that window? Here, in the city, within the city's behavioural confines, it was already hard to believe. And yet he also had a vivid memory of the two women confronting each other, Margaret and Rosemary, each certain that she could claim a special relationship with him, as confidante, helper or saviour; or perhaps, in Margaret Gillespie's case, as rather more . . . One-legged violinist! The warmth of Isobel's thigh roused him as he stroked it.

Isobel put her hand on his to restrain it, and raised her glass to him. 'Shall we have one of those gorgeous sticky puddings on the trolley?'

'No, you'll get fat.' Julian touched his glass to hers. 'Drink up and let's go home. Quickly!'

Margaret had gone over the details again and again in her

mind. She thought she could remember every look, every moment, every one of the few words that had been spoken. She could catch the smell of the bathroom steam and of damp silk dressing gown. And once, there was also the acid wet stink in her nostrils of sodden peat, and she felt again her fear as she confronted Rosemary.

Mentally, she railed at herself and at Julian, and alternately longed for and was repulsed by the remembered feel of the soft skin of his neck and the roughness of his cheek. The memory of his cold, pale chest with its sparse carpet of wet hair made her shudder, and yet she also saw herself, as in a painting, crouched palely before him, her white face staring up in profile, her hand reaching up and resting lightly against that chest. Was that touch tender, or comforting? Or was it a gesture of restraint, or of submission? Each time she relived Sunday's events, her interpretation altered, until she was worn out and sickened by her delusions and fantasies.

There was, too, the additional strain of ensuring that her thoughts were completely veiled from Iain, so that, when she awoke on Tuesday and, dressing, remembered again the panic of dragging on her clothes while Rosemary patrolled below, she decided that she must never think of that day again. She would cease visiting Julian's house, cease her housekeeping and intimate good works, otherwise she would be sure to give herself away.

So determined was she on this course of action that, when she opened the white envelope, so elegantly addressed in black ink, she was quite unarmed. Julian's observation that he would have 'plenty to think about' with regard to his future struck through her like a lance and made her sink, gasping, on to the stairs.

But the stairs were too static to contain her agitation, and she leapt up and strode into the dining room, the letter still in her hand, and hurried around the room, blowing at imaginary dust, moving ornaments and shifting chairs.

Finally, she stopped and put her head on her arms on the back of a dining chair, and cried, in great wailing sobs. Words bubbled out of her with her tears.

'No, no, no. We can't . . . I can't do it! No, I don't know what to do! . . . Julian!' She carried on babbling, feeling the terrible tension dissipating.

Her tears had smudged Julian's note and when she was calm again she hid it deep amongst the rubbish in the kitchen bin, where Iain would never see it. Then she made herself a pot of jasmine tea and sat down to consider what she should do. She didn't allow herself to think about Iain; he was too real, and too important. Her attempts at rational thought drifted rapidly into fantasies, all of which were gentle, introspective scenes in which she and Julian were laughing or talking softly, holding hands or lying together arm in arm. She would be perpetually discovering new depths, gaining new insights; she was his confidante and carer, loving him, ministering to him. In return, he was (although this was rather more shadowy) tender and courteous, gently humorous. She felt again his arm around her shoulder, and how they had stood cheek to cheek and – although her memory tended to want to skitter around the fact – his embarrassingly increasing hardness. She knew that he wanted her and would make love to her with great tenderness (the question of *how* he would make love to her was not allowed to enter her mind).

But then her muted excitement was rapidly turned into self-disgust, not only at her undeniably pathetic, unrealistic daydreams, but also at her body which, although still slim, was visibly creeping into middle age. More as a distraction than out of genuine interest she went into the small downstairs lavatory and investigated her incipient wrinkles in the small mirror above the basin. And then her buzzing thoughts seemed to stagnate and her mind shut down on the topic of Julian, as though in protection, and she went back to the kitchen to worry about the evening meal.

By the time Thursday arrived, her usual morning for 'helping Julian', Margaret didn't know whether she wanted to fly there on the wings of love or to make excuses to keep away. She did know, however, that she was in a ridiculous and most undignified state of mind for someone of her supposed maturity. It seemed that the only way to stop the rocking of this seesaw was to go to Julian and see on which side his weight would lie.

Chapter Seventeen

Julian leant against the banister for a moment to catch his breath. The girl who had let him in was still hovering in the downstairs hall, ostensibly sorting through the post. She looked up when Julian stopped climbing, and he nodded and smiled at her. She smiled back and returned to the pile of free newspapers.

He resumed his ascent, pausing again on the landing by a bathroom that had a wet and dirty floor, and then carried on up to the top of the building. He rapped on the door with the head of his stick and heard a flurry of footsteps inside.

'Brandy!' he gasped as the door was opened. 'Give me brandy – and oxygen.'

'My God! I heard you coming – at least, I guessed it was you. I've been trying to tidy up. Who let you in?'

He shrugged. 'Some girl from downstairs. She arrived just as I was about to press your doorbell. She said she recognised me and would let me in, so I thought I'd give you a surprise!'

This was only the second time that he'd been up to Isobel's bedsit and he had forgotten (or perhaps tried to forget) what a slum it was. How awful student rooms could be! Isobel slid her arms around him and kissed him.

'I was about to be angry with you, because the room's such a mess – I'm a mess, too. But you look exhausted! I'm afraid you'll have to make do with tea. I'm out of brandy and oxygen.'

He lay down on the bed with a groan and stared round at

the room while Isobel filled the kettle and washed some mugs.

'Hah! Scheherazade! Now that's a use I hadn't anticipated!'

She looked at the gauzy scarf that was draped over the shade around the bedside light, and blushed slightly. 'It's so pretty, it seemed a shame—'

'It was merely a fantastical notion on my part. Don't worry. I apologise completely for my poor taste.'

'Your taste in *scarves* is excellent!' She yawned and stretched. 'I'll be glad when these wretched resits are over. But I feel much more confident now, so it's probably been good for me to have to go over all this work again. I've been able to concentrate better this time!'

She brought his tea over to the bedside table and sat next to him on the bed. 'You look good. That neckscarf goes well with the denim.'

'Thanks.'

Julian took her hand and held it against his chest, smiling lazily up at her. They stayed like that quietly for a while, then Isobel put down her mug and lay down on her side next to him. There was a rare calm between them, and it seemed that they lay like that for ages, arms around each other, Julian staring at the ceiling, Isobel, unfocused, staring at his profile. The silence was long and comfortable.

Eventually, Julian asked, 'How was work?'

'All right. Quite interesting. There's one cheeky little lad – he smacked me on the bottom a couple of days ago. What's he going to be like after he reaches puberty!'

'Hmm. I've got competition, have I?' Julian looked at her through sleepy eyelids and walked his fingers down to her buttock.

'Mmm.' Isobel wriggled closer. 'Mmm. You know, one of the nurses was telling me that the hospital arranges for plays and puppet shows and – oh, concerts, folk music and so on – for the children in the wards. Isn't that a fantastic idea? Apparently the children really love them. The entertainment takes their minds off their aches and pains. They all get wheeled along to the big dayroom, so there's a change of scene, a great novelty.'

'Mmm.'

'I bet there was nothing like that when you were little. Was it very tedious and restrictive? I bet you were a brat, too – probably hit all the auxiliaries on the bottom with your stick!' She laughed softly and snuggled more closely against Julian.

'Hmm. I try not to remember too much about it. But you imagine correctly that I was not a model patient! Parents are allowed to stay overnight these days, aren't they? I'm damned glad that wasn't possible when I was in there! My mother would probably have tried to reorganise the whole hospital for my benefit!'

'I'm not sure I want to meet your mother – not that you have ever offered! But you would have enjoyed concerts or plays, though, wouldn't you? Especially violin concerts?'

'I don't know about violins. I was not very enthusiastic about violin-playing at that time . . . Should I suspect a reason behind all this questioning? I don't think I quite like what you seem to be working up to!'

He rolled over so that they were face to face, and Isobel wrapped a hank of her hair around his neck.

'I thought it would be stimulating for the children if someone local – and famous! – could go and play to them. Someone like you, for example.'

'Oh no, Bella, not me! In hospital! Playing to sick children a few choice excerpts from Bartók and Beethoven. Oh no!'

He pushed himself upright, jerking her hair, and scowled down at her, but Isobel reared up and kissed him.

'Not classical, Julian – fiddle music, Jools! You could play Scottish fiddle music, couldn't you? They'd love it! And the staff would love it, too.'

'No, no and no! I do not want to perform to a ward full of sick and incapable children. You're as bad as that wretched man who runs the festival for disabled children. He kept pursuing me, he was like a terrier. He wanted to use me as a role model! Aaagh!' Julian thumped the bed with his fist.

'What are you talking about? I don't see the relevance.'

'He was someone I met at a dinner party months ago. I know when!' Julian suddenly brightened. 'I met him the night that taxi broke its leg. The night I first met you!'

They looked at each other in amusement.

'And my period had started and I was feeling sorry for myself and was snivelling. I'm surprised you want to remember!'

'You were not looking your best, it was true. But I could see you had potential!'

'Hmm! But go back to what you were saying before, the role model business.'

Julian explained what had been required of him, and his revulsion at the idea, and he was thankful that Isobel seemed to understand his point of view. Margaret Gillespie would have been appalled, he reflected. No, hurt, disappointed – appalled was too strong an emotion. She would have seen the festival as a way for him to Give!

'But that's not at all what I'm suggesting. These children are quite different. Many of them aren't even sick, they're often only temporarily out of action. They're not interested in imitating you, they don't want to even think about being permanently damaged. They want to have a good time and to be entertained. You could do that!'

Julian thought for a moment, trying to imagine what such entertainment would be like, then shook his head.

'No. I don't want to do that sort of thing. I'm not the right kind of person to jolly along a group of bum-whackers.'

'You could if you tried. Or you could find your weird friend Tom to come and help. Don't think about yourself so much, Julian, think how much good you could do for those children.' She nuzzled his neck. 'It would probably be very good for you, anyway. You'd be able to reach a new audience, and it would be good publicity.'

'No, I can't do it. I don't even have any suitable music.'

Isobel smiled at him, and stretched again. 'Oh well, at least I tried! Anyway, you haven't yet explained to me why you came round to ring my doorbell.'

'I was going to take you out for a drink, but I don't think I can be bothered now. It's so much more interesting lying here. Especially from down here, because then I don't have to see what a slum your room is! You know, Bellissima, there are so many evenings when I wish you didn't have to leave me to come back here.' He sighed and wove her hair through his fingers. 'But when I see this room, I can't imagine how you and I could ever co-habit tidily!'

'I can't imagine how you would ever let me have time to get on with my work either! You're so demanding!' she teased. 'Anyway, it's better to live apart because then the anticipation's greater!'

She sensed, though, despite his earlier words, that she'd won the battle for the children, and she laughed, pleased with herself, and rolled towards him.

I'm no better than Pavlov's dog, Julian thought later in self-disgust, as he sat in his music room and drank a brandy. And the dog even went one better because he learnt to respond to an irrelevant stimulus! Or does that make the dog more stupid? I don't know. But at least the dog is well known.

He put down his glass and got up to fetch a cardboard folder that lay on the table. The file was garishly patterned in red and green tartan – he hadn't been able to resist buying it. Inside were two books of fiddle music that he had bought soon after he came home from the ceilidh. Although it was late, nearly midnight, he took out his violin and checked the tuning, then, softly so as not to disturb his neighbours, tried out one of the tunes. He repeated it again, and yet again as his confidence grew, trying to imbue the music with the sounds and atmosphere of the ceilidh.

He could probably do it. He would buy some tapes, and listen and learn, until he was confident that he could play in public, to the children's ward. He turned off all the lights except the table lamp and returned to his chair. There were deep shadows in the corners of the cluttered room, but he knew them well now and was unafraid.

He need have no fear about playing to the children. It would be a simple and innocent pastime, the provision of light-hearted, even joyous, entertainment. There were no personal demons still waiting for him in a hospital ward, no hopes for improvement or salvation. All that was required was that he should dress appropriately (should he grow a ponytail?) and walk in. *Walk* in? There were no hills to be climbed. He didn't have to promise redemption to all who imitated him: 'Look at me! You, too, shall overcome! Ye shall be made whole!' For that was not the Truth, Julian, was it? That was the Tempter, offering the unattainable. Listen instead to that other Voice: 'Suffer, little children!' For that was the *true* meaning. Feel the laying-on of hands, hands that made his skin tingle with their power. 'Suffer, Jools! You must feel the pain of reparation. The Agony, Jools! It's your punishment – and your Gift! And feel the ecstasy in the giving. Feel yourself being immersed, total immersion, waves of sound, beating, beating overhead, drowning, covering you – smothering you . . . and him. You're drowning, Julian. Kick your legs and you shall be made whole.'

The spasmodic jerking of his legs, and the damp trickling of brandy on his thigh, woke Julian in his chair, and he fought off the images and the echo of a cry. Canon Bothwell, or was it Tom, had been holding his hand and pushing his wheelchair through the trees towards the river. But the trees had arms and legs and were, after all, crying children, and their crying was a wild music that made him want to faint with love.

Chapter Eighteen

The little boy with the sandy-coloured hair had caught at the nurse's skirt as she passed and had whispered something. The nurse looked at Julian and then whispered back, 'Are you sure?' The boy nodded, and then turned shyly away and hid his face.

'What did he say?'

'He thinks his granny knows you,' she smiled.

'Oh? And who's your granny?'

The boy was silent for a few seconds, but then he whispered again to the nurse.

'His granny used to clean your house,' the nurse relayed.

Julian stared. 'Mrs Gillespie? You're Margaret Gillespie's grandson?' He didn't think Margaret's – Iain's really – grandchildren lived locally. But the boy had burrowed away into his chair and shook his head.

'Ah! She *used* to clean for me. Mrs Knight, of course. So Mrs Knight's your granny?'

One blue eye was turned briefly in his direction and there was a small nod. This information pleased Julian for some reason; grandmother Knight would be most surprised.

'Does she come and visit you? Is she well?'

But the grandson had exhausted his quota of bravery and had retired into mute deafness.

Julian had forgotten about the heat, and the hospital smell. He was already sweating inside his leather jacket as he clumped along the corridor after the almost-scurrying nurse.

'We've put you in the dayroom,' she said, as they came to the door of a large carpeted room, with big windows and easy chairs, in which toys were corralled within playpens, and where low tables were heaped with piles of books and games.

'We found a stool – I hope it's safe!' She looked doubtfully at the flimsy metal and plastic construction. 'And you wouldn't believe how much discussion has gone on about your little concert – such meetings, and notes and telephone calls!'

'I would! I began to think it would never happen! However, I'm here at last. Thank you, this looks just fine.'

'Anyway, it's a lovely idea, Mr Kersland—'

'Oh – Julian. Jools, actually.'

'It was your friend, that medical student, that first suggested it to us. She is your friend, isn't she? Isobel? She's a lovely girl, worked so hard, too. The children are really looking forward to it. Do you want to put your things over here? We'll start bringing them down now, shall we – the children, I mean? Funny, you knowing little Niall's granny. It'll give him such a boost, knowing the star of the show! I'll just go and tell Sister we're ready . . .'

And still chattering and exclaiming, she scurried off, her bottom in its white uniform bobbing like a rabbit's tail.

Julian ran through the likely captions in his mind. 'Handsome –' no, 'Debonair J. K. entertains young fans with his wit and magical fiddle.' A bit down-market – who on earth wants 'young fans'? *Blue Peter* presenters on television, maybe, but not famous fiddlers. How about 'Miraculous recovery by sick children after Kersland's dazzling concert at hospital: "I knew my fiddling would raise their spirits," he said. "Astounding!" say doctors.' Nice overtones of Lazarus, there. A pity, though, to miss out 'debonair', but the photograph should speak for itself! No need to state the obvious. Julian smiled compassionately, once again, as he looked down into the adoring eyes of the small fair-haired girl who rested against his knee.

'Thanks, Julian. That should do.'

The photographer began to pack up his gear, and Julian thankfully released the fidgeting child and pushed her gently back towards her chair.

'Right!' He grated his bow across the strings and produced a few earthy chords. 'The interval's over, ladies and gentlemen! Take your places,' few of them, in any case, had moved, 'for "The Road from Kilnacraig". Does anyone know where that is – Kilnacraig?'

No one did.

'It's near Dumbarton.'

'No, it isnae. It's down Largs way.'

'No. You're all guessing,' Julian said. 'It's nothing but a cottage on the edge of a loch, way up on the north-west coast.'

In fact, he hadn't the faintest idea, nor did he care, where Kilnacraig was.

'It's a ruined cottage, now, all tumbled down. I went over to look at it myself last summer, to see if I could find any trace of the beautiful woman who had lived there. But she was long gone, and all that remained were the roses that she had planted beside the door – because, you see, this tune was made up by her handsome lover. He was a soldier who'd been hurt in the wars—'

'Was that the war with the Germans? My dad—'

'No, no. Long before that. The wars with Napoleon Bonaparte, in France.' Careful, Jools, lots of inconsistencies creeping in; keep it simple! 'This was a soldier who rode a horse – his horse had been hurt, too – and the horse came limping all through the Highlands with his master on his back, returning to find the beautiful young woman. But when they finally arrived at Kilnacraig, tired and hungry and sore – the cottage was empty! But the garden was full of roses, big pink scented roses, and the soldier stuck one in his buttonhole. Then he rode slowly back along the road, stopping everyone that he could find, to ask about his beautiful ladyfriend, and they all told him the same story. That she'd waited and waited for him, but had finally heard that he was dead – and she had planted the roses in his memory. That's why the tune that I'm going to play is so sad – remember it's called "The Road *from* Kilnacraig". The lady, of course – in the manner typical of beautiful ladies – eventually married someone else, whom she didn't really love, because she was so lonely and sad. Or so she said. Actually, the bloke was probably loaded with money.' (And raped her then carried her off across his pommel to be his slave.)

Julian was enjoying recounting these stories and anecdotes. A few were true – he'd managed to discover some of the background behind certain tunes – but what he couldn't find out, he just made up. He'd practised, too – not only the music, that was becoming easy – but the gestures and the dramatic pauses, in the storytelling. Isobel would no doubt be surprised when she heard about this from her nursing friends. She was furiously upset that her annual interview with the Easton Scholarship committee had been arranged for today, of all days. It was probably fortunate, because he might have found her presence inhibiting. She didn't know about these stories. The songs had been her idea, though.

'I can't do that, Bella!' he'd expostulated. 'Can you imagine me leading community hymn-singing?'

But he had seen the sense of her suggestion when he had started to put together a programme. He couldn't just perch there for an hour or so and play. Isobel had taught him two local songs. He had played one already, the 'Jeely Piece' song, and the children had soon relaxed and joined in. He'd had to play it twice, in fact; it had helped set the mood.

'And now let's have something lively to cheer us all up after that sad, sad story. "Hamish McBean's Jig". Now, Hamish was a rock-climber . . .'

Nurses, auxiliaries, the occasional junior doctor, wandered past the open door of the dayroom and stopped, smiling, to listen. Two ladies in neat suits pushed a clanking trolley, laden with magazines and sweets, along the corridor, and several of the children turned to stare and whisper but were hushed by the nurses, with promises of ice cream at the end. A young man with orange crewcut hair, whose pale face seemed familiar, drifted in and squatted down next to the girl with whom Julian had been photographed, and she whispered excitedly to him and held his hand. He gave her some sweets and kissed her, and then moved away to stand for a while, leaning against the doorframe, his expression blank but intensely watchful. Eventually, he slipped away.

He had scarcely left before Julian went straight into the tune of the final song. Two or three of the children laughed and started to clap or try to sing the words, and he grinned and raised an eyebrow.

'I see you know the song. And I hope none of you will *ever* try to do this to your granny. Ready?'

With much giggling and clapping and bobbing up and down, nearly everyone joined in:

> Oh, ye cannae push yer granny aff the bus.
> Oh, ye cannae push yer granny aff the bus.
> Oh, ye cannae push yer granny,
> For she's yer mammy's mammy,
> Ye cannae push yer granny aff the bus!

After two repeats, Julian wiped the sweat off his forehead and cried, 'Enough! You've finished me off! The end!' and he slid down from his stool and bowed, rejoicing in the excited chatter and giggles.

What a revelation! There had been so much interaction, so much give and take. It had been gratifying, stimulating, the way the children had responded. It had been a bit like the ceilidh. I was made to feel part of the experience, Julian exulted, not just the donor but a recipient, too! All this time, I've been playing only to formal audiences, they've soaked it up and *given* nothing . . . But when he finally laid the fiddle back in its case, he wasn't quite able to escape the quiet voice inside his head that whispered, 'Not bad, Jools love. You're improving – but you can't stop here.'

A muscle in the thigh of his right leg spasmed briefly, so that he closed his eyes in silent pain and, perhaps because he was in the hospital, there was a clear image in his mind of a hand held out in comfort. His own fingers clenched involuntarily as he wished that it were true.

Margaret had chosen a light lunch, olive bread with tomato and lentil soup. She wasn't really very hungry but she could hardly come down to the crypt and sit in front of a conspicuously empty plate. As she turned away from the cash till, she caught sight of Rosemary talking to someone by the door. Rosemary waved and pointed to a table.

'I've saved it for us,' she called softly over people's heads. 'I'll join you there.'

Margaret nodded and smiled, secretly delighted; Julian, too, would join them there. She sat down and shrugged off her coat, conscious that her wine-coloured silk shirt fitted her well, then she tucked her hair behind her ears and unloaded the food and cutlery from the tray. She had bought a glass of white wine, too, and took a sip as she looked around. Two acquaintances were organising themselves at a table across the room, and she smiled and mouthed 'hello'. Rosemary was still talking, and Margaret felt conspicuous sitting on her own. She spread out her programme and looked again at the leaflet that had been enclosed within it. 'Welcome to the new season of lunchtime concerts by the Kersland Ensemble,' it said, in large black print. 'We hope you will be entertained by our new programme which, this year, offers a much wider mixture . . .' Oh, and we *are* entertained by your new flamboyant look, Margaret thought. What a contrast to last season's neat, stark simplicity of black and white; such a *flowering* of richly coloured shirts, waistcoats and bodices, fuchsia, magenta and bottle green. There had been quite a few whispers when the musicians filed in, and some of the players had looked slightly embarrassed in their finery. And Julian – where had he found that astonishing waistcoat?

She took another sip of wine and then saw that Julian had come into the crypt. He was talking to Rosemary, but looking Margaret's way. There was a rapid flush of warmth inside her, so that she held her breath for a moment, then smiled and lifted her hand slightly from the table in acknowledgement. He had looked her way, he had sought her out amongst the throng, he had smiled back at her. But was it her imagination, or was his smile broader, warmer, his greeting more enthusiastic, with those women over there?

Margaret continued to watch him surreptitiously as he turned back and spoke to Rosemary, who looked surprised but then nodded and continued collecting food on to her tray. People waiting in the queue stood back to allow Julian to pass; he eased his way between the tables to talk to an elderly woman wearing a jaunty beret. His stick clunked against a table leg as he squeezed through to greet a group of students. Margaret watched his flashing smile, the way his hand gesticulated, the way his face changed as he spoke and laughed. How handsome, even glamorous the students must find him, she thought. And I'm the only person in this room, in the audience, who has seen him hurt, or half-naked, who knows that there are strange fears hiding beneath that smooth charm. There'll be one or two people here who have experienced his bad temper and selfishness, but nobody else knows that this music they have just experienced derives from that shattered knee. That Julian Kersland has been taught to believe that his crooked leg is a means unto an end. She stared at the boy with the orange crewcut who was standing quietly at the back of the student group: you don't know that, do you – and you never will! But I know it, and I know him – and I care for him, better than anyone here! (This line of thought was self-indulgent, and she knew it but revelled in it.) I have held him! I have comforted him! The warmth that spread through her now was almost sexual, and she had to look down at the table in case her triumph was too obviously displayed.

'What are you smiling at?' Rosemary asked as she thumped down her tray. 'I hope you're not laughing at our Leader's glorious apparel!'

'It *is* glorious, isn't it? The sum of all the lesser parts! Oh, I'm sorry, that sounds awful! I didn't mean to imply that *you* were a lesser part!' Margaret hoped her red cheeks would be attributed to her gaffe.

'Too much of me for that, I'm afraid! No, he persuaded me to make it for him. I had to collect up scraps of material from as many of the other players as possible. I'm quite pleased with the end result, actually . . .'

'How clever of you! It's beautiful.' Margaret was jealous, although she was herself no seamstress. 'I really like the new look – and the programme is very impressive, especially with all the interesting notes.'

'Yes, Julian *has* been a busy boy this summer. He did a lot of the research himself, you know.'

'Oh, so that's what all those piles of books were for—' She had nearly said, 'that I've had to dust,' but had stopped herself in time.

'And, of course, he has a friend who's a music historian, and one of the fiddlers is quite an academic, too. Still, Julian's made a very good job of it, and we've got some interesting concerts coming up. Oh!' Rosemary tapped the table and laughed. 'What did you think of his gig at the hospital last week? Wasn't it a lovely photo?'

'Sorry – what was this?'

'The little concert he gave for the children. Apparently they all loved it. Didn't you know?' Rosemary looked at Margaret's blank face and was confused. 'I'm sure he was going to tell you all about it . . . especially since I gather, from what you were all saying that weekend, that it's really thanks to you that he got interested in fiddle music. The ceilidh, and everything.'

'No, I didn't know. How exciting!' Margaret felt sick. 'I'll be able to ask him all about it when he brings his lunch.'

Rosemary looked even more embarrassed. 'Oh, Julian's not staying to lunch. He just came down to show his face really, to talk to a few of the old regulars. You know how they like that. It brightens up their week!'

'Yes, I'm sure it does!' She tried not to sound as bitter as she felt. 'In which paper did you say the photo was?'

He had seen her at Rosemary's table, and he must then have decided that he'd rather starve than sit beside her. Oh, damn him! Margaret saw again how he had looked over at her, and how he had stopped Rosemary from picking up his food.

The chestnut trees were turning, she noticed; their leaves were frayed and crinkled at the edges. She picked up a conker from the grass, and sat on a bench to watch the ducks. The conker was smooth and glossy in her hand, but it gave her no comfort and she looked quickly round to make sure no one was watching, then threw it at a mallard. She missed, but the duck squawked anyway and paddled off furiously.

Vanity and an overactive imagination had led her to this: trailing around after Kersland and believing that she knew and understood him. She knew nothing! Despite visiting his flat twice a week, despite her intimate interferences with his belongings, despite conversations around the coffee cups, she knew – or had been permitted to know – *nothing*! All these weeks, during which she had been imagining that she and Julian were growing ever closer . . . She thought of the various subterfuges that she had used to try to coax him to talk to her about his ideas. She wanted so much to continue to demonstrate her care and affection, but she was too frightened to do so, and – although she analysed every move – he was not sending her the right signals but was clearly holding back. Yet he hadn't sent her away: he had told her, when she asked, anxiously, if she should still keep coming, how glad he was that she came to help. Nor did he avoid all mention of that Sunday at the cottage. He had laughed with her about wearing Iain's clothes while Rosemary 'took tea'; he had even complimented her on her agility in descending to the ground, and for appearing so cool. (But he had not explained why he hadn't let Rosemary in.) He had, however, avoided all mention of the boat, although she longed to discuss the incident with him, his grim and silent fear, and she had been careful to choose a photograph to give him that did not include the island. He'd been pleased with that photograph: Iain had taken it one spring from the hills across the loch, and the cottage stood out, small and white, dwarfed by the hill behind. Part of the village was in the picture, too, two houses and the village hall, and the beach at the head of the loch. The photograph had been taken in the evening light, and there were long, thin shadows that accentuated the relief.

Julian had propped the photograph on the mantelpiece in the music room, and she had been happy that he so obviously cared for the memento. She hoped that it reminded him of their shared experiences.

But he had not told her that he was practising folk music, or that he was booked to play to the sick children. Margaret dug her hands into her pockets and stared at the oily pond. Poor, silly, misguided Margaret Gillespie! You've made a fool of yourself. But at least no *harm* has been done. You haven't made a fool of yourself *in bed*! And I do love Iain – in fact, I've felt closer to him recently. Somehow I've loved him more, ever since . . . Oh, Julian! She thought again of Julian dragging himself up on to the rock, hauling himself out, dark from the water. Sick children! That was the key! He had been playing to the children in the hospital as a sort of exorcism, to see if he could return there and confront other crippled children. Of course! She must talk to him about it. He would tell her tomorrow; he was keeping it as a surprise.

She stood up and realised how cold the afternoon had become. But now she could hope again and, although her eyes still looked tired and strained, her expression was livelier as she walked briskly back to her car.

'Good concert?' Iain looked up from the Sunday paper. 'You were gone a long time. The lunch must have been good.'

'I had a quick walk around the park afterwards to see the autumn colours. Here's a conker for you.'

He laughed as she handed it over. 'That's a beauty. I hope you've got one for yourself – we can have a competition! Oh, by the way, your dear friend Zoe phoned.'

'Oh no!' Margaret groaned. 'What did she want?'

'Nothing, actually – or at least nothing intelligible. She was burbling about Kersland dancing "Strip the Willow" in a hospital ward, or something odd. I didn't quite get it.' He grinned. 'Anyway, she wanted to know if you knew what it was all about since you're "the expert on Kersland affairs". Impossible woman! I was to pass on to you that Mrs Knight's grandson had been there. Does that mean anything to you? Sounds as though our ceilidh has gone to Kersland's head!'

Chapter Nineteen

Thank God! The committee of the Easton Trust was prepared to fund her for another year from the end of March. Isobel slipped the letter into her pocket and carried on upstairs to her room. She hadn't even allowed herself to think what she would have done if her funds had run out halfway through the academic year; it was ridiculous to treat her like a farm labourer, hiring and firing on Lady Day, and she had had to contend with complicated financial juggling to enable her to work an academic year. That interview with the committee hadn't gone well, either. They hadn't been pleased about her examination failures, even though she had subsequently obtained very good grades in the resits. 'You have a grave responsibility, Miss Hutchison,' et cetera, et cetera. But her sober clothes and her tutor's supportive letter must have convinced the committee of her worth. She could not afford to make any more mistakes through carelessness and distraction, though.

And yet . . . these self-exhortations were very noble and pure-hearted, these pledges to pursue the Holy Grail – or was it Asclepius' staff? – but the serpent of temptation was very big and fat. The image made her snigger. Until she read that letter she had been fretting and muttering because her social life with Julian was so limited. Ten minutes ago, she thought, I was feeling frustrated because I know hardly any of his friends. I don't think they even know I exist. Oh, the band knows, and that woman Rosemary, but I never get invited to dinner parties with him, or weekends in country cottages. All we ever do is go out for a drink or a meal or a drive, or go to bed. Sex! There has to be more to our relationship than that! We don't even talk about . . . anything!

But that wasn't entirely true. Their meetings were not short of conversation or humour, it wasn't that which was lacking. It was just that she felt that, by not sharing completely in his social life – or even his musical life, because she didn't go to rehearsals any more since she was so obviously in the way, and she rarely went to the concerts – there was a large part of Julian of which she was probably entirely ignorant. She wanted to know his friends, and to be known. She wanted, in fact, to be recognised as Kersland's girlfriend, not merely to be faintly acknowledged as his 'little bit on the side'.

Isobel sat at her table and stared out of the window. Why, though? Why did she want to be seen to be his girlfriend? Why, even, did she want to be his girlfriend? Why did he want her? The questions went round and round. Is it because you want to share his glory (for there is excitement in being attached to someone unusual and well known), or do you want to show everyone that you're his partner, in everything? (How many people know, I wonder, that I arranged that concert for the kids?) To share: as a subordinate or as an equal? We are equals, aren't we? Not in age, perhaps, but in intellect. Yet we're also subordinate to each other in the other's field of expertise. I'm his subordinate socially, too – and I always will be unless we share. Is Julian ashamed of me? This unpleasant thought had occurred to her before, and whereas previously she had managed to shrug it off, this evening it continued to irk her, even as she tried to work, so that she eventually thumped down her pen and determined to abandon her studying for the evening in order to go and discuss her unease with Julian himself. Unless this problem was confronted, she would not be able to concentrate: the Easton Trust's letter still lay on the table as a reminder that her personal future was not permanently secured. And perhaps, if she were truly honest with herself, it was the Easton Trust and her future in medicine, that were really at the bottom of this general malaise.

Julian, however, was in a buoyant mood, fidgeting around the music room, overactive. He picked up the letter yet again and shook it in the air.

'But don't you see the significance?' Why was Isobel looking so sulky? She ought to be delighted at his good fortune. 'They're recognising that we're an innovative baroque band, and that we have a broad range. And a good audience, too. And two of the pieces they want to record are violin concertos! With me as soloist, of course! It's working, Bella – it's all going according to plan!'

'But . . . I don't really understand. What plan?'

'For Christ's sake, Isobel! This whole new concert series that we're doing, for example. Christ knows, I've put enough effort into the programmes – or have you been too absorbed in other people's navels to notice? If you spared the time to come along to a few more of the concerts you'd see what we're doing. What *I'm* doing. It's proving very successful, too – good reviews. "The excellent Julian Kersland, who seems to have come out of nowhere . . ." and such like. Fixtures in London and Birmingham. Even the old "groupies" seem to like it, find it "stimulating", old Mrs Roberts told me. Poor old things. I'll have them all begging for more when the series ends.'

'Perhaps you should make a video, like all the rock bands, not just a recording. Then they'll be able to see you and drool over you, too.'

'Why are you being so sarcastic?' Julian's enthusiasm was not to be suppressed. He came over to where Isobel was sitting on the piano stool. 'Aren't you pleased for me?'

'Yes, *of course* I am! I'm sorry, I came over because I wanted to talk to you about something, but it doesn't matter. It's the wrong moment.'

Her smile was unconvincing. Julian carefully folded down the lid of the piano and, resting on it, bent forward to kiss her.

'Let's celebrate first, then I promise I'll listen.'

'But I don't want to go to bed,' she said feebly, pulling back.

'I thought that was what little children said! And who said anything about bed?'

'Well, it's cold in here.'

Julian sighed, and limped over to the fireplace, pulling a handle so that the gas fire, previously on low, poured out a hot orange glow into the room. Then he dragged a wooden chair near to the fire, sat down, and held out his hand. There was no tactful way by which she could refuse without creating an awkward scene whose repercussions could last for days, so Isobel stood up, reluctantly, and came towards him.

When she lifted her arms, a few minutes later, so that he could help her remove her camisole, Julian suddenly laughed at the picture that had come to mind. But when she looked down, startled, he couldn't tell her about the Sikh.

'Remember the wooden bench in the jungle?' he asked, and she looked puzzled, then blushed and laughed aloud.

Later, while Isobel was in the bathroom, Julian was in the kitchen, making coffee.

'Look!' he said, when Isobel appeared in the kitchen doorway. On a small slip of paper was written 'Ginger fairings'. 'Margaret left this in the biscuit tin – just in case I couldn't recognise the biscuits!' He shook his head in exasperation.

'So? Why does it bother you? She seems really kind.'

'The mother of one of my pupils has heard that my previous cleaner, Mrs Knight, wants to come back.'

'But you can't get rid of Mrs Gillespie! What would you say to her? Anyway, I thought she really liked coming here to look after you – God knows why! – and the place always looks spotless!'

'Hmm.' Julian wouldn't say any more. To try to explain that he felt threatened by Margaret Gillespie would only sound absurd, but ever since the summer it had seemed as though she was always trying to encourage him into intimate discussions. Sometimes she looked at him so tenderly, almost as if she were pleading with him – and there were the little touches, on his arm or shoulder. Once, he had even had the idea that he should persuade her into his bed, so that the resulting awkward attempt at consummation (for she'd be sure to be shocked by anything other than a conventional position, wouldn't she?) would end all this stupidity. But the outcome of such an encounter was not entirely predictable – and, also, he was too proud. Could he, though, endure Mrs Knight's return? He must think about this seriously, try to recall the noise and interruptions, and weigh up her bluntness against Margaret's quietly persistent neediness. Meanwhile, Isobel 'wanted to talk'. Why couldn't these damned women just leave him alone?

He took the biscuit tin from her and put it down. 'Right. It's a fair trade. What conversation piece brought you scurrying to my door?'

'Do we have to talk about it in here? I'd much rather go and sit by the fire.'

But even as Julian nodded, the doorbell rang, making them both jump. Coffee sprayed from Isobel's cup and splattered on to her skirt, and she swore and hurried to the sink.

'I'll go. You stay here a moment, and perhaps whoever it is can be persuaded to go away.'

'That's exactly why I'm here,' Isobel called softly after him, as he shut the kitchen door. 'That's why I want to talk to you. Hidden away in the kitchen like a guilty secret!'

She dabbed at her skirt, and then she opened the door a crack and listened. Julian was switching on the light in the front hall, clumping across to the outer door. She heard him open the door; there was a momentary silence, during which the sound of a car alarm came drifting in.

'Tom!'

'Aye, Jools. I found you at last! I told you I would.'

'Come in, come in.'

Isobel shut the kitchen door and tidied her hair, using her reflection in the dark window. Well, here was one friend who would have to meet her, anyway – and this was one she had been wanting to meet.

'Isobel? Isobel, it's Tom!'

The two men were going into the music room as she opened the door, so that she only saw Tom's back and heard the unusual nervousness in Julian's voice. By the time she joined them, Tom was lowering himself into an armchair, but he stood up again as she came in and gave her a long, appraising stare.

'Tom, this is Isobel Hutchison.' Not 'my girlfriend', she noted. 'Bella, this is Tom – I don't even know your surname, Tom – this is Tom, anyway.'

'About whom I've heard a lot.'

'Hi, Isobel. I've almost forgotten my surname myself. Tom'll do fine. And so you've heard a lot about me already! Glad to hear he hasn't forgotten about me.'

Julian laughed uneasily, and they all settled themselves around the gas fire. The wooden chair was in Isobel's way and she pushed it with her feet.

'So how did you find out where I live? Did it take you long?'

'I see you've been fiddling,' Tom answered, indirectly. 'The mate that Chris and I are staying with – you remember my partner, Chris – saved the newspaper. He didn't know who you were and thought we might want to find out more about you! But the hospital wouldn't give away your address when I phoned – or even your phone number – even when I said I was a big fan and wanted to invite you to a gig! They probably get a load of cranks phoning all the time, don't you think, Isobel, asking for the nurses' phone numbers and nights off?'

'They were right not to give away the information,' Isobel

said, a little primly. 'The children loved it, didn't they, Julian? It was my idea, as a matter of fact. Julian wasn't very keen at first.'

'So did you play our tune, then, Jools? The one I taught you at the ceilidh.'

'He called himself Jools, too!' She imitated Tom's drawl, and giggled. 'Jools Kersland.'

Tom pursued his lips and nodded his head assessingly. 'Nice touch, you can't be too formal. And what made you choose the hospital, Isobel? Are you his manager, then?'

'No, she was cleaning wards.'

'No, I'm a medic.'

They both answered together, and Tom barked with laughter.

'Well, there's a lot of stories to be told here, and that's for sure. But you haven't asked me how I *did* find you, since the hospital was hanging on to your secret.'

'You've hardly given us a chance.' Isobel was tart. 'Do tell.'

She ignored his raised eyebrow and looked into the fire, slightly ashamed and puzzled by her instantaneous dislike.

'It was easy, Jools – I just got the address from the phone book.'

'But there are lots of Kerslands, even J. Kerslands. You can't have visited them all.'

'Of course not! My mate knew which were the fancy areas, so I just made a list of the J. Kerslands with smart addresses, and drove around in the van. There weren't many. And there's only one with a specially modified car with a "Disabled" badge on the windscreen. Not too difficult to work it out.'

'Mmm. So here you are. Have you come to sign on for classical violin lessons, then?'

Tom shook his head. 'Some other day, perhaps. No, I just came to see if you'd like to come for a beer. I want to hear all about this gig. You too, Isobel – of course.'

'That's a great idea,' Isobel agreed quickly. 'We could go to that wine bar that you told me about, Julian, in the centre—'

'I don't know, it's not—'

'I'm more of a spit and sawdust man, myself,' Tom said. 'Isn't there anywhere local?'

'My favourite's the pub just down the road, but Julian doesn't like it – it's not his type of music. Although I thought *every* type was your type, these days! And you said that this bar had plenty of room between the tables, didn't you? More leg room.' She lightly stressed the penultimate word.

'Bella, stop acting as though you're my childminder,' Julian said crossly. 'But yes, the wine bar's quite a good place to go, Tom. We can talk there without having to shout. And you can breathe, too, unlike in Isobel's pub.'

Julian and Isobel were silent, apart from a few comments on the traffic and the route, as they drove into the centre of the city, and they waited in the car until Tom had found a parking space for his van. The wine bar was, indeed, spacious and discreet, a suitable talking place for the young money-people from the nearby Exchange, or perhaps for couples on lunchtime assignations. The floor was carpeted, bottle green, and high-backed settles with green cushions divided the interior into a large number of small booths. Green curtains hung by scalloped edges from brass rods above the back of each settle, to further hide the sight and sound of the booths' occupants, and faces were made strange by the shadows cast from the green-shaded brass lamps upon each table. Isobel thought that she would not have been surprised to feel the floor rising and falling rhythmically, or to hear waves hissing and thumping against the walls. A waitress in a short blue-and-green tartan kilt swam out of the aqueous dimness towards them, her white notepad held before her like an underwater torch. She nevertheless stumbled against Julian's outstretched leg, and giggled embarrassed apologies as she wrote down their orders.

'Do you come here often? It's not the sort of place that I would have associated you with,' Tom asked Julian, when the waitress had gone. Isobel had wondered about that herself, but Julian shrugged deprecatingly.

'Once or twice, that's all. Business. But anyway, tell me what you've been doing. How are the others – Euan, wasn't it, the flautist? – and Chris?'

Tom gave an account of the past few months, his travels, the village halls, the pubs, and the folk festivals, both in the capital and the islands. He was concise, with an eye for the absurd. Isobel, sipping her white wine, listened to his rough voice and occasionally, when he wasn't looking directly at her, observed his rather harsh features, wondering if the activity of his hands, that waved, pointed and gesticulated, compensated for the immobility of his face. Then, suddenly, as Julian was beginning to relax, Tom switched the conversation back to him, and caught him unawares.

'So you think you're ready to help us form the MacDonald Ensemble now, are you? I wasn't sure you cared!'

Julian was astonished to feel his face flush, he felt as awkward as a ten-year-old asked to give an account of his aspirations by a little-known aunt.

'It's all part of Julian's scheme to reach out to the masses, bringing music into the lives of people from all walks of life, et cetera.'

'Is there anything wrong with that?' Isobel's sarcasm had surprised Julian, and he responded coldly. 'Is it wrong that a man and a musical instrument should stand up in front of a group of people, whether they are young, old, sick, happy, miserable, conventional middle-aged – or even upcoming business people – and, by the right choice of music, hold their attention? That he should be able to show them something *new* and entertain them, so that they are cheered, and . . . enlivened? And for a moment, they can forget pain or worry or work. They may even be shown something *beyond* their ordinary, run-of-the-mill routines. And the player may be shown something in return. And allowed to share. I don't see what's wrong with that. Do you?'

Isobel was quiet, absorbing what he had said. Then she asked, 'Do you see your fiddle-playing in the same terms, Tom? Do you see yourself as some kind of musical homeopath for the ailing, repressed and limited populace?'

Tom answered without emotion, his face expressionless. 'It's a bit different for me, I only play at gigs or ceilidhs and the like, none of the charity stuff or straight concerts. So I'm always playing to folk who like my kind of music. They expect to hear a certain sound, and they get it. That's what they come for, and that's how I earn my bread and beer. The music can be quite emotional – but they expect that, too.' He paused. 'I like this idea of Jools', though, about opening up new experiences. So what about those kids at the hospital – how did they react? Did you feel you'd helped them, Jools?'

Julian frowned and shook his head, twisting his wineglass on the table; then he smiled as he started to remember what had happened.

'They were all pretty excited – happy – by the end. It was a bit slow at first, I couldn't be certain that I was reaching them. They were a bit shy, perhaps, because we were physically rather close, packed into the room with all the chairs and beds and so on. They liked the stories, the stories hooked them in to the ideas of the music.'

'You told them stories?'

'Yes. I was rather proud of the story that I'd devised about "The Road from Kilnacraig" – do you know the tune, Tom? I told them about a dying soldier back from France, and his dying horse, and pink roses.'

'Shit, man! Of course I know the bloody tune! You can't go mucking about with history like that – that's a song about an Orangeman. You'd probably have been shot if you'd been playing in a Belfast hospital!' Tom was really shocked. 'You'd better join up with me and let me do the talking – or at least let me give you a few private lessons!'

Julian shrugged. 'What the hell, Tom, it didn't matter. They enjoyed the story. This was about enjoyment, not political accuracy and the communal memory. And the stories involved the children emotionally, so that they came to have a greater empathy with the music. They were tapping their feet and tapping their fingers, nodding their heads – whatever was physically possible. Which, in one or two cases, was a pitiably small amount. You know, there was one girl who had been wheeled through in her bed, and she was almost completely unresponsive. I don't know what she felt at all. Probably she was too uncomfortable to care very much about anything, poor girl.'

He had forgotten about her until now, had pushed her out of his mind in his post-performance euphoria.

'With short dark hair?' asked Isobel.

Julian nodded.

'That was Claire. Her brother died when a joyrider crashed a car. They were standing together outside a shop, and the car got him but only scraped her. Her ribs were cracked, nothing very serious physically. But I know the nurses on the ward were very worried about her.'

'She'll not forget that, will she?' Tom said. 'Poor kid, she'll keep seeing that. I don't suppose there's any way of wiping that picture out of her mind. Not even music can do that, Jools – or stories. Here, your glass is empty, my round, I think. What do you suggest, Dr Isobel – would stories help?'

But the medical course on the workings of the human mind had so far only concerned itself with theory, and Isobel merely grimaced and shook her head.

They were all silent while the waitress, this time making a pantomime of looking down and stepping over Julian's foot, came to write down their orders. The bar was filling up, conversation and laughter buzzed and hummed around them.

Isobel and Tom watched as the latest arrivals, a couple in their late forties, dressed conventionally and without inspiration, sat down at a central table. The woman looked around and whispered to her husband, perhaps about their so much greater age, because then the man looked around, too, then smiled and put his hand over his wife's as he replied. His circling glance had caught Isobel's and she looked away, embarrassed to have been seen intruding on a privately shared moment of anxiety. She wondered how long it took for a couple to find mutual understanding and support, equally, instead of each seeking supremacy and trying to impose his or her will or ideas; the equal balance must be only slowly, and rarely, attainable. She looked at Julian out of the corner of her eye and saw the strange fierceness in his thin, angular face, as he stared at the table. Tom was looking at him, too, and his voice was surprisingly gentle.

'What's wrong, Jools? Thinking up another story?'

Julian sat up, and his voice was hard. 'Did I ever tell you the story about how I damaged my leg?'

'Yes, you told me – the first day we spent together. Don't you remember?' Isobel smiled, and nudged against him, aware that she was trying to impress Tom with their togetherness. 'After we'd had our picnic, and cream tea, and had gone back to your flat . . .'

The surprises and excitement of that day came back to her strongly. But Julian pulled away from the pressure of her arm and twitched his shoulder irritably.

'No! That story was a fiction. I'm talking about the real story. You don't know the real story.'

The waitress had returned with their drinks and they waited while she took up the empty glasses. The pressure to tell the truth was building up inside Julian, and with it, his anger and bitterness. He didn't know whether he was angry with himself, or with Isobel and Tom. He wanted to shock them; he wanted to hurt Isobel, to show that he was stronger than he seemed. He didn't know why, or care. And he wanted to impress Tom. Through his anger, it struck him that he was frightened of Tom, and this possibility thrilled him and fuelled his anger further, so that he clamped his hand on to Isobel's leg, his fingers digging into her inner thigh.

'Your comment about that girl, always seeing that accident in her mind, has just reminded me of the story that I have tried to forget.'

'Hey, Julian, steady. We don't need to know.'

'But I *want* you to know, Tom. You're going to have to hear. The fiction, Tom, is that I broke my knee when I jumped out of a tree to save a friend. Andrew, he was called – he lived on a farm. I used to visit him sometimes. He was drowning, you see. He'd fallen into the burn, and couldn't get up. And I jumped down from my tree – it was an old oak tree, very easy to climb, by the way – I leapt down, regardless of my own personal safety, to go and drag him out. Very heroic, don't you agree? Especially for an eleven-year-old.'

Tom was puzzled. 'But I don't suppose you thought of it in heroic terms. You just *do* these things, don't you? It's a natural response. You don't just sit there. Anyway, I don't see what . . . Oh. You hurt your knee. You didn't reach him in time.'

The picture of the boy lying beneath the tree, writhing and clutching his leg, probably screaming, while another boy, quite still and quiet, was washed with water in the burn, was very clear.

'Quite. I couldn't reach him. He drowned face-down in a shallow burn. In a narrow burn, to be even more exact. Only his head and shoulders were awash, he should have been able to get up, stupid boy, all he had to do was put out his hands and push himself up. But he just lay there, you see, the water sloshing over his head. And I watched – and waited for him to push himself upright. And then I broke my knee.'

Julian's face was pale and grim as he stared at Tom. He

knew that he had Tom's attention. And Isobel's, too; he gripped her leg more tightly and heard her short, sharp exhalation. A strange violence was growing inside him, he wanted to hurt her physically, here in the booth, to . . . to show Tom. To show Tom. The thought sickened him and he relaxed his grip. Isobel shifted away along the bench.

'But – but that story's not much different from what you told me,' she said, uneasily. 'I realise it's terrible –' she looked briefly at Tom, who nodded, '– but nothing was your fault.'

'It's a bad picture, though,' Tom said. 'It stays . . .'

'You aren't thinking, either of you, are you? Why didn't Andrew get up when he fell into the burn? You haven't asked that, have you?' Julian waited.

'He knocked himself out?'

'There was a bruise on his head, yes. That might have accounted for his failure. But I heard them say later that he had asphyxiated on his vomit. Isn't that language beautiful, roll it round your mouth – asphyxiated on his vomit. No doubt the water also asphyxiated him. And do you know why? He was an epileptic. My friend Andrew had had an epileptic fit. Do you know, I was laughing. I was sitting in my tree, king of the castle, and I was defending it against him, and jeering, taunting him to come and take it from me. If he could touch the trunk, our rules said, then the tree would be his. Easy, you might think. But I had lots of ammunition – not just acorns, which would have been . . . ecologically correct, but pieces of rotten branch. And stones. Andrew was dashing to and fro, dodging, trying to get in behind my view, but I always saw him. He was getting angry, and I was – laughing. Making him feel helpless and a fool. He was running to the burn, perhaps to get some stones to retaliate, and he made a strange sound. And he fell into the burn. I laughed, Tom – I carried on laughing at his stupidity, watched him twitching. And then it was too late. Heroic, wasn't it?' Julian swigged down the last of his wine.

Isobel remained silent, repulsed (as he seemed to have intended) by Julian's behaviour, yet her mind was full of questions. Had Julian known his friend was an epileptic? Did the boy's parents know what Julian had done? But it wasn't as though he had murdered the boy, had he? Boys do these things, taunt each other, have battles. And why had he told the story now, in this place? What had all this to do with Tom? It was as though Tom had somehow been necessary as a catalyst to reveal this darker, frightening side of Julian. She realised, then, how little she really knew or understood Julian; perhaps, indeed, how little she had wanted to understand Julian. Curiosity had led her into this relationship, but her curiosity hadn't been deep or explicit enough. She didn't know this man. She didn't know where to begin.

'You couldn't have known that Andrew would have a fit. You shouldn't blame yourself.'

Julian looked at her, for the first time in several minutes. 'That's what my counsellor, my clergyman, told me, too. Although he also said,' coolly, almost sneeringly he repeated the words, 'that the damage done to me was a penance, and a blessing.'

Abruptly, he was tired of the story, of the melodrama. He felt weakened and empty and he bent down and picked up his stick. He didn't want to answer questions and explain.

'I'm going home.'

'Why did you tell us your story, Julian?' Tom asked.

Julian curled his lips downwards and shrugged. 'I wanted you to know.'

Then, as he heaved himself to his feet and turned away, he added in a strangely pleading voice, 'Come and see me, Tom.'

Surprised, Isobel looked at Tom, but he was still watching Julian thoughtfully.

''Bye, Tom,' Isobel blurted hastily, slithering along the bench to catch up with Julian, who was already on his way to the door.

Tom raised a hand and watched them as they left, Julian lurching, stick thumping, Isobel trailing in the rear. He sighed and caught the waitress's eye, but when she came over he changed his mind and shook his head. Instead, he picked up his jacket and pushed his way through an incoming gaggle of people, and out into the brightly lit dampness of the street.

Julian's car was beaded with raindrops, and the wipers smeared the windscreen as they swept the persistent drizzle aside. Fluorescent signs and streetlights were dulled by the falling droplets, young men lounged against doorposts and under the canopies of shops, and pedestrians walked briskly with bent heads, faces averted from the rain. The traffic light turned red ahead of them, but Julian accelerated the car and sped across the junction, narrowly missing an over-eager pedestrian who had anticipated the crossing signal. Isobel gasped and clutched at the door.

'Why are you so angry – and *horrible*? Why did you have to spoil the evening? Tom had gone to so much effort to find you. And after all that, you tell him, practically order him, to "come and see me, Tom". I doubt you'll ever see him again!'

'That just shows how little you understand.'

The car was caught in slowly moving traffic, and Julian turned his head to look at Isobel. Her skin was putty-coloured in the orange light of the streetlamps and her massive breasts were hidden inside a chunky jacket. Slumped in the passenger seat, she seemed diminished and uncertain, and his taut irritation fell away, so that he sighed heavily.

'Bella, Bellissima. Beauty and the Beast. I'm the Beast.'

'I know,' she said quietly. 'I don't understand.'

I was obsessed with her, he thought. A green and purple sign, 'La Trattoria', blazed in briefly as they passed, illuminating their chests and thighs. Breasts spot-lit in the headlights, remember? Remember that first sight, such exquisite perfection, and the warm softness, the invitation?

Oh, remember! He felt sad, disorientated; he needed to reassure himself, to know that he could look upon Isobel and experience those feelings again; to remember why it had seemed so important; to go back, back to the beginning, here, in the car. At the next crossroads he turned left, then right, into the maze of backstreets and gardened squares, where the lighting was dim and large, old trees cast deep shadows.

'Where are we going?' Isobel asked, vaguely alarmed at this further evidence of odd behaviour.

'You'll see.'

There was a single space in the line of parked cars. He pulled up and reversed the car on to the thick brown carpet of crushed leaves, and switched off the lights.

'Bella.' She was looking at him uneasily. 'Bella, I don't know why I told the story and behaved like that. I'm sorry. Believe me.'

He undid his seatbelt; he didn't care at that moment whether she believed him or not. He undid her seatbelt, too.

'Isabella. Nobody will see us here. Let's recreate our first day again, just part of it. You were reminding me of it in the bar – it was so very good.'

He reached across and drew her head towards his, to kiss her; she resisted at first but then responded, unenthusiastically.

'Take your coat off. Please. Like the first time, do you remember? Please, my Bella – please!'

Isobel could feel his hands inside her coat; he was kissing her, muttering short, disconnected phrases. Feebly, in the confined space, she struggled out of her jacket, Julian pushing the heavy material out of the way. She didn't know what to do. Why couldn't she be sensible, why wasn't there time to think this through? He was relentless, uncaring about her discomfort. She suddenly saw him, pursuing his prey with thrown sticks, laughing . . .

'Oh no, Julian. No, not here.' She twisted her face away. 'Someone will see. No!'

He had pulled up her jumper, pulled it up under her chin, he was scrabbling at her blouse, tugging at it. She could feel the cold air on her body. She was exposed. Cheap! Exposed and degraded! She couldn't believe that Julian's needs could be so out of tune with her own.

'No!' She pushed him away. 'No! Don't! Stop it!'

She pushed him again and he sprawled, shocked, against the door. His elbow had caught in the steering wheel so that he looked disjointed, almost broken. Isobel dragged her jumper down over her gaping blouse, and opened her door.

'No, Julian, I can't bear it, not like this.'

Reaching back in for her jacket she saw that Julian looked crumpled, no longer frightening, and, horrified by the explosive climax to the evening, she leant forward quickly and touched his untrapped arm.

'I really am sorry. Drive home carefully.'

And then she closed the car door quietly, and hurried away over the squelching softness of the wet leaf mould, into the deep shadows. There was a dark alleyway between two streets, a place where she wouldn't normally go at night, but it had cast-iron bollards at each end and was safe from following cars, so she pulled on her jacket and stood, shivering, against the wall. After several minutes she heard Julian start his car and drive away. She waited for a few moments, and then came out of the alley and started to walk home.

Old wet leaves smelt dank. Orange light was caught and trapped by the bare, shiny limbs of the trees. Occasionally cars passed, or a pedestrian. Isobel thought only of getting home. The road ahead was too dark and quiet, and she turned right on to a brighter street that led towards a busier road.

There were two figures in the road, one crouching and hunched, and another man, taller, standing over him. She stopped at once, thinking she was witnessing a violent act, wondering whether to shout for help or run. Then she saw that the bent, subservient figure was, in reality, handling an object in the road, trying to lift it up; an object that was soft and heavy, like a cushion or a small bag of clothes. The taller man had his hand on the other's shoulder, and was stooping to help him pick up the bag. But it was not a bag: it was a dog, a small, limp dog. And the old, bent figure wore a bobble-hat.

'Paddy! What's wrong?' Isobel hurried forward. 'What's happened to Terry?'

The old man, cradling the soft body of his only companion, oblivious of the blood, looked towards her, and the lights made the tears glitter on his cheeks.

'Isobel?'

The tall man's voice was quiet and astonished. It was Dave. Isobel couldn't even feel surprised, too much had already happened this evening.

'I thought you were in the States.'

She reached out to touch the soft flank of the little terrier in Paddy's arms, although she had spoken to Dave.

'This weekend. Is Terry dead? I . . . I can't tell, by looking. And Paddy won't let me examine him.'

Paddy was standing motionless, crying silently, his coat already stained with blood.

'Paddy.' Isobel bent slightly to look into the old man's face. 'Paddy, will you let me look? I'm a doctor,' – 'almost,' she added under her breath.

He unbent sufficiently to let her see, but the dog's head flopped unnaturally and blood dripped from its mouth. Isobel had no idea where a dog's pulse could be found, but she held her hand against Terry's chest, and felt only the stillness of death.

'Paddy, I'm afraid Terry's dead.'

'Terry!'

The old man's mouth was black and toothless as he whispered his little dog's name.

Isobel looked at Dave; in other circumstances, they would have smiled at each other and said, 'So he can speak after all.'

'What on earth should we do?'

'The driver didn't even stop. I thought he was going to hit Paddy, but he swerved. He was going so damned fast. I wish I'd got his number, but I hardly realised what was happening.'

'Did you see what sort of car?' The certainty of what Dave would reply made her feel sick.

'It was a Mini, hard to tell what colour in this light, but dark – dark blue or red, perhaps. The man had dark hair, too – but that won't help. We could never prove he'd done it.'

'No. Perhaps he didn't even realise what he'd done – the driver, I mean.' Could Julian possibly have failed to feel the thud and bump? Or would he really have been so callous, or cowardly . . . ?'

Dave had his arm around Paddy, and was leading him along the pavement.

'Come on, Paddy, let me take you home.'

'Do you know where he lives?' Isobel found that the situation was totally beyond her. 'Were you with him? What do you do with a dead dog in the city? He can't take Terry home – look at it! We'll have to find a bag or box to carry Terry in!' She realised her voice was becoming shrill. 'I'll look by the dustbins over there.'

'Just stay with him a minute,' Dave said. 'I'll find something, it's all right, Isobel.'

He dived into a back court through a broken gate, and she could hear him rummaging; in a few moments he returned with a battered cardboard box.

'Here, Paddy – let's put Terry in here, then you'll both be more comfortable. Isobel, have you got a handkerchief or something, for Terry's head?'

What use was a handkerchief, she thought wildly, but she hunted through her bag and pockets, and she and Dave lifted the little dog from Paddy's arms and laid it in the box, cushioning its dead, battered head. Isobel had some paper tissues, too, and she took Paddy's hands and wiped them clean, then held them in her own.

'Paddy, I'm so sorry. We'll help you get another dog. We don't want you to be on your own.'

'It's all right, Iso. I'll sort it out. Show me where you live, Paddy, I'll help you home with the box.'

'Will you send me a note of his address, before you leave? Somebody may need to help . . .'

'Why don't you go down to the pub? They're still all there for my farewell do. Actually, you could tell Jim, behind the bar. They're sure to organise a collection, they'll look after him. I left early to go and pack. Lucky I did. 'Bye, then, Isobel. Take care of yourself.'

He was already leading Paddy slowly away, half supporting the box that the old man carried. Isobel stood and watched them for a few minutes. When they were about to turn the corner, she could bear it no longer.

'Dave!' she called. 'Dave – will you send me *your* address?'

He waved and carried on, and Isobel, feeling like a criminal, walked slowly to the pub to break the news.

Chapter Twenty

The warm, sweet smell of freshly baked cherry cake was strong at the top of the stairs. Margaret opened the drawing-room door, letting the smell drift in; it was, after all, her alibi. Iain was sitting in his armchair, reading; he had lit the fire against the dank chill of the evening and, with the curtains drawn, the room was warm and mellow. The gas flames flickered ceaselessly, failing to devour the imitation coal, and their changing patterns of light made the sea, in the picture opposite, seem to shift and flow. Guilt stabbed Margaret briefly, but she had made her decision during dinner, she had worked out what she should do.

'I was just on the phone to Zoe,' she said, 'about tomorrow's hospice sale. She wants me to take that cake over to her house tonight, so I may as well do that now, before I get too comfortable by the fire.'

'What – now? Does that woman never stop disordering other people's lives!'

'Actually, I think she was afraid you'd eat it because I once told her that cherry cake was your favourite! It's not too much bother – and I've other things to do in the morning.' She smiled at her husband, ashamed at using Zoe as a scapegoat. 'I won't be long – unless she ropes me in to help. I'll just go and put on something a bit smarter.'

'But you look smart now. You're always smart!'

'Oh, you know what Zoe's like,' she said cryptically. 'And I smell of cooking.'

Iain shook his head ruefully. 'Well, if you must – though I can't imagine what's so urgent about a cherry cake.'

'Ah well. "Life is just a bowl of cherries," or something equally apposite. "You can't have your cherry cake and eat it", perhaps?' She laughed as she went out of the door, and into the bedroom to change.

She exchanged her jumper and skirt for a soft silk shirt and woollen trousers, natural, warm fabrics that were smart yet soft and informal. She would put on her coat so that Iain wouldn't see exactly what she was wearing, and be curious. Ah! – the cake! She'd nearly forgotten to take the cake. What would she do with it if Julian wasn't, after all, at home? She'd have to put it in a rubbish bin. Imagine the binmen's surprise – or the totters', hunting for odds and ends to fill their carrier bags! In any case, she would have to bake another cake in the morning to give to Zoe. Well, she wouldn't give this cake to Julian. It would be absurd to arrive in the evening with a cake! She was not going to his flat to bring him a cake, she was bringing him – herself! Her lightheartedness faded slightly, and she shuddered a little at that idea. She took a deep breath to calm herself. Sometimes it was amusing to test out such ideas in her head, and sometimes quite interesting fantasies could flower from the exploratory thought. But she knew now that these fantasies would always remain as such: unattainable, even unwanted. The reality, the physical reality, would be too awkward and embarrassing; nor would it blend with the reality of her life.

She often puzzled about that episode at the cottage, but what puzzled her even more was that she had persisted with that particular fantasy for so long afterwards and had, apparently, suffered (yes, suffered was the right word for that obsessive torment) from the illusion that love and empathy would grow out of sexual contact: a postcoital Julian whispering his physical and mental anguish into her receptive ear. Silly fool that she was; silly, middle-aged fool! It was not the *sex* that she wanted, it was his confidence and trust, and she would only earn that when she and Julian had time to talk. Recently, it seemed that they dodged each other around the flat, and she could never catch him in a relaxed, confiding mood. He was so busy these days and she was proud of him. It was difficult to refrain from dropping his name into conversations with her friends. It probably wasn't wrong to be proud, secretly, that she had helped his career to expand.

This evening they would have time to talk. She was sure he would be at home; yesterday they had both discussed a documentary about modern Celtic folkgroups that would be on television tonight, and he had been keen to watch. It would finish in ten minutes, and she would be there, at his front door.

Margaret wrapped the cherry cake and put it in a bag, then hastened upstairs to put her head around the door and say goodbye to Iain.

She parked the car around the corner from Julian's flat because she felt it was more suitable to arrive on foot, less easy to be sent away. The terrace was ahead of her, and she counted along the bay windows, numbering the houses in the dark. There was a light on in Julian's front room, the music room, where he would have been watching television. Fine droplets of rain dampened her cheeks, and when she ran a hand over her hair she found it was quite wet. She hoped she looked all right – it was crazy to be walking in the rain.

She hadn't thought of an excuse. Perhaps she could say that she couldn't come to clean on Thursday, so she'd dropped in to tell him because she happened to be passing . . . Feeble, unconvincing. Somehow she would have to ensure that he invited her inside. Why hadn't she planned this initial step more carefully? She had felt confident that she would think of something suitable to say, when the moment arrived.

She would spy on him first, while she thought of a plausible reason for the visit. From the pavement across the road she would possibly be able to see into the front room. Pupils would be standing, wouldn't they, so she would at least be able to see if he had an unscheduled evening lesson. (And she could take the cake to Zoe, who would be most surprised.)

Margaret walked slowly along the pavement, looking across at the windows of the terrace. Some were dark, or curtained, but others were lit and exposed, showing mirrors, pictures, posters or pot plants. Julian's room was dimly lit, perhaps by that orange table lamp; the memory of the sea urchin skeleton and the loch shore came back forcefully. And Julian on the shore, Julian behaving strangely when she mentioned climbing the hill.

She stood opposite his window and looked in, at first unable to understand the picture that she saw. A fair-haired girl was facing the window. Her head was thrown back and her eyes were closed, her hair flopped and jerked across her face as she rhythmically rose and fell. The girl's hands were gripping the back of an upright chair, her throat and neck were bare. As Margaret watched, the girl opened her mouth and writhed and arched, and then was still.

Numbly, Margaret watched as the girl bent forwards and then stood straight. A pair of hands reached up to support her huge pale breasts, and the girl pressed against them and bent down to kiss the owner of the hands. The owner had dark hair.

The images sorted themselves into a strongly drawn, unambiguous picture. Margaret thought she was going to faint. There was a sudden pressure in her head and ears. She breathed deeply and looked around for a missile. An open Coke can stood upright on the wall behind her. She grabbed it, feeling the weight of undrunk liquid inside it, and hurled it towards the glass, a philistine in an art gallery. But the distance was too great and the liquid made the can unstable. It struck the door of a parked car, denting it slightly and spraying Coke. The impact triggered the car alarm, and the car began to wink and bleat pathetically.

No one would suspect a smartly dressed solicitor's wife of such vandalism! Margaret made herself walk casually away. At the corner, she looked back briefly. There were no faces at windows, there was no worried car owner, no naked blonde or spent musician. No one cared: night noises in the city, as natural as the owl and fox in the countryside.

'You're back quickly. Zoe must have been more than usually brisk and efficient!'

Margaret picked up the newspaper and sat down by the fire. She tried to smile. 'Oh, that's Zoe! Always in a rush!'

She'd forgotten about the cake; it was still in the car. She had to wedge her elbows against the arms of the chair because her hands still wanted to shake, making the newspaper rattle and magnify the effect. She scanned the news for fifteen minutes, barely registering even the headlines.

'Shall I make a cup of tea?' Iain stood up and stretched, and his sudden action triggered Margaret to speak.

'I've been thinking – I'll probably stop cleaning Julian Kersland's flat. I always feel I'm in the way. And Zoe said that his previous cleaner wanted her job back. The woman needs it more than I do. I'm depriving her, really, aren't I, of her income?'

Iain looked down at his wife. Her face was pale and set. He didn't want to know, or even speculate upon, the incident that had led to this decision, but he could guess at the turmoil within her. How he loved her; her gentle attractiveness, all her anxieties.

'That's a kind thought, Meg my love. Let's just hope Kersland will have her back. Didn't they have some sort of argument?'

Margaret nodded, worried. She could never go there again; Julian *must* take the woman back.

'Anyway, even if he doesn't,' Iain comforted her, 'it's not

your problem. You were always free to leave, and you've done far more than you needed for him. You've been your usual generous, kind self. And I love you, even if he doesn't!' he added, jokingly.

Margaret looked at him, startled, but he was smiling and relaxed.

'Anyway, I'll go and put on the kettle. What a pity you took that cake away, I could really have enjoyed a slice!'

Later, they discussed their plans for the remainder of the week, and Margaret allowed herself to be persuaded that she would enjoy being released from the responsibility of worrying about Kersland's wellbeing.

'Because you have been worrying about him, haven't you? And I don't suppose you were ever given any thanks!'

She nodded slightly, her face bleak. It was true, it had all been a pointless waste of time and energy – but the ache would take a long time to diminish. And how would she now fill in her empty days? Go back to Zoe and the hospice stalls?

Iain must have read her thoughts (How many other thoughts had he read? she wondered. Had she become so transparent?) because, as he stood up to collect her cup, he said, 'You know, you're wasted, my love, on all this charity work. I admire your persistence, but you would probably enjoy something a bit more sociable, wouldn't you? A bit more stimulating, perhaps? I happen to know the Opera are looking for someone part time to help with administration. I'm not quite sure what, but you could phone and ask.'

He bent and kissed her forehead. 'Think about it. And by the way, I've got Thursday off. Why don't we go somewhere nice for the day?'

Margaret looked up at him and then, on impulse, caught his free hand and held it to her cheek.

'You're such a good man, Iain,' she said, and smiled at him, but his face was unfocused through her tears.

Iain took the tray downstairs and checked the windows and doors, then he went into his darkroom and hunted through the filing cabinet. Between some files was a page from a tabloid newspaper. He looked at it in surprise, wondering why it was there, then crumpled it and threw it into the bin. Eventually he found the large, unmarked envelope for which he had been searching. He took out several prints and switched on the anglepoise lamp to give more light. The top print was of a tree-covered island in a loch; there were fish pens in the distance, and a small working-boat, and the feet of hills. Nearer to the camera was another boat, nudged up against a large smooth rock by the island.

The other photographic prints were enlargements, each one larger than the one before. There were two figures standing on the rock above the boat, two figures against a background of dark trees; a man and a woman on a rock, a woman embracing a half-naked man.

Iain picked up a magnifying glass and stared at the two faces. Then he took each photograph and tore it into shreds, and pushed the pieces deep down into the centre of the rubbish bag. He turned out the light and was about to leave when he saw the skull on top of the filing cabinet. As a final, rather foolish, gesture, he crushed the gannet's sightless skull under his foot and threw the fragments in the bag.

Chapter Twenty-One

Julian riffled through the small pile of papers on his desk. Fortunately his late-afternoon pupil was ill, so that he now had some extra time in which to catch up on the backlog of business. He pulled out a financial report from Guy, the Ensemble's treasurer. Guy was leaving the band because his wife had finally left him for her viola player. It was a pity, because he was a good cellist, but it was understandable – and Julian had another cellist lined up, a keen young lad who'd trained in Amsterdam. The accounts were looking very healthy, the new-style concerts were proving very popular.

He checked through his diary because he had a feeling that they hadn't yet finalised the programme for the second Chamber Music session in April next year. There were the evening concerts on Wednesdays in the New Year, and a recording session, in addition to the Chamber Music and the regular Sunday bookings. And another gig in a pub with Tom and Chris, and the flautist Euan. Tom had arranged that. Tom had given him a new stick, too. It was an old battered stick that he said he'd got from a farmer friend of his; Tom said that Jools' sticks were too *urban*, and that this was an early Christmas present.

Two weeks to Christmas! Julian groaned and looked up from his papers; his reflection was pale against an already-darkening window. He stood up and dragged the curtains across, then lay down on his bed, staring at the ceiling. He ought to do his final Christmas shopping tomorrow. The presents for his mother and for Rosemary were already purchased and wrapped. He wouldn't need to buy a present for Isobel, anyway. Strange, when he thought of her now it was with surprise, surprise that they had ever had a relationship, surprise that he could have so completely desired her. Now, only a few weeks later, his dominant memory was of those final moments in the car as he had tried to recapture his initial desire. But now he merely felt something like revulsion as he saw again the incongruous band of pale, soft flesh oozing out, sandwiched between her dark, rucked-up jumper and the waistband of her skirt. And the revulsion was not only at himself. And then he'd nearly driven into that old fool lurching across the road – an accident had been frighteningly close. As it was, the car had gone over the old chap's bag or whatever it was, probably newspapers or rags to keep him warm when he dossed down. Julian screwed up his eyes and pulled a face. In many ways, that had been an awful evening; although the results had eventually justified the means.

As for Isobel, he had of course sent her a letter of apology; he'd even arranged for flowers to be sent to her, white carnations. She had written back, too, thanking him for the flowers and for 'the many good times' they had had together. It had been a civilised letter, apportioning blame equally without being entirely explicit, and she had mentioned that committee that funded her, explained that she was working really hard . . . Superficially (and that was really all that mattered now, wasn't it?) there had been a civilised agreement that they would have nothing further to do with each other. Julian wondered if Isobel's revulsion was equally deep.

So, no Christmas present needed there. Nor one for poor Margaret Gillespie, God bless her yearning soul! She'd delivered a letter (his life that week had been full of valedictory letters from erstwhile female fans) explaining that she had 'given careful thought', et cetera . . . 'other commitments' . . .

'delighted at his successes, Iain and I wish you well', and so on; and suggesting the recall of Mrs Knight. 'Mrs Lutyens will mediate.' (Robbie, incidentally, was coming along rather well, he was becoming a real pleasure to teach. Odd, because there was no history of musicianship in his family, no fiddle-totin' great-aunt.) So Mrs Knight still wanted to return! He'd think about the Knight problem next year, one day next year, a Knight problem in daytime, day problems, night problems – no problems, really. Problem-free days and nights.

Perhaps he would buy himself some presents, buy some new clothes – bright batik silks and 'ethnic' weaves. Julian shifted on the bed to get more comfortable and closed his eyes, relaxing, planning where he would shop.

He jerked awake and looked wildly at the clock. Past five o'clock – five o'clock in the evening, what was he doing lying here? The doorbell rang twice and he realised what had woken him. He half fell off the bed and hobbled along the hall to the front door, blinking his eyes.

He didn't immediately recognise the boy because he had changed the colour of his hair so that it was almost white. The boy, who had started to smile as Julian opened the door, stopped, and looked at him uncertainly.

'Hello . . . er . . . Julian. You remember me? I'm Mike. We've . . . er, like . . . talked after the gigs . . .' His voice croaked slightly, and he swallowed.

One of the students, of course; the one who sometimes spoke to him.

'Of course! Mike! You used to have orange hair – and you're the one who often brings a score to pick up on our mistakes!'

'Oh, er . . . not often. Only now and again. The score, I mean – not the mistakes.'

'And you were at the hospital, weren't you? Hell, yes! What were you doing there?'

Julian looked at Mike more closely.

'That was my kid sister I was with. She was in because . . . she told me that . . . that you were going to play.'

Mike's voice was causing him some trouble, almost fading away, and there was a strange clicking as though his mouth were dry. Then, he spoke in a rush, and held out a large padded envelope.

'I brought you a present. You don't really call yourself "Jools", do you?'

Julian, who was holding the door open with one hand and holding his stick in the other, wondered if he should take the package in his mouth.

'Come in, Mike, come in. There's no need to stand out here on the steps. Go through there, the open door. Hang up your coat there, look.'

He followed Mike into the flat and then led him into the music room. Mike stopped inside the door and looked round.

'I always imagined it like this . . . you can see . . . I can see . . . quite a lot from outside.'

He walked over and touched the piano. Perhaps the feel of something familiar gave him confidence.

'I'm not a student any more, you know. I graduated last summer.' He nodded to the package that he had at last succeeded in giving to Julian. 'I wrote that for you. You can open it.'

'You've written a piece of music – for *me*?'

Julian was astonished. He sat down on the arm of a chair so that he could use both hands to open the envelope. To have music written especially for him, to have inspired someone . . . ! But what if it was awful, how would he be able to extricate himself? He looked quickly at Mike before he pulled the manuscript out of the envelope. He was very aware that this boy, this young man, would have invested not only time but the agonies, uncertainties, and joys of his own soul in this music.

'I'm scared to look,' he said simply. 'Will you tell me about it first, to prepare me?'

Mike frowned at him, and then came over and took the package from his hands.

'You don't have to be scared,' he said kindly, almost as though he were an adult comforting a child. 'You *will* like it. It may be technically difficult but we can work on that. You'll be able to do it, though, because it describes you. Although it's called *Cityscape*, it's really about you.'

Julian watched as Mike pulled out the manuscript books.

'There are five sections, five scenes, really, for solo violin – you – and orchestra. Modern orchestra, not baroque – although in the third section there are only a few instruments, and they have to sound thin and muted like baroque. That section's called "Sunday Lunch".' Mike grinned, and his face was transformed. 'Good, isn't it? A direct reference to the Kersland Ensemble but also churches, Sunday papers, gentility, visiting relations for lunch, all very subdued and polite. And then there's "City Lights", and one about the river – you can help me think of a title when you've played it – and—'

'I'd like to see it now,' Julian said. 'Can you play it on the piano? I'll sit next to you and read it as you go. Will you bring that chair across next to the stool?'

And so Mike began to work his way through the handwritten score, picking out here the melody, here 'the viola – look! – and the oboe takes it up, and look what you are doing. You *can* do that, can't you?' Soon Julian was fetching his violin, and his fingers stretched and leapt from the low notes to the high, sometimes across enormous, seemingly impossible spans, with drifting pianissimo at the top. He was expostulating, sometimes exasperated, sometimes laughing. But as he played, and began to hear and understand, an excitement, a warmth, began to build up inside him; a realisation that this was what he had been waiting for all this time.

'What does this remind you of? Listen, it'll soon be only a memory. Do you hear steel plates in the shipyards, and the cranes?'

They were halfway through 'Sunday Lunch' when Julian lowered his violin. They had already stopped several times, to allow him to try out and discuss difficult passages.

'Stop,' he said. 'I want to read through that again and to try to hear it all in my head.'

It seemed to him that there was a faint pealing of church bells in there, and the thin, reedy sound of a choir – or was it shuffling footsteps? – that rose and drifted upwards, and still further upwards, into a high, vaulted ceiling; and beneath it all was the quiet, deep continuo of Canon Bothwell's calm and dispassionate voice. Julian stared at Mike and wondered how he knew. But then he saw that the picture was an illusion, and that Mike had actually described the shuffling of postprandial strollers around the fountain in the Tropical House.

'Botanic Gardens?' he asked, but Mike merely shrugged and smiled. 'I can't believe you wrote this – this *wonder* – for me. I'm very honoured.'

Mike swallowed. 'Please . . . please would you try part of "City Lights"?' He turned the pages. 'Try this section here. I think you'll see that it needs a gritty sound.'

Julian peered at the notes, and then laughed and began to play. '"Kilnacraig"! And its ilk!'

'Jools, too. And beer glasses in the background. If you really use your imagination. I only thought of this movement after I'd seen you at the hospital. I hadn't known – I didn't know you could do that, too. And the stories . . . my sister told me . . .'

Mike's mouth seemed dry again, and he stared at Julian, who suddenly found that he didn't want to look away.

'And – and when you smiled at me in the hospital, then I knew you weren't angry . . .'

'Why should I be *angry*, Mike? What do you mean?'

'About the note. I wished I hadn't given it to you. I know it was months ago, but—'

'What note?' Julian was genuinely perplexed.

'After that concert in – oh, months ago. You were talking to a couple of people. I didn't have a chance to speak – I didn't want to, anyway, I was too nervous, so I just gave you the note. Up in the hall – not downstairs . . . Oh hell! Don't tell me you never read it! Oh hell! I've made a mess of this . . .'

Mike was distraught. He pushed back the piano stool and began to gather up the music, then put it back again.

Julian watched in bewilderment. 'Mike, stop! Keep calm and tell me about the note.'

'I can't *tell* you about it. You need to read it. It doesn't matter . . . oh, shit! Keep the music anyway.'

'Wait! Let's talk this through. You can't just run away now.' He spoke gently. 'Mike, this music is incredible. We need to do a little work on it together in some places, but it's basically very, very good. I am . . . overwhelmed by it. Now – the note. If you gave me a note – and, yes, I do remember the occasion' (I was talking to the Gillespies) '– I would have put it in my pocket. Can you remember what I was wearing? I don't suppose so. Why should you?'

'But yes, it was the first time you wore that South American-type waistcoat. But look, it doesn't—'

'OK. I wear that a lot, and I haven't ever found a note in its pockets. The pockets are too small, anyway. Right – where next?'

'*Forget* the note, Julian!' Mike was desperate.

'No, it's essential. I might have taken it into the green room and put it in the fiddle case. But I would have seen it later – unless it got mixed up with the cloth and shaken out. Let's look, anyway, although it's unlikely it will still be there.'

He picked up the case of his baroque violin, and opened it. Mike watched as he looked in the pocket at the neck end of the case, and shook the soft cloth that lay on top of the violin.

'What's that?' Mike pointed at the clear plastic wallet that was pressed down into the neck of the case. 'A photo?'

'Photographs of my grandmother, and a signed photo from her own teacher.' Julian pulled out the wallet, tugging at it because it was tightly wedged at the sides. 'I never look at them, but they're a sort of talisman—'

'There!' Mike darted forward to grab the folded slip of paper that lay beneath the wallet, but Julian jerked it from his hand, and almost overbalanced.

'Don't you want me to read it? I think I need to.'

Mike turned away. He looked at the manuscript books on the piano stool, then back at Julian.

'Yes,' he said softly; and he walked across the room and sat down in an armchair.

'"Julian Kersland. Why do you bother with all this crap? I want to write for you. And I want you to play my music."'

Julian read the words several times. Simple enough to be over-dramatic. So simple.

He walked across to the chair opposite Mike, and saw how Mike watched his twisting, ungainly step.

'Do you want to write for this, too?'

Mike continued staring at Julian's leg. 'To me,' he said finally, 'it's not important. It must be important to you, physically, as a hindrance. But you're not the footballer type anyway. Nor am I. We've got so much to do that it doesn't really matter, does it? It doesn't matter.'

Julian lay back in the chair, holding the note tightly. 'It doesn't really matter, does it?' he repeated silently. Does it really all come down to that? The frenetic searching, the pretence and the despair? Phrases of Mike's music soared inside his head. He thought about the complicated knot of truth and untruth in which his leg had been entangled, and as he repeated Mike's words he saw that finally his leg was free. A tremendous sense of peace came over him. It was true:

until now, everything else had been irrelevant.

He looked across at Mike, who was waiting quietly, watching: young, white-haired Mike, who captured pictures and characters and created them anew within thin black lines – and who had also captured, and freed, the real Julian Kersland. He needed Mike, Mike needed him; a symbiosis, they needed nothing else. Nothing else mattered. They would create together – and how they would fly!

Julian leant forward and held out the note, and when Mike reached out to take it, Julian grasped his hand in his and held it, even though his leg didn't hurt and probably never would again.

'Thank you,' he said.